A Haunted
Guesthouse
Mystery

Old
Haunts

"[A] wonderful new series."
—KATE CARLISLE,
New York Times bestselling
author of the Bibliophile
Mysteries

E. J. COPPERMAN

Author of An Uninvited Ghost

BERKLEY
PRIME
CRIME

$7.99 U.S.
$8.99 CAN

ISBN 978-0-425-24620-7

EAN

continued . . .

Night of the Living Deed

"Witty, charming and magical."   —*The Mystery Gazette*

"A fast-paced, enjoyable mystery with a wisecracking but, no-nonsense, sensible heroine . . . Readers can expect good fun from start to finish, a great cast of characters and new friends to help Alison adjust to her new life. It's good to have friends—even if they're ghosts."
—*The Mystery Reader*

"A delightful ride . . . The plot is well developed, as are the characters, and the whole is funny charming and thoroughly enjoyable."   —*Spinetingler Magazine*

"A bright and lively romp through haunted-house repair!"
—Sarah Graves, author of the
Home Repair Is Homicide Mysteries

"[A] wonderful new series . . . [A] laugh-out-loud, fast-paced and charming tale that will keep you turning pages and guessing until the very end."
—Kate Carlisle, *New York Times* bestselling
author of the Bibliophile Myseries

"Fans of Charlaine Harries and Sarah Graves will relish this original, laugh-laden paranormal mystery . . . [A] sparkling first entry in a promising new series."
—Julia Spencer-Fleming, Anthony and Agatha
award-winning author of *One Was a Solider*

"*Night of the Living Deed* could be the world's first screwball mystery. You'll die laughing and then come back a very happy ghost."
—Chris Grabenstein, Anthony and Agatha
award-winning author

Berkley Prime Crime titles by E. J. Copperman

NIGHT OF THE LIVING DEED
AN UNINVITED GHOST
OLD HAUNTS

Old Haunts

E. J. COPPERMAN

BERKLEY PRIME CRIME, NEW YORK

THE BERKLEY PUBLISHING GROUP
Published by the Penguin Group
Penguin Group (USA) Inc.
375 Hudson Street, New York, New York 10014, USA
Penguin Group (Canada), 90 Eglinton Avenue East, Suite 700, Toronto, Ontario M4P 2Y3, Canada
(a division of Pearson Penguin Canada Inc.)
Penguin Books Ltd., 80 Strand, London WC2R 0RL, England
Penguin Group Ireland, 25 St. Stephen's Green, Dublin 2, Ireland (a division of Penguin Books Ltd.)
Penguin Group (Australia), 250 Camberwell Road, Camberwell, Victoria 3124, Australia
(a division of Pearson Australia Group Pty. Ltd.)
Penguin Books India Pvt. Ltd., 11 Community Centre, Panchsheel Park, New Delhi—110 017, India
Penguin Group (NZ), 67 Apollo Drive, Rosedale, Auckland 0632, New Zealand
(a division of Pearson New Zealand Ltd.)
Penguin Books (South Africa) (Pty.) Ltd., 24 Sturdee Avenue, Rosebank, Johannesburg 2196,
South Africa

Penguin Books Ltd., Registered Offices: 80 Strand, London WC2R 0RL, England

This is a work of fiction. Names, characters, places, and incidents either are the product of the author's imagination or are used fictitiously, and any resemblance to actual persons, living or dead, business establishments, events, or locales is entirely coincidental. The publisher does not have any control over and does not assume any responsibility for author or third-party websites or their content.

OLD HAUNTS

A Berkley Prime Crime Book / published by arrangement with the author

PRINTING HISTORY
Berkley Prime Crime mass-market edition / February 2012

ISBN: 978-0-425-24620-7

BERKLEY® PRIME CRIME
Berkley Prime Crime Books are published by The Berkley Publishing Group,
a division of Penguin Group (USA) Inc.,
375 Hudson Street, New York, New York 10014.
BERKLEY® PRIME CRIME and the PRIME CRIME logo are trademarks of Penguin Group (USA) Inc.

PRINTED IN THE UNITED STATES OF AMERICA

10 9 8 7 6 5 4 3 2 1

To Cosmo, George and Marion,
but also to Jessica, Josh and Eve, who
are the best there ever were

AUTHOR'S NOTE

I am, you should know, absolutely grateful to the readers of the Haunted Guesthouse Mysteries. Everyone who's ever read and enjoyed any of my books—consider me a friend. Anyone who's ever read and gotten in touch to tell me how much you liked it, I am in your debt.

To my author buddies: Julia Spencer-Fleming, Jennifer Stanley (in any of her incarnations), Lorraine Bartlett (in any of *her* incarnations), Chris Grabenstein, Rosemary Harris, Leann Sweeney, Jack Getze, Jeff Markowitz, Kate Carlisle, Roberta Rogow, Meredith Cole, Jane Cleland and anyone whose name I'm blanking on at this moment—you are incredibly generous and open. I only hope I'm half as good a friend.

At the risk of sounding like a broken record (for those who remember records), my eternal gratitude to my editor, the incomparable Shannon Jamieson Vazquez, who always tortures me with my mistakes by being right about each and every one and inspiring me to come up with better solutions. I love you dearly, Shannon, and someday, I'll get you for making me work so hard.

Major-league thanks to the indefatigable Josh Getzler, of the Hannigan Salky Getzler Agency, for being an agent who is honest, supportive, dedicated and amiable, which doesn't sound like much (no, wait—actually it sounds like quite a bit!) but is very rare among humans and extremely valuable. Thanks once again to Christina Hogrebe, who is all those things too, and who got this whole ball rolling to begin with.

Long-overdue thanks to Dominick Finelle, the artist who creates the Haunted Guesthouse covers, and Judith Lagerman, executive art director at The Berkley Publishing Group, who developed the design and overall look of the series. Without the two of you, I'm sure not nearly as many people would have stopped to take a look.

If this is the first book of mine you've read, welcome. If it's the ninth, the sixth or the third, thanks for sticking around. Thanks for taking the trip with me. Tell your friends. Tell your enemies. Tell total strangers. And know that I'm with you there, every step of the way.

One

"Careful!" I said. All right, shouted. "We can't afford to drop this."

It wasn't so much that the sheet of wallboard Maxie, Paul and I were holding up was so expensive it couldn't be replaced; it was more that hauling another heavy sheet up here in the attic of my massive Victorian home and guesthouse would be enormously difficult.

Renovating the attic into a bedroom for my ten-year-old daughter, Melissa, during breaks from my duties as hostess and overall ringleader of the house at 123 Seafront Avenue had seemed like a good idea when I'd come up with it in April—it would give Liss a little privacy from the flow of guests in the house, and would free up another bedroom downstairs to rent out, thus generating more income. It had seemed like a practical and logical idea. In April.

Now it was July on the New Jersey Shore, and the attic was not yet air-conditioned. Heat, in case you haven't heard, rises.

It was about 15,000 degrees up here, even with the windows open.

Sometimes, my creative instincts overcome my common sense. I really should watch out for that.

"*You* can't afford to drop it," Maxie answered. "It's not our money."

"No, it's not," I agreed. "But you were in favor of this plan, and practically forced me into it. So if you don't want the construction to go on indefinitely—"

"It wouldn't matter to me," Maxie cut me off. "I've got nothing but time."

That was true. Paul and Maxie were going to stay in the house for a very long time.

They were dead.

Perhaps I should explain.

Paul Harrison and Maxie Malone had both died in my house, a little less than a year before Melissa and I moved in. They'd been murdered, and although there's quite a story involved with that, it's been told elsewhere, at length. Suffice it to say, they seemed bound to my property, and I was, in essence, stuck with them.

When I finalized my divorce from Melissa's father, whom I charitably call The Swine, I bought this great big old house, knowing it was in need of repairs in pretty much every room. But I didn't know it was haunted. It wasn't until a rather questionable accident gave me a massive headache and the ability to communicate with my two nonpaying boarders that I gained that information. When I'd discovered my mother and my daughter had actually been able to see them all along, I had been relieved that I wasn't going insane, but not that pleased Mom and Melissa had been keeping their abilities from me all those years. Turns out that though most living people can't see ghosts, obviously, most of the females in my family can—I was the rare exception, until recently. Go figure. My mother and Melissa could see pretty much every ghost they encountered, and my abilities were developing slowly.

Anyway, today I had an almost-full roster of guests downstairs, a heavy sheet of wallboard I was trying to attach to the studs on a slant, and I was putting my resident ghosts to work hanging drywall.

"Just a couple seconds longer," I told the ghosts as I secured this particular sheet in place with my cordless drill. Maxie seemed not to be exerting any energy at all, but Paul was visibly flagging—his ability to interact with physical objects was improving, but he was not able to do it as well as Maxie. There don't seem to be any "rules" regarding ghosts—it's not like they all have the same abilities, apparently. Paul tells me that some ghosts can roam freely, and I've seen that happen, but the two of them couldn't leave my property. They didn't know why. And we haven't been able to figure out why some dead people show up as ghosts and others don't. (The whole "unfinished business" thing is a good theory, but there seem to be a ton of exceptions.)

Frankly, the whole afterlife didn't seem very well organized, in my opinion.

"I'm not sure how long I'll be able to hang on," Paul said, "breathing" heavily. And sure enough, a second later his fingers seemed to fly up into the wallboard—the ghost equivalent of dropping something.

Luckily, Maxie was stronger and more "solid." "I've got it," she said, "but don't take all day."

The drywall screws went in fairly easily—if you do something enough times in your life, you get good at it—and then I could tell my two nonalive assistants to relax. Once all the wallboard was hung in the room, I could work joint compound into the cracks and the screw holes, and after sanding (my least favorite part), I'd paint the room. Assuming Melissa ever decided on a color she liked.

I checked the wallboard for fit, and it was fine; a quarter-inch short on the bottom, but the wainscoting I was planning to add would more than compensate for that. The next piece we hung would have to fit around the window I'd installed the week before, so I began to measure for the fifth time, despite having memorized the dimensions. I'm never comfortable until I can actually see everything fit in its final state.

"What are you thinking about for the ceiling?" Maxie asked. Maxie was trying to be an interior designer when she died, and still has opinions. Since she couldn't go anywhere but my house, all her opinions were about 123 Seafront. You can't possibly imagine how thrilling that was to me.

"The ceiling?" I asked, as if I didn't know what she meant. I was stalling for time. Typically, the way these things work is that I suggest a traditional—but classy—design element, Maxie scoffs and counters with something that sounds outrageous and absurd, and I reject it. Then I think about it for a moment, realize she's actually on to something, and end up grudgingly doing things Maxie's way. We have a slightly dysfunctional relationship, but it works for us. Which I suppose technically makes it functional.

"Yeah. That thing that hangs over the rest of the room—remember?" Maxie thought she was witty. Spending eternity with a witty ghost was probably some kind of Chinese curse.

"I figured I'd just paint it white," I said. There was no use in trying to delay the inevitable. "It's already pitched at an interesting angle; that should be enough of a visual statement." I braced myself for the coming withering condescension.

It never came. "You're probably right," Maxie said. "The dimensions of the room are the feature. It would be a mistake to add too many elements to that."

"You're agreeing with me?" I asked. "How does that work into our usual dynamic?"

We were both distracted by the sound of the doorbell. I have an old-fashioned one on the house, loud, and even up here, it was as clear as a . . . what it was.

The idea that someone was using the doorbell was odd; the front door was unlocked until all my guests were inside at night, and on a hot afternoon like this, it was as likely as not to have been left wide open so as to better allow out the conditioned air and drive up my energy bill.

With two flights of stairs between me and the front door, the prospect of traipsing all the way downstairs to find a meter reader or misguided UPS deliveryman was less than appealing. Especially since I was soaked in sweat from spending my afternoon performing construction in an un-air-conditioned attic,

"Would you mind taking a look and seeing who that is?" I asked Paul. The ghosts, after all, don't have to worry about things like walls and ceilings—they zip right through solid objects—and don't so much walk as glide through the air. Going downstairs was hardly an exertion for Paul.

But he shifted his gaze to Maxie. "Would you do it, Maxie?"

"Why me?"

Paul raised an eyebrow. "Because I went the last fifteen times," he said.

"What are we, six years old?" But Maxie disappeared through the floor, not looking in any special hurry. I'd probably end up having to go down there myself anyway.

I gave Paul a significant look as soon as Maxie left. "Okay, what was that all about?" I asked him. "You didn't ask her to go downstairs because of some juvenile scoring system. You wanted her out of the room."

Paul looked away. His polite Canadian upbringing and his British roots probably made him feel embarrassed for having emotions.

"I have a favor to ask," he said, unable to make eye contact. My mind immediately raced through the possibilities of things a deceased person could ask me to do . . .

Oh, no. Not *that*.

This part is complicated: Before my guesthouse was offi-

cially open for business, I was approached by a man named
Edmund Rance, representing a firm called Senior Plus Tours,
which books tours with "special experiences" for senior citizens. Rance had heard the rumors of hauntings at my house
and asked specifically for eerie, ghostly happenings at least
twice a day to astound his clientele.

Before I could agree to the deal, which guaranteed me a
profitable season, I had to convince Paul and Maxie to "put on
a show" a couple of times a day. At first, this had consisted of
them moving a few knickknacks around to give the guests a
look at "floating" objects, and they still did that, but we'd
added some other features. For one, Paul, who said he'd been
in a band before his murder, would play music on a few instruments (cheap ones) I'd bought for the shows. And the ghosts
had decided between themselves to surprise me every once in
a while by floating some unexpected object around to get a
reaction out of me. Maxie took special delight in selecting
things from the toolshed or the basement, and although they
were never living (or dead) creatures, they could be pretty
slimy. There had been some I could not identify. This surprised me, not so much the guests, who were, to my disappointment, amused by the hijinks. Ghosts. You can't live with
them, you *can* live without them, and I'd recommend it.

The ghosts also could make objects "appear out of thin
air." This was accomplished simply by hiding whatever they
liked in their clothing (a pants pocket or inside a jacket) and
then removing it at a strategic time. The ghosts seem able to
keep material objects with them, hidden from sight, as long as
they carry the object in a pocket or under their clothes. I've
seen Maxie secret things in her endless supply of T-shirts, for
example. Lately, they (okay, *Maxie*) had also taken to doing
annoying things like mussing my hair or my clothing while I
was talking to the guests. I had gotten her back by scheduling
the spook shows randomly—which had the added advantage
of helping us avoid guests who were "civilians," or not in on
the Senior Plus deal, who might be alarmed to see invisible

people juggling fruit. Maxie didn't like the unpredictable aspect of a random schedule.

When the offer from Senior Plus Tours had come, I hadn't known the ghosts for very long, but I knew better than to approach Maxie with the proposition. I talked to Paul instead, and ran into a condition: Paul, a former private investigator, wanted to keep his mind occupied with the occasional case, and he needed me to be his "legs." I reluctantly agreed to sit for the private-investigator exam and obtained a license, hoping Paul would be content with the effort and not actually ask me to investigate things.

It hadn't worked out that way.

"I'm not investigating another crime," I told him firmly now. "I've had my and Melissa's lives placed in enough danger. It's not going to happen again."

Paul turned back toward me with a strange grin on his face. "Oh, it's not that, Alison," he said. "It's something considerably more . . . personal."

That threw me—personal? What could be personal to a dead guy? I mean, you could see right through him. Literally. "I don't understand, Paul," I told him.

"It's something . . . I've been meaning to ask since I met you," Paul said. He turned away again, but I could see that even the slightly transparent tone of his face was reddening a little. Who knew a ghost could blush? "I've really come to know you now, and I'm just beginning to feel that you won't think I'm foolish."

He reached into his pocket, then extended his hand and opened his fingers. He was holding a small jewelry box covered in velvet.

Oh, my! There had always been an odd sort of attraction between Paul and me, but we'd never said a word about it, because it is impossible to act upon unless I die, which I'm not really willing to do for a guy. Call me selfish.

"Oh, Paul," I said, "you know I care about you, but this is far too much."

Paul's gaze went from the box to my eyes in a nanosecond. His eyes narrowed, then widened, and he smiled broadly.

Then he began to laugh. And he didn't stop. It seemed he *couldn't* stop. And that went on for a full minute; I know because after a while, I checked my watch. Okay. I had clearly misinterpreted something here.

"Come on, it's not *that* funny," I finally managed to get in. "So what were you going to ask?"

Paul's laughter ended gradually, and his face took on that sad, serious look he gets sometimes when he's forced to acknowledge that he is, in fact, dead. "It's something I'd like to ask you to do for me," he said.

But he didn't get the chance to tell me anything more than that because Maxie levitated up through the floor and grinned at me. "There's a guy downstairs looking for you," she said, looking more wicked than usual. "He's cute, too."

Perfect. A cute guy comes to see me while I'm here basting in my own juices. Story of my life. I'd been on a total of three dates since my divorce from The Swine, all with Melissa's history teacher, Ned Barnes. But Ned and I had decided to take a break from each other for a while because Liss was weirded out by the idea of a teacher dating her mom. So now, the possibility of an attractive stranger downstairs was both interesting and daunting. I hesitated a moment, trying to calculate how quickly I could change my clothes.

Finally, I decided I'd have to face the music as I was, since no man worth cleaning up for would want to wait as long as it would take me. Besides, if he didn't see my inner beauty, the heck with him anyway. You can rationalize these things.

I did use the rag I had in the attic to mop up a bit, then made my way back into the air-conditioned part of the house, which helped. And by the time I'd made it all the way to the ground floor and the front entranceway, I felt more presentable, even if I didn't look that way.

And that's when I realized it didn't matter how I looked, because the mysterious man in question was kneeling in my foyer, a big crooked grin on his damned handsome face, his sandy hair carefully mussed just enough to make it look casual. He was hugging my daughter tightly, and she was purring, "Daddy!"

I groaned (if there were any guests within earshot, they probably thought it was a "spook house" effect). The very last person I wanted to see had traveled three thousand miles to visit my house and, no doubt, disrupt my life. My ex-husband, Steven Rendell.

The Swine.

Two

"What are you doing here?" I rasped when I had absorbed the sight.

Steven started as if shocked, looked at me, and patted Melissa on the shoulder, the universal signal to detach from a hug. Our daughter, ten-year-old traitor that she was, squealed at me, "Look, Mom! Daddy's come home!"

Terrific. Almost two years of seeing to her every need, and Melissa was about to switch sides on me based on her father's ability to walk through the door? Since he had walked through a similar door going in the other direction with a curvy blonde on his arm the last time I'd seen him, I was less impressed with this talent.

It sure was a good thing I wasn't bitter, though.

Steven extricated himself from our daughter, who was currently cute-ing herself out of any inheritance *I* was going to leave for her, and folded his arms across his chest after he stood. For those of you keeping score at home, that's a typical defensive posture. But his face gave off nothing but warm smiles and a hint of—was that sadness?—in his eyes.

"Alison. You look terrific."

Oh, please. I knew very well that I looked horrendous—I was covered in sweat and dust—but that really wasn't the argument I wanted to have just at the moment.

"I said, 'What are you doing here?'" I'd fallen for his charming act once before, and ended up married. Then divorced. Then I started seeing ghosts. If I thought about it hard enough, my entire current situation could be seen as The Swine's fault.

"I suppose I deserve that kind of welcome," Steven said. "I know I didn't treat you very well, but I want to try to make up for that."

Melissa held up a small box. "Daddy brought me an iPod touch!" she chortled. Make no mistake, kids can be bought. Mine has a higher price than most, but all kids can be bought.

Before I could get another word in—and believe me, it was going to be a doozy—one of my Senior Plus Tours guests walked in from the den and smiled in my direction. Mrs. Fischer, who was here with her sister Mrs. Spassky, was a darling little lady easily in her mid-eighties who would have been described as "jolly" if she were forty pounds heavier.

"Alison, dear," she began, leaning on her elegant cane with the carved eagle on its handle. "Can you recommend a good local dealer in antiques? I do so love the quaint atmosphere around this town, and I'm hoping to take some of it home with me."

Luckily, having lived in Harbor Haven most of my life (except for that period during which I was married to The Swine), I knew almost all the storekeepers in the area, and had deals with some for a commission on purchases from those customers I sent their way. I do this only with those I know to be the best at what they do, you understand. It's not about the money. Mostly.

"Why yes, Mrs. Fischer," I told her. "Amber Lion is a wonderful antiques dealer, and they're not far at all. Let me see if I can find a business card of theirs . . ." Like I didn't know I had a collection in the side table right here in the foyer. I opened the drawer and made a show of looking.

"Nice to see you, Melissa," Mrs. Fischer said. She'd been here less than four days into an unusually long two-week Senior Tours booking and had already struck up quite the friendship with my daughter, who had told me the older lady was "adorable."

"This is my father, Mrs. Fischer!" Melissa gushed.

I quickly "found" the card for Amber Lion and turned abruptly back toward my guest. "Here it is!" I said a little too loudly. "Would you like me to call you a taxi?"

"Alison, you didn't mention your husband," Mrs. Fischer said, walking over to Steven, who reached out and actually kissed her hand. Boy, he was good.

"A pleasure to meet you," he crooned.

"*Ex*-husband," I said.

Mrs. Fischer must have caught the tone in my voice, because she smiled uncertainly, said, "Of course," and walked out onto the front porch.

"You've become a good businesswoman, Alison," Steven said, approaching me.

I held up a hand in warning. "Not another step until I know why you're here," I said.

My ex-husband had the nerve to look offended. "Don't you think it's possible I wanted to see my daughter after more than a year?" he asked.

It occurred to me that even low-fat fake butter wouldn't melt in his mouth. *Liquid* butter wouldn't melt in his mouth. "No," I said. "I don't think it's possible."

"Mom!" Melissa, like most children of divorce, probably held a hope that her parents would reconcile and wasn't thrilled with my attitude. I'd have to put on a better front until Steven and I were out of her earshot.

"I'm sorry," I said, more to my daughter than to The Swine. "I'm having a difficult day. Why have you come, Steven?"

Maxie poked her head through the ceiling and grinned hungrily at my ex. Normally, I might be disturbed by such an image, but the interest of a dead woman, especially one as, let's say, difficult as Maxie could be, was just what The Swine deserved. I grinned back at her.

"I told you," he answered, looking up at the spot to which I was smirking like a fool. "I wanted to see you and Melissa."

"Of course. And where's . . . What's her name, again?" I knew perfectly well the name of the woman who had been— what do the lawyers call it?—the co-respondent in my divorce.

"Amee is still in California," Steven answered. Amee with a double *ee*. Also her cup size, presumably. "We're . . . spending some time apart."

Melissa scowled a bit at the mention of Amee. She knew about her, but mostly in an intuitive fashion. I hadn't explained the circumstances of the divorce other than to tell her that it was unequivocally not her fault in any way. But she knew that once Steven had started regularly mentioning the woman for whom he was traveling three thousand miles west, there had to be something more to this than Mommy and Daddy having a disagreement over his leaving the toilet seat up again.

"Oh, I'm sorry to hear that," I told him, although I'm sure my voice sounded about as sorry as if he'd told me he was giving me six million dollars in a trust fund for our daughter. "I'm sure you'll work things out. Every relationship doesn't end in a divorce like ours, you know."

"A divorce like yours!" Maxie crowed, floating down a little and coming to rest halfway between the ceiling and the floor. "This is your ex?"

Melissa knew not to react to Maxie when a "civilian" like Steven was present, but her eyelids flickered a bit. She clearly saw that the reunion she'd been picturing was going somewhat differently than in her plans, and she offered to show Steven the room we were building for her in the attic. He did his best

to feign interest, and let her pull him toward the main staircase by the hand. I followed, if for no reason than to make
sure Steven didn't give her a new Porsche once I was out of
sight.

"It's gonna have a flat-screen TV right on the wall, and a
dock for my iPod touch, and it's going to be painted green,
and—"

"You decided on green?" I asked. "Last I heard it was
going to be yellow."

Melissa rolled her eyes. I could be *so* embarrassing. "Green
is a much happier color, Mom." No, not embarrassing—I was
an idiot. That was it.

We arrived in the attic, and I noticed to my consternation
that Steven wasn't even breathing hard from the climb. He
must have started exercising regularly, and all I could think
was that the entire time we'd been together I'd never seen him
do so much as a push-up.

He looked around the attic, having climbed the pull-down
stairs (I was going to have to figure out another access point
soon) and stood on the recently installed plywood floor.
Granted, the space didn't look like much yet; I'd just started
with a few sheets of wallboard so insulation was visible almost
everywhere, and the skylight was not yet cut into the roof. In
short, it looked like an attic.

"This place is amazing," Steven said, authenticity oozing
out of his voice like the filling of an overstuffed Fluffernutter.

"It *will* be," I answered. "See, there's going to be a skylight . . ."

"No, I mean it, Ally," my ex said. "I can't believe how great
it is you're doing this for our daughter. And your handiwork is
fantastic."

Now I *knew* there was something he wanted from me. Steven had been adamant about my not doing any physical labor
when we were married. He'd made me quit my job at a home-
improvement superstore, then used a business connection to
"find" me a desk job when I'd insisted on going back to work

the year Melissa turned five. It had been the beginning of the end of our marriage. Well, that, and Amee.

"Okay," I said. "Who are you, and what have you done with my ex-husband?"

Maxie wafted up from the plywood floor and hovered where she could get a really good look at The Swine. "He's not bad," she said. "How'd you get him to marry you? Were you pregnant?"

Melissa, knowing we shouldn't acknowledge the ghosts with Steven in the room, gave her a sharp look. For that matter, so did I.

"I'm just here to see you and Liss, Ally," my ex said, still doing his best to sell the tone in his voice. "I know that's not what you would have expected, but I'm willing to wait you out until you trust me again."

Something was definitely up. This was the exact attitude The Swine had used when he was trying to charm me, back when we first met.

"That might take a long time," I told him. "Where are you staying while you're here?"

He looked stumped, as if the question had never entered his mind before. "I sort of figured I'd stay . . . here," he said.

"You did, huh?"

Melissa gave me a look that begged for leniency. I did my best to ignore it.

"Is that a problem?" Steven asked.

"It is if you think it'll be like when we were married," I said. "But if you want to stay here as a paying guest, I have a room that's open. The going rate is a hundred and sixty-five dollars a night."

The Swine raised his eyebrows, feigning either surprise or offense. It didn't matter which. "For me?" he asked.

"You're right. For you, a hundred and eighty-five."

"Mom . . ."

Steven grinned, and reached into his back pocket for his wallet. "You *have* become a good businesswoman," he said. "You take credit cards?"

I nodded. "I know better than to try to cash a check from you, after the last child-support one bounced . . . When was that, again?"

This time The Swine outright laughed. "Put that on the card, too, if you like," he said. He handed it to me.

Maxie sat down the way the ghosts do, bending her body into a sitting position, but still hovering over the object upon which she was sitting, in this case a box of ceiling tiles. She happened to glance at the floor, where I'd laid out newspapers in anticipation of spreading joint compound into the gaps between drywall sheets. And suddenly, her eyes widened noticeably, and she drew in what would have been a breath in a living person.

"Oh my god," she gasped. And then, she seemed to be crying. No tears fell—there's no moisture in her—but she shook and shuddered, and closed her eyes. She repeated herself a number of times. I'd never seen her look like that before.

I handed Melissa her father's credit card. "Go downstairs and ring him up, please," I told her. Liss was looking at Maxie, and must have realized I wanted to be able to talk to her in private. She nodded, and took her father by the hand. "And charge him the full amount," I added. "I'm going to check."

Steven looked strangely at me but didn't say anything as he let Melissa lead him back to the pull-down stairs and the lower floors. Just before he disappeared down the stairs, he gave me a look I knew, which said, "We'll talk later."

As soon as they were off the stairs, I walked over to the sobbing ghost. "Maxie," I said, "what's wrong?"

She couldn't speak. She just pointed at the newspaper on the floor. So I knelt down and looked at the open page.

" 'Property Taxes Go up Four Percent?' " I asked. "What do you care about property taxes?"

Maxie shook her head violently and pointed again. Wrong article, I guessed.

" 'Human Remains Identified'?" I read. "Is that it?" Maxie nodded. I started to read.

The article began, "The remains of a man found at Seaside Heights two weeks ago have been identified as those of Robert Benicio, an Asbury Park native reported missing for more than two years. County detectives now believe Benicio was a victim of foul play."

I looked at Maxie again. Her chest was still heaving, but less severely than before. "Did you know this Benicio guy?" I asked.

She gulped a few more times, and nodded.

"Was he a friend?"

Maxie finally made eye contact and seemed to contain her emotion. Her voice only wavered a little when she said, "He was my husband."

Three

I don't know how long I stood there, staring. After regaining the power of speech, I managed to squeak out, "Your husband?!"

Maxie looked at me darkly. "You're surprised?"

"You've never even mentioned that you were married. When I asked if there was anyone you wanted me to contact . . ."

She tilted her head, an admission that perhaps she was being imprecise. "Okay, so maybe we weren't exactly husband and wife anymore. Big Bob and I only got married for a couple of days."

I couldn't decide whether to react to "Big Bob" or "a couple of days," but I came down on the latter after a moment. "You were married a couple of *days*?"

Maxie waved a hand. "Yeah. I knew him from when I used to go to this biker place in Asbury Park, the Sprocket, maybe three years ago. And we took a bike trip to Vegas on his hog.

Took a few days to get there. We went out the first night with a couple of his buddies, and the next morning, we woke up married. It was pretty funny, really."

She grinned at me and the look of what must have been total befuddlement on my face, then she went on. "It was a real good joke for a couple of days, but then it was time to go home, so we got a divorce or an annulment or something. We went home, but we kept calling each other 'wife' and 'husband,' you know. Drove my mom crazy. She hated Big Bob."

"Why?"

"Oh, you know mothers." Maxie smiled, but the sadness didn't leave her face. "He wasn't good enough for me, he borrowed money, he hit me . . ."

I took in a breath, one with actual air in it. "He hit you?"

Maxie looked abruptly in my direction, as if she'd forgotten I was listening. "Just once. We were both drunk, and we had this fight. He didn't hurt me, or anything, and he was real sorry afterward. It never happened again."

"Never?"

She shook her head. "No, but there wasn't any opportunity. It was after we were, you know, annulled or whatever, probably three years ago. I made the mistake of telling Mom, and she made me leave Big Bob the next day. I never saw him again." Her eyes turned back toward the newspaper on the floor. "Until now."

"So what happened to him?" I asked, pointing to the article.

"It says blunt trauma to his head," Maxie answered. "I guess somebody got mad at him."

"I guess so."

Paul's face appeared in the floorboards. He seemed like he was going to say something, then saw the expression on Maxie's face. "What happened?" he asked.

"You don't get to find out unless you come all the way up," I said. "You're creeping me out even more than usual."

Paul levitated directly up to a "standing" position, crossing his arms. "Is this adequately normal for you?" I nodded. His innate politeness mixes with a general disapproval of my native language, which is Sarcasm. I grew up in New Jersey.

"Is something bothering you, Maxie?" he asked.

Maybe I could run interference for her. "Maxie might prefer not to tell—"

"Yeah, my ex-husband died," Maxie told him. So much for needing my interference. "Somebody smashed in his head."

"How long has he been dead?" Paul asked her. Paul, the private investigator in life, was unable to kick the unsolved-crime habit And he wasn't above using me and my newly acquired PI license to supply him with his brain teasers.

"Longer than us," Maxie answered. "I'm surprised we haven't heard from him already."

Paul tilted his head and raised an eyebrow in a "you never know" expression. "Not everyone who dies ends up like us," he reminded her. "And it's not like we mingle with everyone who does, either. Do you want me to see if I can locate him?" Paul has the ability to connect mentally, or something, with other ghosts. He and I call it the "Ghosternet," but it doesn't always work. For instance, he hadn't reported any luck communicating with my father, and although my mother apparently sees Dad on a semiregular basis, she'd been no help to me in that area either.

"Try, would you?" Maxie said. She still looked shaken but was becoming herself again. "I'd like to know what happened to him."

"As soon as I get a moment alone," Paul told her.

"You're a ghost," I said. "You can have a moment alone whenever you want."

"You and I still need to talk," he said.

"I need to go tend to my child and my ex-husband before they work out a deal where he doesn't have to pay for his room," I told him. "We can talk later."

"Alison . . ."

But I was already on the pull-down stairs. I needed to get

past the embarrassing moment I'd had with Paul when he extended the jewelry box, and to be brutally honest, I didn't want to leave Steven and Melissa alone long enough for her to start liking her dad better than me.

Now, by any analysis, Paul could have certainly followed me downstairs. He can, after all, levitate and move through solid objects, so it wouldn't be at all a stretch to say he could easily have beaten me to the ground floor. But he didn't. Maybe he understood that I needed a little time to regroup.

So I made it to the front room without any interference and found The Swine there, apparently holding court with some of the guests. He was sitting on the sofa with Don Petrone, a seventyish gentleman of impeccable manners and tailoring, wearing a tie and blazer even in this heat, while Lucy Simone, a rare non–Senior Plus guest, was sitting on the facing easy chair. Lucy, an attractive woman in her early forties, was gazing at The Swine with a smitten look. I could relate—it was easy to fall for Steven when he wanted you to do so.

Both guests, in fact, were listening to Steven with something approaching rapture.

Melissa, surprisingly, was nowhere to be seen. I'd have thought nothing could tear her away from her father. (I later discovered that she'd run back to her room to excitedly text her BFF Wendy about her dad being "back home.")

He, of course, was grinning from ear to ear and gesticulating with enthusiasm. "So we check into the honeymoon suite, and Alison goes to take a shower," he was saying. "I want to make the atmosphere as romantic as possible, but I can't think of what to do. And I remember seeing movies where they spread rose petals in a path leading up to the bed. Now, I don't know where you go to get rose petals, but then I see the hotel has provided us with a bouquet of, waddaya know, *roses* right there on the table. And I figure they won't mind if I borrow a few. But here's the thing . . ."

"The hotel left a bouquet of roses for you?" Lucy asked. "I haven't seen so much as one flower since I checked in here."

Perfect; now they were comparing my humble little guest-house to a four-star hotel.

Wait a minute—I'd been so caught up in Steven's story that it hadn't occurred to me it was a new one. I didn't remember any rose-petal story associated with our honeymoon. In fact, our honeymoon had been essentially an overnight stay in a local motel because Steven had needed to be at work the following day at the investment firm that would, eventually, steal his soul.

I sidled up behind the couch and leaned over to whisper in his ear. "This story isn't about us," I hissed. "You've got the wrong honeymoon."

He ignored me and addressed his audience. "Well, Lucy, I'm willing to bet we spent a great deal more per night at that hotel than you're spending here, and we didn't get many of the extra touches that a guesthouse like this can offer."

"Well, there are plenty of towels, I guess," Lucy responded, seeing that The Swine wanted her to like the place. She'd accommodate if necessary. "But it's spooky. Sometimes I think I hear things."

Don Petrone gave me a look. He knew, as did all the Senior Plus guests, that the spirits in the house were not to be discussed with "civilians." The seniors seemed to enjoy the exclusivity of the knowledge. I nodded just a tiny bit at Don.

I couldn't see Steven's eyes from behind the couch, but I could picture his expression. I hadn't mentioned any ghosts to him, but I knew they were more or less the talk of the town in Harbor Haven. He might have heard something before he'd arrived.

Anyway, he didn't react. And I didn't give him time to finish his enthralling tale. "I'm sorry to drag him away," I told the assemblage, "but my *ex-husband* and I have a lot to discuss." I sort of grabbed The Swine by the arm and pulled him to his feet.

"Are you sure?" Lucy asked with great breathiness. "I wanted to hear the end of the story." Or any other story he was selling, no doubt.

"Maybe later," I said, but that didn't seem to console her much.

I finally managed to extricate Steven from the room and into the kitchen, which the guests rarely entered because I don't actually serve food. I barely cooked for Liss and me as it was.

"Okay, Melissa's gone," I told The Swine. "So will you finally tell me what's going on? Why are you here?"

"I told you, Amee and I are taking a break, and I wanted to see you and Lissie." The Swine even managed to look sincere while saying that. "Is there a problem with that?"

"There's only one problem—I don't believe you. Come on, Steven. You walked out of our lives almost two years ago, and we've barely heard from you since then. Now that your pre-midlife-crisis blonde has turned you out, all of a sudden you feel the need to fly three thousand miles and come visit unannounced? Or don't they have working cell phones in California?"

Steven leaned back on the counter and did his best to look thoughtful. "I understand why you feel that way, Ally," he said.

"Don't call me 'Ally.'" I can be petty when I have the opportunity. I'm not proud of it, but it's true.

He held up his hands, palms out. "Absolutely, *Alison*."

"And don't patronize me. You understand why I feel this way? That's big of you. *You're* the reason I feel this way. I don't trust you, I'm never going to trust you again, and I'm going to ask you one last time: Why are you here?"

The Swine bit his lower lip. "I missed Melissa. Okay? I'm a father, and I wanted to see my little girl. Is that really so far out of your experience with me that you can't believe it?"

"Why didn't you call ahead?" I figured I could poke a hole in his explanation.

"Because I thought you'd tell me not to come."

Damn. He was right.

"Okay, so I would have told you not to come. Can you

blame me? Did you see how you've disrupted her life? Can you see how she has that gleam in her eye now, that hope that Mom and Dad will get back together? How can you do that to her?"

Steven closed his eyes a moment, then took a deep breath. He looked at me. "Because maybe I have that gleam, too," he said.

Four

"That's what he said?" My best friend Jeannie Rogers, seven months pregnant and great at being astonished, was outdoing herself at the moment. "He wants to get back together with you?"

We were walking from our favorite bakery café, Stud Muffin, and heading toward the neighborhood greengrocer, Veg Out. I needed a few things for a salad I probably wasn't going to make tonight, and Jeannie wanted to get in her walking for the day, determined as she was to gain only baby weight and no Jeannie weight. Having given birth ten years earlier, I was perhaps a bit skeptical about her chances of that, but I was grateful for the company, since I needed to vent to someone, and telling my mother about Steven's return was not high on my to-do list. Luckily, Steven had taken Melissa to the boardwalk in Seaside Heights in his latest attempt to convince her that he was the good parent out of the two, so I had a good few hours (between the randomly scheduled spook shows, today to include a hideous substance—rubber cement, which rubs off easily—slithering down the walls) to do my venting.

"He didn't say those words exactly," I answered. "But he was certainly delivering that message. What do you think I should make of it?"

"What do I think?" Jeannie replied. "I think you shouldn't have let him back into the house when he showed up. I think you should boot him out before he gets a chance to hurt you again. I think you should leave him alone in a room with Tony and come back after we've had a chance to clean up."

As we crossed the street, I saw two men walking away from us into the intersection. They were semitransparent. A car passed through them. This ghost thing was getting to be routine; I barely even started at the sight, and Jeannie didn't notice my reaction at all. I was getting to be a pro, even though Mom and Melissa insisted I was capable of seeing only about 20 percent of the ghosts floating among us on a daily basis. But I thought they were just being spirit snobs.

"Let's keep your husband out of this situation, and out of jail," I suggested. I had introduced Jeannie to her husband, Tony Mandorisi, after he and I had become friends when I was working at the home-improvement superstore. Tony is a licensed contractor, and helps me out on my more difficult projects around the house. Although we were still working on finding a practical means of access to the attic.

"I just can't believe you let him back into your house," Jeannie said. Jeannie is a wonderful friend who doesn't know when to quit.

"Technically speaking, he'd never been in that house before," I pointed out. I know when to quit, but that doesn't mean I will when I should.

"Either way," Jeannie said. Don't feel bad; I don't know what it meant, either.

We probably would have gone on for a good deal of time, but we walked by the office of the *Harbor Haven Chronicle*, the local weekly newspaper, and Phyllis Coates, the owner/

publisher/editor/entire staff of the paper, opened the door and called to me.

Phyllis and I have known each other since I was a thirteen-year-old delivery girl for the *Chronicle*. She seems to think of me as her protégé, and I think of her as a good old friend. Phyllis went into the newspaper business when it still wasn't quite thought of as respectable for a woman, and has lived it on her own terms. I respect that. Also, she always knows everything that goes on before anybody else. It can get a little unnerving.

"Alison," she said now, a cup of steaming coffee in her hand and some unedited copy in the other. "I hear your ex has come back to rekindle the marriage."

See what I mean?

"He's just here to visit Melissa," I insisted before Jeannie could offer an opinion. "He's not staying, and we're not rekindling anything."

"That's not what I hear."

"Maybe you need a hearing aid," I suggested.

Phyllis laughed. "More like I have to go back and check my sources," she said. "Hey, mind if I join you two for a bit? I need to get out of the office for twenty minutes every six hours, or my doctor says I'll die of stagnation, or something."

She fell into step with us as we headed up the street.

"So what's going on in town?" Jeannie wanted to know. Jeannie is a dedicated, serious gossip, and admires Phyllis for her ability to get to the truth and her willingness to pass it along.

"The usual stuff," Phyllis answered. "Mayoral election coming up in November, so the boards are going nuts. Planning, assessors, schools—you name it. They all find stuff to talk about when the politics in town starts to heat up. Everybody thinks they're a big shot."

Jeannie looked disappointed. She prefers something a little more lurid. "No sex scandals?" she asked.

Phyllis shook her head. "It's summer, honey," she explained.

"Everybody's too busy trying to make a buck because we were smart enough to start a town near the only beaches in the country that make you pay to get on."

It's true—New Jersey's beaches often require badges for admittance, and the badges require fees. Most other shore areas in the country don't, but ours are more . . . beachy, I guess. Harbor Haven is one of the quieter towns on the beach (real New Jerseyans say "down the shore"), but if you want to swim near a lifeguard—and you should never go in without one nearby—you're going to buy a badge.

"How about some crimes?" I asked Phyllis, just to cheer Jeannie up. If she couldn't find out who was sleeping with whom, maybe Jeannie could hear about a rash of bicycle thefts or a genuine convenience store holdup. "There must be some crime."

"Nothing," Phyllis lamented. "It's gotten to the point that I'm running a story on crime outside of town. Those bones they found in Seaside Heights. Sounds like a good mystery, anyway. Apparently, somebody bashed the poor guy's head in."

Big Bob, then, was making news miles from where he was found. I told myself there was no way I was going to get involved this time. I guess, technically, Maxie was a friend, but murderers tend to be violent, unpredictable people, and I find it comforting to stay away from such types.

"Ooh!" Jeannie perked up. "What's that one all about?"

"A man named Robert Benicio was killed in Seaside Heights, probably about two years ago," I said. "Like Phyllis said, someone hit him hard in the back of the head. His body was buried in the sand, but far from the water and down deep enough that the remains weren't discovered until recently. Dental records and fingerprints confirmed his identity, and now the county prosecutor's major-crimes division is looking into the killing."

I kept walking and was suddenly aware that I was walking alone. I stopped and turned around to see Phyllis and Jeannie staring at me with the same expression on both faces—amazement.

"What?" I asked.

"Are you holding out on me?" Phyllis demanded. "You getting back into the PI business? Are you investigating this case?"

"Me? What? No!"

"Then how did you know all that?" Jeannie chimed in. Thanks a heap, Jeannie.

"I read it in the paper," I said.

"But I haven't run a story about it yet," Phyllis said. They started to walk again, more slowly, something for which I was grateful. It was getting hot out, even at only nine in the morning.

"I don't want to hurt your feelings," I told Phyllis, "but the *Chronicle* is not the only newspaper I read."

"I'm crushed," she answered.

"Don't be. It's just there are six days of the week when you don't publish."

"So what caught your eye about this case that you did so much reading?" she asked. Phyllis's reporter's mind is rarely at rest, and she never accepts the easiest answer to any question without some skepticism.

"Nothing special," I tried. "I just noticed the story on a newspaper when I was hanging some wallboard in the attic, and the headline got me." That was sort of close to the truth—it had been Maxie who'd noticed the headline, but I was *there*.

"What about it?" Phyllis probed. She'd do whatever she needed to do to improve her headlines and get more people to read them.

"Just the subject, I guess," I answered. "You know, people do just read articles casually once in a while."

"Bite your tongue."

We arrived at Veg Out, which was bustling on this July day. An open-air section (normally part of the parking lot) was devoted to the latest from local farms, and both Harbor Havenites and some vacationers—and after spending enough years in town, you knew which was which—picked through the Jersey corn and tomatoes, and even the occasional peach.

I started my quest for vegetables I'd theoretically put in a salad for dinner tonight, knowing full well that I almost never cooked and would probably end up ordering a pizza. But I'd made a New Year's resolution to reverse that trend, and it was only seven months into the year. Time to begin.

"I see watermelon," Jeannie said, and before I could suggest that lugging one around might be problematical, since she was pretty much already smuggling one under her belt, she was off to check out the possibilities.

"I guess it's just you and me," I told Phyllis.

"Sorry," she replied. "I was just out for the walk. Gotta get back to the office. Stop in sometime, and bring in Melissa. She's almost ready to start delivering papers." And she, too, vanished before I could protest. I was starting to wonder if I had properly showered that morning.

I started looking at some bunches of broccoli. That's a good vegetable—green, with vitamins and beta-carotene and things like that. High intake of broccoli is also said to lower the risk of some aggressive cancers.

See? Wikipedia is good for some stuff after all.

The problem was, I would be making a salad for just Melissa and myself, and these heads of broccoli were tied together in bunches of two, and each one was quite large. This was, in short, more broccoli than I would probably need in the next six months. But the ties were strong, and I wasn't sure that Mrs. Pak, the grocer, would mind if I removed them.

But my dilemma was eclipsed when I heard a deep voice very close to my left ear. "I have a knife," it said.

I drew in a deep breath and tried to remember if under such circumstances it was better to scream or to fall to the floor in a dead faint. Unconsciousness was definitely leading when I turned to see a man next to me. A large man.

A very large man. In a black leather biker jacket and dark sunglasses. And a mustache, which was both a little retro and a little menacing at the moment. I summoned what little voice I could find, but decided not to scream. A man with a knife could move before anyone could get to me in this crowd.

"I beg your pardon?" I squeaked. Oh, like you would have come up with something more defiant.

"I have a knife," the man repeated. He raised what looked like a very effective blade attached to a black handle. "If you want me to cut through the bands on that broccoli."

"Oh. Oh!" The idea that my life was in fact not in immediate danger was just starting to leak through to my reasoning center. "Is it okay to do that?"

The man took the broccoli from my hand, rather gently I thought, and severed the thick ties on the vegetable with what appeared to be no effort at all. "They want to sell the broccoli," he said. "Are they going to argue with a paying customer?"

"You're clearly from out of town," I told him. "Mrs. Pak is not to be reckoned with."

"Trust me," he said.

Sure enough, when I brought the newly liberated broccoli to the cash register, which Mrs. Pak herself was operating, there was absolutely no drama at all. "Two fifty," she said. I provided the cash, she provided a bag, and everyone's view of the transaction appeared to be favorable.

"Thanks for the help," I told the man, who was no longer brandishing his lethal-looking knife.

"No problem." He extended a hand. "I'm Luther Mason."

I took his hand. "Alison Kerby."

Luther nodded. "I know."

"You know?" What the hell did that mean?

"I've been following you since you left the *Chronicle* office," he said. Suddenly, my new friend seemed menacing again.

"Look, don't take this the wrong way," I said, "but you're

scaring the living daylights out of me. Why would you follow me to the greengrocer?"

Luther's eyes seemed to squint a bit behind the dark glasses. "You don't need to be scared," he said. "It's just that I heard you talking about the body they found in Seaside Heights."

That had an ominous ring to it. "So?"

"So, Big Bob was a friend of mine. We rode together."

This was coming at me too fast. "You . . . rode together?"

Luther nodded. "Yeah. On our hogs. Big Bob was in my bike club."

"I don't understand," I said.

"We rode motorcycles together," Luther said, speaking slowly as if to a relatively stable mental patient.

"No, I get that. I don't understand how that adds up to you following me."

He smiled. For a man who looked like he could tear Mount Rainier in half with his bare hands, he had a gentle smile. "It's simple," he said. "I heard your friend say that you're a private detective, and I want to hire you to find out who killed Big Bob."

I felt my bottom teeth come up to bite my upper lip. "Are you sure you wouldn't just settle for some broccoli?" I asked.

Five

In the end, I invited Luther back to my house. For one thing, I wanted Maxie to vouch for his story—I wanted to make sure she'd seen this guy before—and to hear what he had to say.

But it was all I could do to convince my seven-months-pregnant best friend that she should *not* hop on the back of a motorcycle with a man we had just met.

"It's perfectly safe," Jeannie protested. "I've done it before."

"Then you won't mind missing out on this chance," I countered. "I'm not explaining to your husband why you and your unborn baby were seen tooling down Ocean Avenue on the back of a *hog* with a stranger."

"You're no fun anymore," Jeannie pouted.

"I never really was," I said.

It was that way the whole drive back to the guesthouse. With Steven and Melissa out of the house, I could meet Luther by myself. I explained to him that the kitchen, being a sort of off-limits area for the guests, was our best place to speak privately, but I didn't notice either ghost lurking about on the way inside, which was unusual. And a little worrisome, since I had also insisted on Jeannie going home to protect her, in case my instincts about Luther turned out to be mistaken.

"You don't want me to investigate Big Bob's death," I told him as soon as we sat down and I put the broccoli in the fridge, where it looked lonely. "I'm really not a professional investigator. I just sort of got my license on a lark."

"But you have it," he answered. "You can do stuff the cops aren't going to do. Look. I knew Big Bob. I knew his ex-wife Maxie Malone, and I'd heard she bought a house in Harbor Haven. So I was going to the newspaper office to see what I could find out about Maxie when I overheard someone say you were a PI. I need a PI. It's kismet."

"It's crazy, is what it is," I countered. "You don't know me at all. I'm not a real investigator. And I'm sorry to tell you, but I knew Maxie, I was helping her fix up this house, and she died about a year and a half ago. I bought the place out of respect for her." (I'd used this line on people before, and preposterous though it sounds, given Maxie's temperament, it never failed to convince people.)

This time was no exception. Luther nodded. "I found that out this morning. When I couldn't find Maxie, I went to see her mom."

"I know Kitty," I told him. "So she must have told you that Maxie was dead. Why come all the way from her house in Avon to Harbor Haven when you knew that?"

Luther shrugged. "I don't know. It threw me. Maxie was dead—she'd been murdered, like Big Bob, and not that long after him. I started to wonder if there was a connection. The only mention I could find of Maxie's death was online, an article from the local paper here, so I came to the newspaper office to talk to the reporter, but the office was closed."

I knew there was no connection, but explaining that without mentioning that Maxie was available for corroboration would be tricky. "Maxie's murderer was caught," I told Luther. "It had nothing to do with Big Bob." Okay, maybe not so tricky.

Paul stuck his head down through the kitchen ceiling and looked confused. Glad to see him, I mouthed the name "Maxie" at him. He nodded, and vanished back up through the ceiling.

"Are you okay?" Luther asked. "Does your jaw hurt or something?"

"I had something stuck in my teeth," I told him. I had to stall just a little so Maxie and Paul could hear the whole conversation.

Mrs. Spassky stuck her head in through the swinging kitchen door. "Sorry to bother you, Alison dear," she said.

"No bother, Mrs. Spassky. Do you need something?" Keep talking until Paul and Maxie get here, okay? Nice guest.

"The name of a store where we can get salt-water taffy. My sister says you can't vacation at the beach and not bring home salt-water taffy." Mrs. Spassky's eyes rolled just a bit; she clearly thought Mrs. Fischer was being silly. Then she caught sight of Luther, and examined him closely. No doubt she was comparing him to Steven, whom she still saw as my husband.

"I know just the place," I told her. "Sweet Tooth, at the corner of Harbor Avenue and North Haven."

Mrs. Spassky gave Luther a few more ogles and nodded without making eye contact. "Thank you, dear." She left the kitchen just as Paul and Maxie appeared through the kitchen wall. Paul still had a quizzical look on his face, but Maxie stopped in what would have been her tracks if she'd been walking. Her hand went to her mouth.

"Luther," she whispered.

Luther's head turned a little, as if he'd heard his name spoken. But he just blinked, and looked back at me.

"You came here to talk to Phyllis at the *Chronicle*," I said, to distract Luther. Didn't want him thinking he might have heard a voice. "How did that lead to your looking for a detective?"

"I wasn't looking for a detective," Luther said. "It hadn't occurred to me before your friend mentioned you had a license, and then it seemed the logical thing—you have a mystery; you hire a detective."

"There are plenty in the phone book," I said. "I'll recommend one." I didn't actually know any, but I could pick a name out of the Yellow Pages as well or better than most.

"No, it has to be someone who cares. You told me before a little bit about your connection. Maxie owned this house, and now you own it. That's too huge to be a coincidence. It's magic, or luck, or Maxie's spirit, or something."

Maxie grinned at me and mouthed the word *spirit*. She clearly found that hilarious.

"It's just a coincidence," I said.

Luther shook his head. "I saw Big Bob just before he disappeared. He said he was coming here to Harbor Haven." Luther still looked a little spooked (pardon the expression), but was focusing again on my question. "Something about visiting his ex-wife."

Maxie gasped.

"Why?" I asked.

Luther nodded, and took off his dark sunglasses. His eyes were narrow, as if constantly squinting into the sun. And he was facing away from the window. "I'm not sure," he said, "but he always felt bad about the way it ended. He'd just found out Maxie was here, and he said he was going to go see her, maybe he could make things right."

Maxie was listening with an expression of incredulity. She appeared to be crying, although there were no tears falling from her eyes.

"He wanted to reconcile with his wife?" I asked. That had seemed the way Luther's story was headed.

"I don't know," he answered. "He said it was all about just making it up to her about the way they'd split, but he might have wanted to start back up again. He really loved Maxie. If you knew her, you'd understand."

"I'll bet," I said before I thought about it.

"Bet your ass," Maxie retorted, her voice scratchy.

Luther looked at me. "You don't believe me?" he asked.

Snap back, Alison. The man doesn't know Maxie's here in the room with you. "Oh, I believe you, Luther," I said. "But I'm still not the person you want investigating Big Bob's murder. The police are really good at that sort of thing."

Luther stood up, as if being burdened by the chair was now far too limiting a condition for him. "The cops don't care about some biker getting himself beat to death," he said. "To them, it's like a gang killing. One less biker to worry about. They'll pay lip service to it, stuff it in the cold case file, and nothing will ever happen. I need someone who won't give up on it."

Maxie nodded her head—yes, that was the way it would be.

"That's not me," I argued to both of them, noting that Paul, standing a foot or so off the kitchen floor in one corner and stroking his goatee, wasn't being any help. "I have to run this guesthouse. I have paying guests here."

"You've done it for people you barely knew," Maxie said quietly.

Luther didn't react to her voice this time. "Just take a look," he said. "Spend an afternoon on it. I'll pay you."

Senior Plus had booked a number of rooms during the summer, and there had been some money when a low-budget reality-TV show called *Down the Shore* had shot its second season in the house, but my guesthouse was still far from being a gold mine. I had expenses, not the least of which was my mortgage on the house. I had to save for Melissa's education. And The Swine's child-support payments were, let's say, sporadic. A paying job was not something I could turn down flat without a really good reason.

"I'm afraid of violent people," I told Luther (and by extension, Maxie). I thought that was a really good reason. "And I'm not interested in getting someone who has already killed a great big man mad at me. I don't have that kind of dedication, Luther." For some reason, Luther smiled at the words "great big man." "You don't want someone like me investigating a violent crime."

"I'm not asking you to catch them, just to find out," he argued. "It happened two years ago. Whoever did it is probably long gone. But I need to know what happened. The man was a friend of mine. A good friend. Can you understand what it's like to have someone like that just vanish?"

It probably was unfair of me to think of The Swine, but I nodded.

"Then certainly you can understand how I feel," Luther said.

"Maybe I do, but that doesn't make me the right person for the job. I'm not a great investigator, Luther; I'll tell you the truth. And if I take on this job for you, I'm more than likely to mess it up. It means too much to you to allow that. Don't ask me."

Paul, who had raised his eyebrows at the phrase "not a great investigator," shook his head and said, "You're not being fair, Alison."

Luther's voice was surprisingly gentle when he said, "But I *am* asking you. Please, Alison. Spend a day, an afternoon, and see what you can find out. If it's nothing, then it's nothing, and I'll move on. But if there's a chance I could know what happened to Big Bob, it's worth taking."

"You have to," Maxie said. She wasn't looking at me. "You just have to."

"Do I have to say it again?" I asked. "I'm afraid, okay? I don't want to do this. I've done things like it before, and I ended up terrified. I don't want that again. Please."

I walked out of the kitchen and into the den—which I had converted from a dining room to discourage any thought of food being served here—where all five of my Senior Plus Tours guests were presently gathered.

Mrs. Fischer and Mrs. Spassky were just heading out the door on their taffy expedition. Mr. and Mrs. Westen, who had insisted I call them Albert and Francie, were sitting on the sofa, reading. She had the latest Harlan Coben thriller, and he was reading *The Bridges of Madison County*. Don Petrone sat looking elegant in his blazer and long pants (and not sweating, which was remarkable even in the air-conditioning). The man should have been wearing a captain's hat.

Lucy Simone, the youngest of the current group, was out with friends from the area. She wasn't one of the Senior Plus guests—she was a native New Jerseyan who'd switched coasts after college. It was not a beach vacation for her, since the ocean wasn't exactly a novelty for someone from California. The Swine was taking up the last available room.

The five of them in the den all looked up when I walked in. I must have had a look of despair on my face, because they all appeared concerned when they saw me.

"Are you all right, dear?" Mrs. Fischer asked.

"Just fine," I said, even though I felt like I was being pressured into something I really didn't want to do. "Just trying to hold onto my convictions."

"Convictions?" Francie, a sixtyish woman with flaming-red hair reminiscent of Lucille Ball or Bozo the Clown, asked. "Are you an ex-con?"

"No, Francie," Don, who was even wearing an actual ascot in the mid-nineties weather, admonished. "Convictions, like in your principles."

I winced, anticipating a follow-up comment from Francie about the state of public schools' administration, but luckily, she remained silent. From behind me, however, I heard Maxie's voice, and it didn't sound happy.

"You won't do this for me?" she asked.

Immediately, I did a mental inventory of the guests. Everyone in the room had come via Senior Plus Tours, which meant they had come looking for ghosts. I could in fact be seen speaking to someone who wasn't visible and still stand a chance of not being considered a raving lunatic. So I turned and saw Luther in the doorway to the kitchen, looking pained. Above his head was Maxie, hovering over the kitchen door, wearing a black T-shirt with "Good to the Last Drop" emblazoned on her bust.

I couldn't talk to Maxie in front of Luther, but I could talk to Luther. "I won't do this for you," I said, looking just a little above his head. He must have thought I had some strange astigmatism.

And, of course, that was when I heard The Swine's voice from the entrance to the foyer, behind me. "Which one of us are you talking to, Alison?" he asked.

"You'd do it for anybody else, but not me?" Maxie demanded, as if there was no one else in the room. Maxie didn't much care about anyone else being in the room. She could see them, she could hear them, she could even sort of touch them, but for the most part, she ignored the guests except during the two-a-day spook shows she knew were necessary to my Senior Plus contract. "I help you out every single day with this little guesthouse of yours, and you can't do this one thing for me?"

"It's one of the ghosts," Francie piped up to Steven. "She's talking to one of the ghosts." Thanks a heap, Francie.

"Ghosts?" The Swine put on a look of absolute bafflement. Melissa, at his side with the inevitable ugly stuffed animal I'm sure Steven had "won" for her at the boardwalk (it looked kind of like a neon-orange goat), looked helplessly at me.

"Ghosts?" Luther echoed. Francie's head turned between Steven and Luther like she was watching a tennis match.

"Sure," Francie went on. "There are ghosts haunting this place. It's why I came here."

Luther did what people do when they hear there might be ghosts in the room. He looked up and scanned the ceiling. I understand it, but they're almost never there.

Melissa, meanwhile, was intent on getting her father out of the room, and if she could, I resolved to increase her allowance. "Come on, Daddy," she tried. "I want to see how the tiger looks in my room." Oh, so it was a *tiger*?

But Steven wasn't buying. "Ghosts, Alison?" he asked.

I was about to suggest we go into the kitchen to talk when Luther walked over to me and looked seriously down at my face. "You sure I can't change your mind?" he asked.

Steven's eyes widened a bit. He was getting the wrong idea. Good.

"Find someone better for you," I answered. "I'm not the right one."

"I think you are," Luther said. "And I don't plan on giving up."

The Swine's mouth dropped open.

Luther, his point made, nodded at me, turned, and left, walking right past Steven and Melissa as he did. My daughter watched him go with a strange look on her face, then looked me in the eye and asked, "Who was *that*?"

"I'll talk to you later," I told her. "Steven, can I see you in the kitchen for a moment?"

Before The Swine could respond, however, Paul rose up through the floorboards to stand directly in front of me. "We need to talk," he said. That wasn't ever a good thing. Both his look and his tone communicated some urgency, and that was even worse. Paul wasn't going to be dissuaded.

"Certainly," my ex-husband said, and started to head for the kitchen.

"Not *now*," I told him. "I meant later, at dinner tonight."

A conspiratorial twinkle appeared in my ex-husband's eyes. "You're inviting me to dinner?" he asked.

"Strictly business," I told him.

Melissa had heard Paul, and knew her father shouldn't find out about our two less-than-alive tenants, so she jumped in, a sneaky trait she did not get from my DNA. "Come on, Daddy," she reiterated. "I want you to see how the tiger looks in my room." She took Steven by the hand and led him, looking bewildered, toward the stairs.

A little late, but a small increase in allowance would be a possibility.

"Now," Paul said, as if I hadn't gotten the message the first time.

I looked at the assembled guests, whose level of intrigue ranged from rapt attention with an expression of salacious anticipation (Francie) to complete and utter disinterest (Albert).

The two sisters, in their eighties and self-assured, were watching, but discreetly, as they quietly began discussing their taffy-shopping plans. Mrs. Fischer and Mrs. Spassky had class. Don Petrone merely looked dapper and said nothing.

"I'll be in the attic if anyone needs me," I said to the room.

"Where will you be if we don't need you?" Albert asked. The man was a laff riot.

I chuckled. "That's very funny, Albert." Yeah, I'm a businesswoman.

Paul rose through the room and vanished into the ceiling. This was his subtle signal that I should get my butt up to the attic pronto. Seeing little choice, I did exactly that.

Once I made it all the way upstairs, thinking all the way that moving my daughter up this many flights might not be a great idea after all, I found both Paul and Maxie waiting to ambush me in my own attic. So I decided, having anticipated this gambit, to do a little work on the construction site at the same time. I think better when I'm doing something with my hands.

"Let's cut to the chase," I said. "I know what you're going to say, and you know what I'm going to say."

"I doubt it," Paul said.

Maxie was hovering near the window, where the light coming in made her harder to see, and she sounded uncharacteristically soft and airy, to go with her appearance. "Is there something I can get you, Alison?" she asked.

I had to squint to make sure it was really Maxie over there; she almost never called me by name.

I turned from the wall I was sizing up and looked at her. "Yeah, a house with no ghosts in it," I suggested.

Maxie didn't even pick up on the comment, which had sounded more harsh than I'd meant it. "I mean, like a bottle of water, or some sandpaper, or something?"

"Okay, what exactly is the scam you're trying to pull, Maxie?"

Her voice took on a slight edge, but it was obvious she was

trying to control it. "I'm just trying to be *accommodating*," she said.

So that was it—Maxie wanted to show off how cooperative she could be in the hope that it would inspire me to be the same. Good luck with that maneuver, but if I could get something out of it . . . "Sure, Maxie. A bottle of water sounds good. It's hot up here."

"Be right back," Maxie answered, and before I got the chance to revel in her obsequiousness, she was gone.

"Okay, what's *your* act?" I asked Paul, who still looked rather stern. He was apparently trying the opposite of Maxie's tactic. That wouldn't work, either, but it was considerably less enjoyable.

"I don't have an act. I just . . ." He stopped when Maxie reappeared through the floor. She pulled two bottles of spring water out of the pockets of her cargo pants (the ghosts can change wardrobe whenever they like, so Maxie had made sure to "put on" something in which she could conceal objects easily).

"Here ya go," she said in a voice so sprightly it sounded like she was in a commercial for floor wax. "Nice cold water. I even put on an extra show for a couple of the guests when I took them out of the fridge and flew them through the den."

"Thank you," I said. I looked back at Paul, expecting him to launch into his pitch for me to investigate Big Bob's murder, but he stood (floated) there, not saying anything and looking irritated. It was odd.

"So?" I said to him. Maxie turned and looked, too. But Paul remained silent, making strange circles with his mouth that suggested he was trying to think of the right thing to say.

Finally, he turned to Maxie and said, "Can you give us a moment alone, please?"

I was a little surprised at that, but Maxie didn't miss a beat. She stole a glance at me, seemed to decide this would ingratiate her with me, and nodded. "No problem. You know where to find me." And she disappeared into the ceiling. Maxie sits out on the roof sometimes, and on other occasions, it's absolutely anybody's guess where she goes.

I put my hand on my hip and scowled at Paul. "I thought she'd never leave," I said with a sarcastic edge.

"You weren't getting it," he protested. "I just wanted to have a word with you, and you kept avoiding me."

"You know, if you want to ask me a favor, there are better ways to get on my good side than making a scene in front of the guests." I started spreading joint compound on the seam between two pieces of wallboard.

"The first time I offered you a ring." Sly English Canadian wit. With my ex-husband downstairs and an unpredictable Maxie trying to get me to investigate a murder, that was the last thing I needed.

"We're not talking about me investigating what happened to Big Bob?" I asked.

"Of course not, although you really should do that for Maxie. No, I want to get back to what we were talking about before." Paul grunted and floated over to where I stood, the better to look me in the eye. "I was trying to ask before if you would help me find someone."

Once the seam is filled with compound, there's a trick you can use: Get a damp (not wet!) sponge and lightly run it over the edges of compound, smoothing as you go. This will save you tons of sanding later. "Find someone?" I asked Paul. "Can't you just send out a Ghostogram or whatever it is you do?"

"This is someone who's still alive," Paul said quietly.

I turned to look at him. His face, always serious, was bordering on sad. "Who are we talking about?" I asked.

"The woman I was going to marry," Paul answered.

I actually stopped smoothing the joint compound and turned to look at Paul, but he had moved so close to me that I was immediately startled. "You were engaged?" I asked.

"Well, I was going to ask her," he said. "Just before I took the job guarding Maxie, I bought the ring I showed you, and once the assignment was over, I was going to ask. I was carrying it around in my pocket for days. And, well, you know what happened." Paul and Maxie had been murdered his second day on the job as her bodyguard, something Maxie rarely let Paul forget. This raised the stakes on his pain a good deal, I thought.

"Why didn't you ever say anything before?" I asked. "I told you I'd get in touch with anyone you wanted, to let them know you were . . . the way you are. You didn't even want me to contact your brother in Canada."

Paul's gaze was so intense it was hard to look at him long. But going back to spreading joint compound seemed sort of rude now, like I'd be insinuating his problem was trivial. He closed his eyes a moment, which helped in an odd way.

"At first, I thought it was best to try to forget her," Paul said. He turned his face away from me. "I figured I was gone and she needed to move on with her life, and I should do my best to stay out of it. That seemed like the thing to do."

"So what changed your mind?"

"It's just short of two years since all this happened," he answered. "And things have changed, surely. I'm accustomed to my current state of being; I've accepted that there is no returning. But there's something that feels . . . unfinished about the way I left Julia. Like I hurt her unnecessarily."

I didn't understand that. "It's not your fault you died," I told Paul.

"I know." There was something in his voice. It sounded like Maxie had before, when she'd found out that Big Bob had died.

My ex-husband was downstairs. Maxie's had been found buried under the sand in Seaside Heights. Paul wanted to locate his ex-girlfriend. It was "Revisit Your Failed Relationship Week" at 123 Seafront Avenue. No doubt Mrs. Fischer and Mrs. Spassky would soon be visited by boyfriends they'd dumped in 1956.

"When you're alive, the idea that you need closure in a relationship seems normal," Paul went on. "People understand that they need to make peace with what has happened and continue their lives. But what happened to Maxie and me . . . It takes a while to absorb exactly how permanent it all is. And now, I just want to know that she's all right. I want to see if she's moved on."

"Will you be able to handle it if she has?" I asked.

"I'd like to think so," he said. "It might be harder on me if she hasn't."

The seam between the two pieces of wallboard was going to be smooth. I might have to do a touch of sanding when everything was dry, but not much. And that was good, because I hate sanding.

"Okay, I'll try to find your . . . Julia for you," I told Paul.

He lowered his head. "Thank you."

"It's what friends do for each other," I said.

Paul turned back to face me. His eyes didn't look any different than they usually did, and his semitransparent appearance didn't allow for tons of color to come through, so I didn't know if they were red. But he looked like he'd been through an emotional ringer. He coughed theatrically, and looked me in the eye.

"If you do it for me, you're going to have to do it for Maxie, too," he said.

"I know."

Six

"I don't know if you've noticed, but I work in Harbor Haven."
Detective Lieutenant Anita McElone (rhymes with *macaroni*)
sat behind her immaculate desk in the squad room of the Harbor Haven Police Department, which is to say the entire
department minus the chief's office. Even on a Sunday morning, she was all business. "This is a murder that took place in
Seaside Heights. Why would I know anything about it?"

"Because you're a detective, and you have a natural curiosity about something that happened so close to home," I told
her. "You'd know about it because you get the dispatches from
the county prosecutor's major-crimes division, probably in an
e-mail on your desktop right now. And I'm figuring you'd
know about it because, well, you're the only cop I know. How
am I doing so far?"

McElone and I have an unusual relationship. I respect her
professionally, and she thinks I'm a lunatic. So far, it's been a
workable enough arrangement, but it has had some hairy

moments. We don't talk about those much. In fact, we don't talk about anything much if we can help it. But my private-investigator's license had gotten me in the door, and I figured if I was going to look into Big Bob's death, talking to an actual cop might not be a bad place to start.

"You have a client on this, or is that little B and B of yours not keeping you busy enough?" McElone likes to prod me, because she knows my guesthouse is not a bed and breakfast. I don't serve breakfast, though I do provide coffee and directions to a local diner that gives my guests a discount. It's win-win, really. No one wants to eat my cooking. Even the broccoli I bought yesterday and then totally ignored was well on its way to becoming compost.

I was ready with a true answer, for once. "I have a client. Luther Mason, a friend of the deceased, wants me to find out what happened to Big Bob." I'd called Luther and told him I'd changed my mind about the investigation, and he had agreed to (hell, he'd practically rejoiced over) paying me my "usual fee." As if I had a usual fee. My first official client had been a ghost.

McElone raised an eyebrow. "Big Bob?"

"The victim, Robert Benicio. He and Luther used to ride together."

The eyebrow came down, and the eyelids dropped to half mast. "They used to ride together," she repeated slowly.

"On their hogs," I said.

I think the detective actually chuckled a bit. "So, out of the entire world of private detectives, an old biker pal of the victim decided to come to the owner of an adorable Victorian on the beach to find out who murdered his pal?"

Well, that wasn't very nice. "Yeah," I said defiantly, or at least petulantly, pushing aside my own doubts. "You got a problem with that?"

McElone ignored the question. "So how come ol' Luther decided you're the PI for him?"

"How come you're the one asking all the questions?"

"Hey, I get paid whether I talk to you or not. I've got a B

and E right here on my desk I could be looking into right now." McElone was such a ham that she actually leaned back and laced her fingers behind her head. "So are you going to explain yourself, or am I going to try to find out who busted into an expensive house during tourist season and stole only a DVD player? Not even Blu-Ray?"

I groaned, more inwardly than audibly, I like to think. "What was the question?"

"What made Big Bob's biker buddy decide to pick your name out of the Yellow Pages?"

"He said he overheard a conversation between me and Phyllis Coates about my investigator's license, and thought I'd be the right person for the job," I told her. "He said it was kismet."

"Uh-huh."

"What do you mean, 'uh-huh'?"

"Let's say a friend of yours disappeared one day, and then resurfaced, literally, in Seaside Heights two years later with a great big bash in the back of the head. You hear some ladies on the street talking, and one of them says she has a PI license. Is that how you'd pick a person to discover the culprit and lay your friend's memory to rest?" McElone's point was not lost on me; I'd been asking myself the same question since Luther had approached me at the greengrocer. Which reminded me to make a mental note to do something with that broccoli tonight.

"All right, there's more, but you're not going to like it," I told her. I was being completely honest with the lieutenant. The next part of the story was not going to be her favorite.

McElone could see it coming; her eyes took on a feral quality, and she sat back in her chair as if pushed. "This isn't going to be another one of your ghost stories, is it?" she asked quietly.

I nodded. "I'm afraid so. See, Big Bob was married—very briefly—to Maxie Malone. Now you'll remember—"

She cut me off. "Maxine Malone was the woman who owned the Victorian immediately before you. The one you said showed up in your house as a ghost and told you she was murdered."

"Well, you arrested the killer, didn't you? After the department had filed the two deaths away as suicides for a year." I'll admit it; that was designed just a little to get under McElone's skin.

"You know that happened before I got here," she said. Good. It had worked.

"Well, Maxie and Big Bob had a quick Vegas wedding— and got divorced a couple of days later. But Luther said that just before he disappeared," I told her, "Big Bob had been planning to come to Harbor Haven to find Maxie, maybe reconcile with her. That's why Luther said he came here, to see if he could find out something about Maxie's death."

McElone, in full cop mode now, was already tapping something out on her computer keyboard, no doubt calling up the file on Maxie's and Paul's murders, or the dispatch she'd gotten from the county on Big Bob's. "You don't think the same killer who got Malone and—what was it, Harrison?—also killed Big Bob, do you?"

"No, of course not."

I couldn't see McElone's computer screen, but she seemed very intent on it. "Well, the county doesn't have much on your pal Big Bob. In fact, he barely registers as having existed." She gave me a significant look. "I don't suppose the ghost of his ex-wife told you what happened?" That was sarcasm— McElone doesn't believe in the spirits in my house, and if I were her, I wouldn't believe in them, either. But she's seen enough at my guesthouse to know unusual things go on there. Or as she often puts it, "Your place is freaky."

"No, Maxie doesn't know what happened," I reported. "She hadn't heard from Big Bob for a while before they both died."

"Uh-huh," the lieutenant repeated.

"Is there anything the county told you that can help? Anything that wasn't in the papers?" I asked.

"There isn't much," McElone admitted. "You have to keep in mind this is a two-year-old case, and nobody's been looking for him for quite some time."

"And he was a biker," I said, remembering what Luther had told me.

McElone looked up sharply. "What is that supposed to mean?" she asked.

"Luther said the cops weren't going to care too much about one dead biker. They'd figure it was just some random violence between two transients who wouldn't be missed."

She scowled. "*Luther* is wrong," she said. "The county cops and the Seaside Heights cops are both going over this thing with a fine-toothed comb. They can't help it if nobody found the body for two years. There's been complete decomposition; there's been all sorts of environmental factors; there's been enough time for the killer to move to Mars if he felt like it. The police aren't indifferent, and we don't choose which crimes we investigate, but the body's been there two years."

I had gotten the very reaction I'd been hoping for, so I decided to use it. "And I'll bet that when Big Bob disappeared two years ago, a code-red alert went out, and the state police were mobilized to search, right?"

Now, I have received many a dismissive look from Lieutenant McElone in the short time I've known her. But this one clearly took the Dismissive Derby. "Maybe they would have," she said, "if somebody had reported him missing."

That didn't add up. "Nobody filed a missing-persons report on Bob Benicio two years ago?" I asked.

McElone shook her head. "Nobody. The only reason they were able to identify him was because he'd been busted for possession four years prior to his death, and there were fingerprints and dental records on file from when he'd been in the service. So if your pal Luther was so concerned about his close personal friend, how come he never bothered to tell the cops that someone was missing?"

That was a good question. I'd have to ask Luther tonight when he came by for a progress report. And dinner.

Seven

"Who's this guy Luther, and why is he coming to dinner?" Steven wanted to know. "I thought we could make it just us and Melissa."

"It's touching that you're jealous, Steven, but Luther is a client, and he's coming by for a progress report on the case I'm investigating for him." I had decided that since there would be company for dinner, it was a poor choice for me to cook, so I was searching through the take-out menus I keep in a kitchen drawer, hoping to be inspired to make the appropriate phone call.

"A client." The Swine rolled his eyes. "And how is it you became a . . . what? A private eye? And never told me?"

"Our divorce settlement doesn't require my telling you when I start a new business," I told him. "No more than you had to tell me when you got dumped by the dye job."

"I didn't get . . ." He looked exasperated. "That's not what we're talking about. But a private investigator? *You*?"

"Me. You want to see the license again?"

"It just doesn't make sense." That had been the point he'd been making for fifteen minutes now.

"A lot of things don't make sense. For example, you believing that everything on your girlfriend is the original equipment doesn't make sense. But the bottom line is: I have the license, I need the money, and I take on clients. Luther is one of them." I left out the part about him being my first flesh-and-blood client.

After leaving McElone's office, I had spent a little while searching through the phone book (it's a big paper thing, children, that has the names and phone numbers of all the people who live in your town) for Julia MacKenzie, the apparent love of Paul's life, who had been living in the area when Paul and Maxie died. She was not listed, and a call to Information (it's this number you can call to . . . Never mind) showed no phone number, listed or not, under that name. Yeah, I'm old school.

Twenty years ago, that might have been definitive proof that Julia had left the area, but in an age when people give up their landlines entirely for cell-phone service, it meant a grand total of nothing. And since she could have been listed with any of at least twelve possible service providers in New Jersey, my PI license was going to get me bubkes in tracking down Julia's phone number.

I would have to ask Paul more about his almost-fiancée, which, given his emotional outburst the last time we'd discussed it, was not an exciting prospect.

"Fine," my ex answered, "you go ahead and pretend you're Nancy Drew, but we haven't yet sat down as a family for a meal since I've been back."

"That's because we're *not* a family anymore," I reminded him. "We're a single mom and her daughter, and you're the guy who left. We've spent a long time and done a lot of hard work to accept that. You don't get to change it because the dye job you were dating decided to trade you in for a newer model." I didn't know that was what had happened, but pay-back, despite the common expression, can be quite enjoyable.

"Amee does not dye her hair," The Swine said. Was that the best he could do? "But I realize you're still sore about my leaving. That's my fault, and I get that. I could apologize from now until the end of time, and it wouldn't change anything. All I want is for you to accept that I really am sorry, and whether or not that makes a difference to you, it's the truth." Okay, so that *hadn't* been the best he could do.

I rejected the usual pizza place and the Chinese takeout because we always use those, and Melissa wasn't a big fan of Chinese, although that started to change when she discovered the power of the lo mein noodle. Was I actually looking for something special because Luther was coming for dinner? I'd have to stop and think about that at some point. I probably should have asked him what kind of food he liked, too. Well, he hadn't asked what we'd be eating. I decided that gave me free rein.

"I believe you're sorry," I told Steven. "But that doesn't make us a family again."

He was about to answer when the kitchen door swung open. "Who's not a family?" I heard from the doorway.

My mother stopped dead in her tracks at the sight of her ex-son-in-law standing next to me by the kitchen sink. You have to understand: Mom has believed that everything I've done in my life—absolutely *everything*—has been brilliant, beyond question, always amazing, never anything less than genius.

Except marrying The Swine.

Although Mom hadn't ever expressed disapproval of my marriage—that's just not her style—she had never told me what a wonderful choice I'd made or how Steven was exactly the son-in-law she'd always wanted. From Mom, that was close to being a declaration of war.

Steven had done his best to charm both my parents, and had failed miserably in both cases. It should be noted that my father had not held back the way Mom did, and frequently referred to my husband as a "bum," despite the fact that Steven was (very) gainfully employed doing some financial thing I didn't understand pretty much the whole time we were married. Dad, gone five years now, had not valued a man based on his checking-account balance.

"Steven," my mother said now, her voice dropping almost to the kind of gasp you hear in horror movies when a person realizes she's in the same room as a psychopathic killer.

"Loretta!" The Swine gushed, walking to Mom and spreading his arms for a hug, which my mother stood still for, but did not reciprocate. "It's been such a long time!"

"Yeah," Mom said. She waited until he ended the embrace, then walked toward me, taking off the little backpack she uses in lieu of a real purse. She put it down on the table, eyeing me with questions the whole time. "How long have you been back?" she asked Steven.

"Since the day before yesterday," The Swine admitted, thereby ratting me out as a daughter who doesn't keep her mother sufficiently informed. Granted, he had no idea I hadn't told Mom, but that didn't mean I couldn't blame him for her disappointment in me.

"It's been *really busy* since then," I jumped in. "Haven't had a minute to myself, honestly."

"I'll bet," Mom said. "So what brings you back, Steven?"

My ex smiled his most convincing smile—he almost had me fooled, even—and told Mom all about how he had just wanted to reconnect with his family and see his little girl again. She smiled throughout his spiel, nodding occasionally, and did not so much as glance in my direction, giving The Swine her full attention.

He stopped, finally, to take a breath after this dissertation on the power of family ties and lost chances, and Mom said, "No, really. Why are you here?"

The Swine shook his head a little and used Smile Number Forty-Two, the sad and misunderstood one I'd seen quite often during the last year we were married. "I can see you're just as hard to convince as your daughter, Loretta. Well, I'll have to work twice as hard to win your trust, just like Alison's. But you'll see; the old Steven is gone forever. The man you see before you is the new Steven. I'm a changed person."

Mom turned to me without missing a beat and asked, "What's for dinner?"

In the end—after a short lecture from Mom about inviting people over for takeout—we decided on Thai food for the evening. The small talk after I called in our order was excruciating, as Steven was desperate to show off what a wonderful father he was (anybody can be good at something he only has to do every couple of years), so he called Melissa down. She, also wanting to present her dad in a positive light, was on behavior so impeccable I strongly considered the possibility that aliens had stolen my daughter and replaced her with a cyborg replica programmed for good manners. I wasn't complaining, but it was odd. Then she remembered a computer game she hadn't finished in her room and went back upstairs, saying she'd only be a minute. It had been a lovely show.

Every once in a while, Paul would stick his head into the room, but he scowled whenever he saw The Swine, and retreated before I could acknowledge his presence. Mom, who can both see and hear more ghosts than I can, knew better than to speak to him with Steven in the room, anyway.

Luther arrived before the delivery guy, and introductions were made all around. We went out into the den, where only Mrs. Fischer and Mrs. Spassky were sitting, the other guests no doubt in town to find some supper.

"I haven't found out much yet," I told my client. "Big Bob was dead almost two years, and nobody ever even reported him missing to the cops." I let the question go unasked.

Luther answered it anyway, as I'd hoped he would. "At first, we figured Big Bob had just gone off to find his wife, and maybe they were getting back together." On cue, Maxie rose up from the basement and floated into the center of the room, where she could get the best view of Luther. "By the time anybody started looking for him, not only was Big Bob still missing, but Maxie was nowhere to be found. Turned out she was here in this house, but none of the guys knew it. And now I hear she died just a few months after Big Bob. It's a lot to take in."

"Tell him," Maxie said forcefully. "You tell him what really happened."

I had intended to do so anyway, so I filled Luther in on the real story behind Maxie's and Paul's deaths (though I left out the part about their afterlives, because frankly I didn't see any value in telling Luther about that, and I didn't want Steven to know either) and the investigation that ensued after I took over the house. To his credit, The Swine did wince at the proper times in the narrative, and at one point commented that I should have called him, despite the fact that the voice answering his telephone probably would have been considerably higher pitched.

Luther listened carefully, asked the occasional question, and lowered his head while thinking, as if the weight of the thoughts made it harder to hold it up. When I finished the story, he said, "I wish I'd known that then."

"Nobody knew it then," I assured him. "Even the police didn't know. This all happened less than a year ago."

"It's fascinating!" Mrs. Spassky piped up from the sofa. "What an exciting story!" I hadn't intended for them to hear it, but at least my guests were enjoying themselves, and that's what a good hostess wants, isn't it?

Steven, his eyes agog, seemed incapable of speech. He stared at me for a good thirty seconds without speaking, which was probably a new record for him.

There was a knock at the front door, and before I could move, Melissa appeared at the top of the stairs and launched herself down to reach the door first. It is this way whenever food is present. I'm not sure how she does it (although her bedroom window *does* face the street), but it doesn't make much difference, since I'm still the one who has to pay the delivery guy.

We retreated once again to the kitchen, where Mom had been busy setting the table—*somebody* in this family had manners, as it turned out—and began passing various containers around.

"Is there anything without meat?" Luther asked. "I forgot to mention I'm a vegetarian."

Luckily, there was some pad see ew puck, which I'd gotten simply to have the thick rice noodles Melissa and I favor. Yeah, I'm loading my kid up on carbs. Call the nutrition police. I passed it to Luther.

"I'm sorry I didn't think to ask," I told him.

He waved a hand. "Not important," he said. "It doesn't really fit the rest of the image, I guess. Bikers are supposed to hunt and eat venison, right?" He chuckled to himself.

"You're not a biker all the time, are you?" Steven asked. "How do you make a living?"

"I work at a bike shop," Luther told him. "It's what I know best."

Maxie was unusually silent, watching Luther from her perch near the cereal cabinet. She was wearing a T-shirt bearing the legend "More Than You Think" and an expression of something very much resembling wistful sadness.

She never took her eyes off Luther.

We ate in relative silence for a while, asking for items to be passed and discussing the food itself. Then Luther asked me what the next step in the investigation might be. I looked toward the oven, where Paul was "sitting."

"You need to make contact with the Seaside Heights police or the county unit," Paul said. "And see if you can get a copy of the medical examiner's report."

I passed that on to Luther as if it was my own idea, adding that I might be able to get some of the ME's information through Phyllis at the *Chronicle*, who had a special "friend" in that office from whom she got certain news leaks in exchange for . . . activities it was better for me not to think about.

"What do you think you'll find out?" Melissa asked.

I shrugged. "Can't say. You ask questions. When you get the answers, then you know what you'll find out." Paul nodded proudly—I was an apt pupil.

The Swine shook his head as if to wake up from a bad dream. "A private detective," he mumbled. I ignored him, something I was very good at doing

"So tell me about this Big Bob," Mom said. She believes in understanding the essence of a person if you're going to be involved in his life (or death, as it were). "What was he like, Luther?" But she was looking at Maxie when she said it.

Luther sat back from his dinner, which he had eaten politely but without gusto. He got a faraway look in his eye and smiled a little. "Bob was a funny guy," he said.

"He would always do the opposite of what you expected," Maxie said.

"He didn't tell jokes or anything," Luther continued, "but you just laughed a lot when he was around."

"I almost never saw him in a bad mood," Maxie put in. "I didn't know him for long, but he always seemed to be happy. He liked his life."

Luther, not hearing his friend's ex-wife, overlapped her a bit. "Big Bob. It was a funny name for him. He probably didn't stand taller than five eight. But he had a larger-than-life personality. I'll bet he gave himself the nickname just to make people smile."

"Did he work at the bike shop, too?" Steven wanted to know. He was apparently fixated on everyone's profession. Maybe he wanted to decide what to be when he grew up and was looking for choices.

Luther shook his head. "Big Bob was a short-order cook at a stand on the boardwalk. Took pride in it, too. You asked for your burger well done, and you got it well done."

"He had really nice eyes," Maxie said, her voice sounding

even more distant than usual. "I mean, seriously, even when I married him, I was never in love with Big Bob, but I first noticed his eyes. Big, brown, with lots of emotion in them. There was always something going on behind them that he'd only tell you if he knew you well enough."

"It sounds like he was a really nice man," Melissa said. A ten-year-old can cut through the babbling of adults to get to the heart of the matter.

At the exact same moment, Maxie and Luther said, "He was."

Damn. Now I was actually starting to care about finding out what had happened to Big Bob Benicio (and try saying *that* three times fast). I hadn't planned on that.

Luther left not long after that, and Mom left not long after Luther. I could tell Steven was desperate for whatever bogus family burlesque he'd decided would melt my heart, and, naturally, I was intent on not letting him have it. But before I could deal with that, I had to talk privately with Paul. I gave him a special look as we left the kitchen, as The Swine was saying, "Let's just sit in the living room and talk."

"It's the den," I corrected him. "And in a minute. I'll be right back." I headed for the downstairs front powder room, which was luckily unoccupied at the time.

Once inside, I latched the door and waited. But nothing happened. For a full minute at least. "Paul?" I mumbled. Usually, he can zone in on my voice and respond. This time, I got nothing.

"Paul," I said a little more adamantly.

His face barely came up through the floorboards. His eyes were closed, for some reason. "What?"

"Come in. I need to talk to you."

"Alison," he said, "you're in the loo." Don't you love Briticisms?

"I came in here so I could talk to you," I told him. "I'm not *doing* anything."

"Oh." Paul opened his eyes and rose up, very slowly,

through the floor, stopping just at eye level to be sure he wasn't about to see something he shouldn't. When it was evident he would not, he came all the way into the room.

But he still wouldn't look at me, despite my being fully dressed and simply standing in the bathroom. Paul is easy to embarrass. Almost so easy that it's no longer any fun.

"What is it you wanted to discuss?" he asked, showing an unusual interest in the ceramic tile I'd installed as a backsplash.

"Julia MacKenzie," I said. I watched him for a reaction, and I got one. He forgot his excruciating discomfort and looked at me.

"Have you found her?" he asked.

"Not yet. In fact, there's no one listed in the phone book under that name. Now, that doesn't mean much, but I need to know more about her in order to have an idea of how to pursue this." I sat down on the only logical place to sit. Luckily, the cover was down.

"If I were you, I'd—" Paul began, but I held up a hand.

"I'm doing this for you," I told him. "It's a favor for a friend. I'd like you to see that I can do it myself. Now, if you could just tell me about Julia, I'll see a direction in which I can go."

Paul smiled. "It's a very sweet gesture, Alison," he said. "But—"

"Please."

He nodded. "All right. Julia is thirty-one, about five-foot-seven, has chestnut hair that falls to her shoulders, and brown eyes. She favors blue jeans and work shirts most of the time, and loves to watch American football on weekends."

"She sounds like someone *I* should marry," I said, forgetting the context.

Paul didn't react. "She works, or worked, in the offices of the cable-television company CableCom, in Freehold. That's how we met." He chuckled. "I was exchanging my cable modem for a newer model."

There was a knock on the door, and I heard Francie's voice from the hallway. "Is someone in there?" she asked.

"I'll be right out," I said, then lowered my voice to talk to Paul.

"Where was she living when you knew her?" I asked.

"What?" Francie called.

"I'll be out in a minute!" I shouted.

"In Gilford Park," Paul answered. "I'll get Maxie to write the address out for you." Maxie's skills with physical objects are better than Paul's, and fine-motor-skills tasks like writing are still difficult for him.

"You didn't have to yell," Francie complained.

"Sorry!"

"She was going to quit her job with CableCom after she got her master's degree from Monmouth University at nights and online," Paul continued quickly, realizing I couldn't stall Francie forever. "She was less than halfway through when I . . . back then." Paul still doesn't like to mention that he's no longer alive.

"Okay," I said. "That's somewhere to start. I'll talk to you later." I stood up and opened the door as Paul dropped back through the floor.

Francie stood there waiting, despite there being three other bathrooms in the house, including another on this floor. She gave me an odd look as I got out of her way.

"Were you talking to someone in there?" she asked.

"Do you see anyone in there?" I countered.

"No," Francie admitted.

"Then I guess I wasn't," I said, and walked away as fast as I could.

Mrs. Fischer and Mrs. Spassky had vacated the area, and I assumed they had gone upstairs to bed. I caught a glimpse of Albert waiting for Francie in the doorway of the game room at the other end of the hallway. Waiting for me in the living room were Melissa and Steven, looking like they were awaiting the results of an especially tight election in which someone they knew well was a candidate. Their faces were unusually tight, with identical thin smiles (I'd never realized that Liss had inherited her father's mouth) and slightly widened eyes. They were standing oddly close to each other, side by side, next to the sofa, like soldiers awaiting inspection by a general.

Oh, yeah. The Swine's big family moment. I'd already forgotten during the three minutes I'd spent out of his company. Maybe that should have told me something.

"We've been waiting for you," my loving daughter whined.

"Don't get mad at Mom," my ex admonished her, albeit gently. "She's here now." He was trying so hard; it would be fun to disappoint him in whatever odd gambit this might be.

"We have a surprise!" Melissa said, taking his cue to brighten up. "Daddy got it."

Uh-oh. From what I could tell, given the fact that his bill with my guesthouse had been spread over three credit cards, The Swine's discretionary income was not exactly at its highest point ever. Since the Wall Street bust in 2008, he'd been treading water, just barely. And yet, he never was able to resist spending on . . . anything he wanted. Although it had not been much of an issue when he was earning generously in his brokerage job, that did not appear to be the case now.

"What did you do?" I asked him.

"Such a tone!" he admonished. "This is a gift, Alison. Just relax. I wanted—*we* wanted—for the three of us to have a fun family evening. So I splurged just a tiny bit as a way of saying thank you for letting me back into your lives."

"I'm not letting you back into—"

"Mom," my daughter cut me off. At least, she *looked* like my daughter. She was acting more and more like Steven's daughter, and I was a little peeved at how quickly that change had taken place.

But having standoffs with her father in front of Melissa wasn't going to help my case, so I did my best to relax my facial muscles and let out a breath. "Sorry. So. What's this fun surprise I've been hearing so much about?"

Grinning like a couple of hyenas, each of them took a step to the side and put out their hands like a pair of spokesmodels showing off the latest model of sports car. "Ta-DA!" they sang. And they pointed toward an object on the floor.

It was a small black box sitting in front of a stool. And on the stool, connected to the box by a wire, was a microphone. It looked like . . . Oh no, it couldn't be.

"It's a karaoke machine," Steven said.

It was.

I'd never even been to a karaoke bar in my life, I was running a guesthouse in which people ranging in age up to eighty-six were staying, and my ex-husband—with the collaboration of my only child—was trying to get me to sing easy-listening hits into an amplifier. Surely the man was deranged.

But I had to be delicate in my reaction. Bringing Melissa in on this little ploy raised the stakes—I couldn't destroy Steven with my withering sarcasm for fear of wounding my little girl as collateral damage.

"It's . . . charming," I said finally, forcing a weak smile. "Did you keep the receipt?"

Melissa didn't react, but Steven's grin twisted into something a touch more sardonic. "Give it a chance, Ally," he said. "It's something we can all do together."

"Yeah, come on, Mom!" Melissa urged. "It's fun, and you get to choose the song you want to do." She leaned over to the machine and pushed a button.

Steven grinned at the machine as if he'd given it life all by himself. "It does everything," he said. "It carries hundreds of songs, shows you the lyrics, and even has a record function if you want to keep your performance, or sing harmony with yourself."

So that's what they were calling it these days.

To be fair (which took effort), they had spent some time planning this, since the machine went directly to a particular favorite of mine, "Bad Moon Rising," by Creedence Clearwater Revival. And a flat-screen television, left mounted on a crossbeam after the *Down the Shore* crew had evacuated (with an ominous reference to coming back for another season sometime), flashed to life with the lyrics to the song—as if I would need a prompter for that one.

"Let's hear you, Mom," Melissa said, holding the microphone out for me to take. The sound system suddenly began playing an intro to the song (although it was clearly *not* the original CCR arrangement).

"Oh, all right," I said, taking the mic from her hand and rolling my eyes just a bit, "but just this one." And as I passed Steven to take my rightful place at the center of attention, I muttered to him, "I told you not to call me 'Ally' anymore." His eyes registered hurt, but he nodded.

Seventeen songs later, when Melissa finally managed to pry the microphone out of my hand, we had been joined by all the week's guests except Mrs. Spassky, who, according to Mrs. Fischer, "you couldn't wake up with a jackhammer and a brass band." Even Lucy Simone, who had come in from her night out in Red Bank, applauded when I finished my rendition of "Bad, Bad Leroy Brown."

I took a quick bow and handed the mic over to Melissa, who looked relieved and launched into "Say Hey (I Love You)," by Michael Franti and Spearhead. As I walked back into the "crowd," a little abashed by my own lack of inhibition, Steven sidled up to me near the easy chair.

"See? Not such a bad thing," he said, pointing at how Melissa was holding the audience in the palm of her hand.

"She's a natural," I answered.

"I didn't mean Melissa," my ex said. "I meant spending a little time together just having fun as a family."

"A family of Mom, Dad, their daughter and several senior citizens?"

"It takes a village, Alison," Steven said.

I didn't answer for a while as I sorted out my emotions. "You know I wish I could believe that," I told Steven. Before he could protest, I added, "All I can say is that you never showed this much interest in being Melissa's father until your silicone-enhanced friend showed you the door."

"She's not . . . No. I'm not letting you take me there. Alison, did you know that I've been texting with Melissa at least twice a day for the last year?"

My daughter was just hitting the part in the song where she says that her momma told her "don't lose you / 'cause the best luck I had was you." And I absorbed what my ex-husband had just told me. "She never said anything to me," I told him.

"That's because she's afraid you'd insist she have no contact with me," he answered.

My mouth dropped open. "You know I would *never*—"

"I know," Steven assured me. "But she's ten. And she wants so badly for us to be all together again. Don't we owe it to her to at least try?"

I felt the trap springing around me again. But this time, I shook it off. "Not yet," I told him. "I don't trust you yet. I've spent a long time convincing myself that what happened with us wasn't my fault, Steven. I don't want to look back at this moment someday and think, 'That's where I made my mistake.'"

Melissa ended her song and took a bow, bending her leg behind her like a pro. She held out the microphone and said loudly, "Who's next?"

"You got any Tony Bennett on there?" Mrs. Fischer asked.

"Who's Tony Bennett?" Melissa asked, and there was a groan among some of the older inhabitants of the room. "I'm sorry."

"Don't be, honey," Mrs. Fischer said, looking right in my direction. "It's not *your* fault."

"I'll take the next turn," Steven called, and he bounded over to where Melissa was holding out the mic. He took it from her hand like, well, Tony Bennett jumping on stage and launched into a version of "Stormy Weather." The crowd, especially Lucy, were immediately taken by his charm. I was a little more practiced than that.

Melissa stood to one side of the area between the sofas, which had become the stage section of the room, and beamed at Steven. Maybe she really *did* want us to be a family again, but then, most children of divorce hope for that, according to the therapist I was seeing right after The Swine left for Los Angeles.

Mrs. Fischer wandered over to me as Steven charmed the crowd more with his attitude than any actual semblance of talent. She smiled a motherly smile at me and nodded her head in his direction.

"That's quite a guy you used to be married to," she said.

"Yes," I agreed. "I just wish I knew what he was up to."

Eight

"I haven't been able to find out anything about Robert Benicio," Phyllis Coates said.

I'd gotten up especially early the next morning (and I get up early every morning, so this was *early*) to visit the *Harbor Haven Chronicle* office, still bleary from the late-night karaoke festival (it had gone on until nearly eleven o'clock!), because Phyllis (who's at her desk every day at six) knows everybody on the Jersey Shore and isn't the least bit concerned about sharing information, especially if she thinks there's a good story in it. And if we could get something on Big Bob's murder, well, that would be perfect for the *Chronicle*.

"Nothing on the autopsy?" I asked.

"Well, the county cops aren't exactly making it a priority," she answered. "So far, it looks like a blow to the back of the head with a heavy object like a hammer or a vase or something. And it doesn't sound like Big Bob was the vase type."

"Don't assume," I told her. "I had a vegetarian biker over for dinner last night."

Phyllis looked interested all of a sudden. "Oh really?" she said. "Going through your 'dangerous man' phase?"

I waved a hand. "Hardly. I told you about Luther. He's my client, the one who wants me to find out about Big Bob's murder."

It's so unattractive when a person smirks. Phyllis was being quite unattractive.

"What's that face supposed to mean?" I asked.

"What face? This is my regular face."

"Uh-huh." I decided to move on. Phyllis, after all, was now a valuable source of information; it was time to utilize her. "You ever heard of a Julia MacKenzie?" I asked her.

She stopped and seemed to think for a long moment, then shook her head. "That one's not ringing any bells," she said.

Damn!

"But you know everybody."

Phyllis smiled and put her hand on my shoulder. "I hate to have to tell you this, sweetie, but I'm not infallible."

"All right then, you're a good reporter and—"

She cut me off. "I'm a *great* reporter."

"You'll get no argument from me. So lend me your expertise—I'm looking for a woman who used to live in Gilford Park. Worked for CableCom and was working on a master's degree at Monmouth. She doesn't appear to have had an address, and she doesn't have a phone number, at least not a landline, listed or unlisted. What's my best bet?"

Phyllis scrutinized me closely. "What do you think your best bet is?" she asked. Sometimes talking with Phyllis can be like talking to a therapist. They're supposed to help you, but all they do is make you come up with the answer yourself. It's really annoying.

"I was thinking I'd go to Monmouth University, spread my alumna status around, and see if I could find some student records."

Phyllis applauded quietly. "I have taught you well."

"You haven't taught me at all."

"That's what you think," she said. "But keep in mind that the university will probably consider all student records confidential, since they are, and won't want to tell you anything. What's your recourse then?" She had the temerity to look amused.

"Um . . . I can flash my private-investigator's license?"

Phyllis's mouth flattened out in disappointment. "Yeah, that and a couple of bucks will get you on a bus to Atlantic Highlands. What else ya got?"

"I could turn on the charm. Flirt a little."

She looked me up and down. "When did you become Angelina Jolie? Besides, suppose the clerk you encounter is a heterosexual woman or a gay man?"

"All right, Master Yoda. What's your best strategy for such situations?"

Phyllis took a moment to consider. "I think maybe you need to figure this one out for yourself," she said.

I had never considered frustration a physical sensation before. "Phyllis! This is no time for an object lesson! Help me! I can't ask—"

"You can't ask whom?" Phyllis said.

"I can't ask you any nicer than that," I said by way of recovery. To have told Phyllis that I couldn't ask Paul this time would have raised questions about my house, my ghosts and my sanity. Phyllis and I have not discussed the ghost issue at 123 Seafront. She doesn't like taking things on faith, and I don't like her thinking I'm completely out of my mind. It's a win-win.

She chewed her lower lip for a moment. "I'll tell you this: People always like to help when they think it's about *them*."

When they think it's about them? How could I make finding Julia MacKenzie's student records about the person in charge of student records? Had Phyllis been taking classes in how to be inscrutable?

"That doesn't help," I told her.

"Yes, it does. Think about it."

"That does it. Cancel my subscription to the *Chronicle*." I headed for the door.

"No," she said as I walked out.

The clerk at the provost's office of Monmouth University was, in fact, a petite African American woman in her late twenties, who looked like she had received her baccalaureate degree from that institution roughly a half hour before I showed up to ask about Julia MacKenzie.

"May I see some ID, please?" she asked when I requested Julia's student records.

I produced my PI license from the tote bag I use as a purse, and handed it over to the clerk. She looked at it very closely.

"Are you Ms. MacKenzie?" she asked. The woman was wearing a name tag that read "Miss Sharp," which I could only assume was an ironic comment. I momentarily considered telling her I was in fact Julia MacKenzie, but I couldn't imagine she'd believe I changed my name to Alison Kerby for professional reasons.

"No, I'm not. I'm conducting an investigation, and I need to contact Ms. MacKenzie. She's not in any trouble, or anything; I promise." I widened my eyes just a bit to look more innocent and trustworthy.

Miss Sharp did her best to look sad. "I'm so sorry," she said. "I'm not allowed to give out that kind of information except to the person herself."

I couldn't think of anything to do, so I didn't do anything. I just stood there. It was sad, to tell the truth. I'd had the whole trip over here to come up with a strategy, and I had nothing.

"I really need that address," I said. Yeah, that was going to work.

"I'm so sorry," Miss Sharp repeated.

I stood there for a while longer.

"Really," I urged.

"Sorry," she answered.

I had to think of something before we got down to the single syllables "re" and "sor," but nothing was coming to mind. Finally, I considered what Phyllis had said—make this about Miss Sharp, not about me. Hey, at this point, I'd have given bribery some serious thought if I had any money.

"Miss Sharp," I began.

"Megan," she offered. That was good. It personalized the exchange.

"Megan," I said. "How long have you been out of college?"

"Me? Six years." Wow. She looked younger.

"Did you go to Monmouth?" I asked her.

Megan smiled and shook her head. "No. I went to Brookdale." The community college of Monmouth County.

"No kidding! So did I!" Okay, so that was an out-and-out lie, but this wasn't about me—it was about *Megan*. "I know what that's like," I said.

"Yeah, but you were probably, like, twenty years ahead of me," she said. More like ten, but I wasn't in a position to press the point right now.

"Can I ask you a question?" I said, ignoring the fact that what I had just said was in fact a question itself. I leaned a little over the counter in an attempt to make Megan feel I was sharing something confidential. "Have you ever done something stupid because of a guy?"

Her lips sputtered. "*Have* I!" she said. "There was this one time I shoplifted a pack of Twinkies just because my boyfriend forgot his wallet in the car. Then I look up, and there's this *security video camera* right over my head! I almost had a heart attack!"

"Oh, I know that one," I concurred, despite the fact that I had never so much as considered stealing anything in my life. "I smuggled a Swiss Army knife onto a plane once for my husband, just so he could open a can of beer with the opener." Okay, so that was a complete fabrication, but The Swine had once asked me to sneak an extra large bottle of conditioner in my carry-on, and it had been confiscated by TSA guards.

"Wow. Guys can be real jerks." I was pretty sure I had Megan where I wanted her.

"So, listen," I said, practically whispering, despite there being no one else in the room. "I took this job just because my husband—ex-husband now—got himself into trouble and needs to find this Julia MacKenzie because she's a perfect match for his bone marrow. And if I don't find her right away . . ."

"No kidding!" Megan, despite the holes in that story through which one could fly the starship *Enterprise*, seemed genuinely concerned. "You're doing this even though he's not your husband anymore?"

"I wouldn't want my little son to lose his daddy," I said, changing Melissa's gender out of a strong sense of superstition. "What happened between us wasn't Timmy's fault, was it?"

"Of *course* not!" Megan gushed. "But the rules say I can't give you that information."

Bureaucratic functionaries are exasperating, but predictable because they always tell you the rules have to be followed, no matter how stupid those rules might be. Luckily, they are generally so bound to the letter of the law that you can get around them with just a quick flick of civil disobedience so long as it appears to fall inside the lines. Or did that metaphor just get tangled up?

Observe: "Well, suppose you *don't* give me the information," I suggested. "Suppose you call up the information on your screen, and then you take, let's say, a two-minute break."

"A break?" Miss Sharp was slower on the uptake than a one-armed drummer.

"Sure. Go in the back and get yourself a cup of coffee. Powder your nose. Find your purse and take a piece of chewing gum out of it. Just for a minute, no longer than that."

Had there been an independently powered lightbulb in the area, it would have illuminated over her head at that moment. "Oh!" she squealed. "I get it!" She punched a few keys on her computer keyboard, with the screen facing away from me, and waited for the proper data to appear. Then she looked back at me, winked, and in a voice too exaggerated for a third-grade pageant about Patrick Henry, said, "Well, I think I'll just get myself a cup of coffee. Don't look at that screen, now!"

"Oh, I won't," I promised.

Megan Sharp leaned over the counter and hissed at me, "I really meant that you should, you know."

I nodded. "I know."

She smiled and exited through the door behind her, stopping to wink one more time.

Sighing heavily, I pulled myself up onto the counter and into a sitting position. From there, I could reach Megan's computer screen, and turn it so it could be read. It took me perhaps thirty seconds to copy down the contact information for Julia MacKenzie on a notepad I had in my tote bag, turn the screen back, and hop down off the counter.

I left the office before Megan returned, and only on the way out did I notice the security video camera over the door.

It appeared to be unplugged. If only the place had sold Twinkies.

Nine

I tried the phone number listed for Julia MacKenzie immediately, and found that it had been disconnected. This was not terribly surprising, seeing as how it was obtained through records that were at least two years old. But the residence address in Gilford Park would take me about forty minutes to reach, so would have to be left until the next day. I had to be back at the house for the pre-lunch spook show (Paul was adding a guitar played by an invisible ghost today, in addition to the usual flying objects and "spooky" noises made by Maxie with an old hacksaw I'd found in the basement). I knew I could count on Paul to perform for the guests in my absence, but Maxie was somewhat more . . . mercurial in her moods.

Besides, I had to form a plan to investigate Big Bob's murder, and on that, at least, I could consult the other licensed (if somewhat deceased) private detective in the house.

I got back to the guesthouse at about ten. That left roughly an hour before the next "performance," which was enough time to talk to Paul about a Big Bob plan and perhaps visit with my daughter, whom I had not seen outside the company of her father for days now, except when she was working at her "summer job," which was cleaning some of the guest rooms and sweeping off the front porch, for which she was paid ten dollars an hour, far too high a price. But I was the idiot who'd negotiated the deal, so I couldn't complain.

As if she knew my wishes, Melissa was on the front porch when I pulled up in my prehistoric Volvo wagon, cranky in the summer weather so alien to its native Sweden. That was one reason it had no air conditioner, so I was fairly well drenched in sweat by the time I stopped the car and extricated myself from the driver's seat.

I had hung a glider on the front porch, because that's what you do in front of an enormous Victorian built to look especially inviting during the warm-weather months. I had never seen one of the guests so much as consider sitting on the glider, but in theory, it was a good idea. Melissa sat on it now, not exactly swinging but making sure it stayed vaguely in motion.

"What's up, cookie?" I said by way of greeting. Okay, so I was being more chipper than usual, but I was locked in a battle for the soul of my child, and all bets were off.

"Hi, Mom." A voice that could race molasses and lose. The ten-year-old version of a subtle signal she was feeling sort of down.

"What's the matter?" I asked, sitting next to her on the glider but keeping my feet off the floor so it could continue to glide. "Did you just remember that school is a mere seven weeks away?"

"No, but thanks for the reminder."

"Come on, spill. It's the middle of the summer, you have your friends around and time on your hands, yet you're sitting here looking like someone ran over your pet wildebeest. So what's the problem?"

It was going to be something Swine-related, I knew. And I would have to take great pains to react without anger. Melissa was testing me—Steven was the magical parent who would grant all wishes and never disagree, casting me as the evil witch who forced people to eat broccoli (I would *have* to do something with that broccoli tonight!) and refused to make things exactly the way they used to be, mostly because I actually *remembered* the way things used to be.

"Why did you marry Dad?" she asked me.

That caught me a little off balance. I'd expected something more on the order of, "Why don't you love Daddy anymore?" Maybe this was going to lead up to that, because I had a really good answer all ready to go.

I had to improvise a bit on this one, though. "I loved him," I said. "And he seemed to love me. I was sort of knocking around in my life, I couldn't decide what I wanted, and he seemed like the only thing that was making me happy."

But Melissa was already shaking her head; no, that wasn't what she wanted to hear. "What was it about him that made you want to marry him?" she asked.

"What's this about really?" I countered.

"Answer the question." The world will be deprived of a great prosecuting attorney if this child decides to forgo law school.

"What made me fall in love with your dad? Is that what you're asking?" Melissa nodded, so I went on. "Well, when he wants to, he can be awfully charming. And in those days, he wanted to. Funny, concerned, interested, warm—he was all that. And he was going to work to help people do better in life. He was going to set up really inexpensive investments for people who didn't have much money, so maybe they could have it a little easier. He used to believe in stuff like that."

Melissa nodded, small movements of her head, as if taking an inventory of what I'd said. Maybe she was having a hard time picturing her parents as a couple of idealistic kids just starting out in life.

"Why don't you feel like that now?" she asked. Ah, the question I'd been waiting for.

"Things changed," I said. "Your dad changed. So did I. I wanted to come here and start this guesthouse, and he—"

"He wanted to go to California with Amee," my daughter said, her eyes daring me to treat her like a little child who wouldn't understand such things.

"Yes," I said, biting my lip just a little. "That was the end of it, but it wasn't the whole reason. He started getting caught up in making money, and that made him different. I had you, and that made *me* different. I wasn't interested in the life he wanted, and he didn't have time for the one I wanted. Before we got to the point where we hated each other, we figured it was best to split up."

Again, there was the little nod of her head. She was absorbing. Maybe she'd think it over later and come back with more questions. I couldn't decide whether that would be a good thing or a bad thing.

"That's very interesting," Melissa said. She stood up and started toward the front door. I grabbed hold of her arm as she passed me, and gave her a hug.

"Very interesting?" I asked. "Are you studying us for anthropology class?"

"What's anthropology?"

"Don't worry. You'll find out in college."

She walked back into the house, her eyes a little dreamy. This injection of her father into her life again might have been exciting, but it couldn't be easy for her, and I wasn't sure what to do about it. On the one hand, I felt like things had been a good deal simpler for both of us before Steven had come back. On the other . . . Well, it had been a long time since Liss had a dad. I couldn't deny her that.

And as for any prospect of Steven becoming a permanent fixture in our lives again, he was going to have to do it from somewhere else within a week. Today was Monday. A week from today this crew of guests was going to be gone, and a new Senior Plus Tour was scheduled two days later, with every bed in every room of the house booked. My ex-husband would have to find himself somewhere else to live if he wanted to stay in New Jersey.

Added to my list of things to do: Talk to Steven about his residency plans.

But first there was the spook show, along with strategizing about the Big Bob case. I'd decided to call it "the Big Bob case" to sound more private-eye-like. And it required my attention, which meant it required Paul's attention. I went inside to find him, and to enjoy my very expensive air-conditioning.

Before I could get to Paul, though, I decided to check in on the guests. I didn't want to think—whether it was true or not—that I was neglecting them to concentrate on the investigations.

I toured the house briefly: Nobody was in the game room, which made me wonder why I'd bothered to get the pool table a new felt top. Very few guests ever used it, although my daughter was threatening to become the next Minnesota Fats. Maybe the space would be better suited to something else. I didn't have a license to serve alcoholic beverages; otherwise, the oak-paneled, Tiffany-lamped room would have made a lovely bar, but that was far too expensive to even consider. Yes, I had cold beer and chilled wine in the room, but I did not charge for the drinks, and I made sure no one under twenty-one (not that I ever *got* a guest that young) could have access to them. Melissa and best-friend Wendy or anyone else who dropped by after school would *never* have access. Liss knew that Paul and Maxie were watching when I wasn't around, and she wasn't interested, anyway.

I already had a construction project upstairs to worry about, so the game room would remain a game room for the foreseeable future. I walked into the hallway and toward the library, a former walk-in pantry that had been turned into a sitting room by the family who lived here for decades before Maxie bought the place. I'd lined the walls with bookshelves and filled them with more than two thousand volumes, ranging from classics to the latest mass-market paperback mysteries.

Lucy Simone was sitting there now, reading a book of Emily Dickinson poetry. She looked up and smiled when I appeared in the doorway.

"What's up?" I asked. "Not out enjoying the heat?"

"I'm waiting for my friends to pick me up—they're out renting jet skis," she answered. "They have this idea for the afternoon. You know how you could always do something when you're home and you never do, but once you're on vacation, it becomes a priority? It's sort of like that." Wow—Lucy really was a lot younger than my usual guests. She looked tentative, suddenly, as if she wanted to ask me something but didn't know how.

"Something I can help you with?" I asked.

Lucy licked her lips. "Yeah. I guess. Look, I don't know how to say this, exactly, but I think I saw something a little odd not too long ago."

Something odd in my guesthouse. Who would have expected that?

"Odd?" I asked, as if everything around here was always completely normal.

"I was sitting here reading, maybe twenty minutes ago," she said. "And I would swear I saw something fly by the door."

This is a problem when some of the guests in the house aren't aware of the, let's say, special nature of the house. We'd been varying the times of the "spook shows" for when Lucy was out, and that was one of the reasons I was doing a check of the house now. But it wasn't like I hadn't anticipated this question coming up. The trick was to limit the damage as much as possible.

All I had to do was raise possibilities and let her decide which one to believe.

"You saw something fly by the door," I said calmly, sounding like I didn't want her to think she was crazy. "What did you think you saw go by? Could it have been a leaf, or even just a change in the light from the foyer?"

"It was a laptop computer," Lucy said.

Okay, this was going to be a little trickier than I might have anticipated. "A laptop computer?" I repeated, giving myself time to think.

"Yeah. A MacBook. A real old one." Yep, that was my laptop all right. Maxie must have been taking it upstairs to get on the Internet. She spends a lot of time on the Internet, and since her computer was confiscated by the police when she was murdered, I magnanimously allowed her to use mine. She, of course, never failed to let me know how old and out of date it was, but since I was the one who'd have to pay for a newer model, she'd just have to get by. It was an object too large for her to conceal in her clothing, the only way the ghosts can move physical objects around without them being seen. Maxie did not wear loose-fitting clothing.

"You sure?" I asked. Maybe I could plant a seed of doubt in Lucy's mind.

She nodded confidently. "I work at the Apple Store in San Diego. And I can tell you, I haven't sold one of those in years."

"No, I meant are you sure you saw one fly by? Maybe you were thinking about work and thought you saw something."

Lucy shook her head. "I saw it, all right. It was really strange, like someone was carrying it. It bounced up and down, like the person was taking steps."

That was weird in itself, since Maxie and Paul generally glide, not walk, around the house.

"Oh, *that*," I improvised. If I could convince her it was something normal . . .

"Oh, that?" Lucy asked. "Does that happen a lot?"

"Sure," I assured her. "What you saw wasn't a laptop computer, not a real one, anyway."

"It wasn't?" Lucy, although a sophisticated person, was at least as stupid as I was, and as proof, I offer the fact that she thought The Swine was absolutely dreamy.

I waved a hand. "Nah. Melissa was playing a trick on you." I made a mental note to inform Melissa that she had played a trick on Lucy. "I gave her my old laptop when it died a year or so ago, and she likes to take things apart. She gutted it, put the case back together, and she puts it on wires. Pretends it's walking around the house. She actually has an old broom handle she uses to make it look like it's bouncing up the stairs."

Lucy regarded me carefully for a very long moment. Then she smiled broadly. "Of course!" she said. "I *thought* I saw a wire holding it up!"

Sure she did! "She actually uses fishing line," I said. "It's very thin but very strong."

Lucy laughed, now in on the joke. "She's such a smart girl!" she exclaimed.

"Yes," I exhaled. That was the only part of this whole exchange that was true, so it was somehow comforting to agree with it.

"She must get it from her father. He's so clever!"

I said good-bye to Lucy and walked out into the den.

Mrs. Fischer and Mrs. Spassky were out in town somewhere, no doubt shopping for more mementos of their shore vacation. That left Don Petrone, Francie and Albert as the spectators for the upcoming spook spectacle. *Spooktacle? Make note of that for future brochure to Senior Plus.*

And I had to make sure The Swine wasn't in the house when the fun began.

All I needed was for Steven to find out about the ghosts. Either he'd think I was crazy and sue for custody of Melissa, or he'd try to find an angle to exploit my two squatters for financial gain. Technically, I was doing that, but I was a benevolent dictator; Steven would not be above advertising on network TV to come and see the ghosts in Harbor Haven, New Jersey.

Okay, maybe I had kind of done that, too, when I'd allowed the reality show to film here—but ultimately it hadn't even brought me that much publicity, since McElone had prevailed upon me to seek an injunction prohibiting the production company from using some of the spookier footage they'd shot. The lieutenant felt that it would "compromise any future investigation" into the incident. Trent Avalon, the executive producer of *Down the Shore*, had argued, but lost. He thought it was my idea, and although he said he might want to bring the show back to the house when they shot their next season, he was not a happy camper leaving behind "the best sweeps-month footage we've ever gotten."

I wasn't so sure I wanted them back, frankly.

I found my ex-husband in the backyard, which was still in a state of recovery from the *Down the Shore* television filming experience: While the show was shooting, enormous double-wide trailers had been parked here for weeks while tanned and brash young "TV stars" tried to be spontaneous on cue. It had wreaked havoc with my lawn. The production company had done its best to restore the area to its original state, but right after they left, the hot weather arrived, the rain stopped and we were shortly on drought alert. I had to stop watering, and there was still a certain amount of regrowth that had not yet taken place, even with normal rainfall returning.

Steven was standing in the hot sun, wearing cargo shorts and a T-shirt with a picture of the Beatles on it, along with a straw hat he told me would keep his face from getting sunburned without having to "smear chemicals all over my skin." Living in California, where they know how to deal with both the sun and a fear of chemicals, had changed my ex, and I wasn't sure whether it was in a good way or not.

My mission here was to cook up some errand for Steven to perform that would take him away from the house long enough that he'd miss the ghostly goings-on scheduled for the pre-lunch performance. The trick was to get him to leave without Melissa, since she was gearing up for her "amazing flying girl" section of the aforementioned goings-on, something she insisted on doing at least once a week. It consisted of Paul or Maxie (I usually insisted on Maxie, who could hold physical objects more securely) lifting Liss up at the top of the stairs and then "flying" her down and through the house while she pretended to be horrified, something no guest had ever believed, given the ecstatic expression on my daughter's face as she levitated her way through the house. The giggling didn't help the illusion much, either.

"What are you up to?" I asked him.

Steven, enjoying his "contemplative moment" pose, pretended to be startled by my voice. "Oh, Alison! I didn't see you there!" he lied. "I was just doing some thinking."

That was rarely a good thing. "Thinking about what?"

"I've made a lot of wrong turns in my life," he said with a wistful tone I came close to believing. "Maybe I should have gone for that doctorate you wanted me to get. Maybe I gave up too early on the idea of investment services for people with less disposable income." He turned toward me to make "significant" eye contact. "Maybe I should never have left Melissa and you for California."

Okay, so it was a crock, but reacting with hostility wasn't going to get him out of the house when I needed him gone. "You think so?" I asked, matching him pose for pose. "You weren't happy out there with Amee?" And I would like it noted that I almost said "Barbie" but caught myself at the last second.

He wrinkled his brow, turning specifically toward the sun so he could squint more effectively. Man, he was good. "I *thought* I was, but since I've come home, it's occurring to me that I was just fooling myself. I think this is where I belong."

"No kidding." All right, so I was vamping; I didn't know where to go with that.

Steven grunted a little, a sign that he was becoming even more philosophical. "I don't like who I am out there," he said. "I like who I am here. With you and Melissa."

I would have to take an hour or two later—probably while not sleeping tonight—and ruminate on why I should believe anything this man said. But he sounded so sincere, so truly lost, that I found myself sympathizing.

Then I hardened. No time for this now—I had to get him out of the house.

"You really want to help me?" I asked.

Steven turned and smiled like a golden retriever seeing a stick about to be thrown. "Absolutely! What do you need? Help in your investigation?" *That* was new.

"I need you to go to the Home Improvement Mart and pick up some things for Liss's new room," I said. "Can I give you a list?"

This obviously was not the intimate, husband-and-wife kind of thing my ex had been hoping for, but I was opening the door for him to do something I could at least theoretically consider a favor. Maybe I'd be beholden to him later on (more likely not, but there was no reason for *him* to know that).

He jumped at the opportunity and was gone ten minutes later, in my poor overworked Volvo. Wiping my brow both from heat and relief, I went upstairs to the attic, where I knew Maxie would be lurking. Luckily, Paul was there, too, since he was the one I'd really been looking for anyway.

"I was hoping to find you here," I told him. "I don't know what to do about Big Bob."

"What do you mean, you don't know what to do?" Maxie asked. "Find out who killed him."

"Thanks for the help. And by the way, don't go flying my laptop past one of the civilians anymore, okay?"

She scowled at me. "How am I supposed to know which ones know we're there and which ones don't?"

"The ones who look stupefied to see a MacBook zooming by the door of the library generally don't," I pointed out. "Just hide it under your shirt."

"It makes me look weird," Maxie said.

I avoided mentioning that she *was* weird. "Nobody can see you."

"Big Bob," Paul reminded us. "Where are we in the investigation?"

"Nowhere," I said. "All the ME says is that he got hit in the back of the head. The crime scene could be anywhere, because Bob was probably moved from somewhere else, unless he was buried right where he stood. Plus, it was all two years ago. We don't know what he was doing or why anybody would want him dead. Honestly, Paul, I have no idea what to do next."

Paul stroked his goatee, making him look strangely like a muscular, translucent professor of fine arts. "You've gotten all your information secondhand," he said. "We need something more immediate, something you can experience yourself."

"What does that mean?" I asked. "Unless you have blueprints for a time machine or tickets for 'Big Bob—the Ride,' I don't see how I can experience any of this firsthand."

He smiled on one side of his mouth. "Yes, you do," he said.

Oh, this wasn't going to be good. "I can't," I answered him. "I don't know anybody—"

"You know Luther," Maxie broke in. "You know me. I can help you. The first thing is to do something about the way you dress."

"Paul . . ." I attempted.

"I'm sorry," he answered. "This is one time that I'll have to go with Maxie's judgment."

That was the last thing I wanted to hear.

"First," Maxie said, "get me a piece of paper and a pen. You're going to have to borrow some of my clothes."

Nope, I was wrong. *That* was the last thing I wanted to hear.

Ten

"You know, you're really not the same size as Maxie was."

Kitty Malone, Maxie's mother, read the note her daughter had sent with me (sealed, so I couldn't see it beforehand) and, without questioning it, had led me to a room upstairs in her house that clearly had once been Maxie's. The room, like the rest of Kitty's incredibly immaculate house, was neat as a pin, but it was very Maxie—you'd have thought a heavy-metal band had lived there with a Renaissance Faire convention, the push-pull between outrageous and gorgeous was so strong.

We were standing there, next to a closet with sliding doors, and Kitty was holding various articles of clothing up on hangers next to me, trying to gauge whether I could wear them.

"I really didn't think I was," I replied. I knew exactly which areas of my figure were either larger or smaller than on Maxie, and I was coming away with body-image issues. "It's okay with me if none of this stuff will work."

Kitty shook her head. "Oh no," she said. "Maxie's note

says she wants me to find you clothes of hers to wear, and I'm going to find them. It's really the least I can do, after all she's been through."

Not long after I'd taken possession of the house, I had contacted Kitty with the news that her daughter, though still deceased, was within reach, and could communicate with her. Kitty had been naturally skeptical, but after a while, she'd come by and been convinced. She can't see or hear Maxie, but they communicate in writing and on the computer screen, and seem to have actually improved their relationship. Kitty comes by every week or so to "see" her daughter, and I often hear laughter coming from the room where the two of them have their Bizarro World chats.

"I'm not sure this is a good idea," I said, attempting to put an end to this embarrassing process. I didn't want to dress like Maxie, and I was starting to resent the implication that I should.

Kitty held up a short—no, *really* short—black leather skirt and narrowed her eyes. "This one might work," she said.

"Oh, I sincerely doubt it," I said, but Kitty was already taking it off the hanger.

Having observed Maxie all these months, I could recognize some of the clothing coming out of that closet, and that was eerie enough in itself. But being in this room, which Maxie had clearly decorated herself, with its blood-red walls and a Viking helmet over the doorway (how did she make this stuff *work*?), was somehow considerably creepier than living in a house with two actual, certifiable ghosts. Don't ask me.

"Let's see," Kitty said.

I stood there for a moment.

"Come on," she reiterated.

Unable to come up with a decent argument against it, I took off the paint-stained jeans I was wearing and took the mosh-pit-ready garment from Kitty's hand. She nodded after I'd wriggled uncomfortably into the skirt. "I can let a couple of stitches out of that, and you'll think you were born in it," she said, eyeing me with the practiced eye of a master seamstress—despite the fact that she had been, I was told, the speech and language expert for the Lavallette school system for more than twenty years before retiring and opening a private consulting business.

"I don't know," I said, holding my breath. "I'm pretty sure I was born in my skin, and this is tighter than that."

Kitty laughed. "Don't worry. By the time I get through with it, you'll be able to walk *and* breathe at the same time."

"Bet you a dollar I won't," I told her.

It took another forty minutes, but eventually Kitty managed to (literally) talk me into the skirt, a pair of black leather pants (if anything, more embarrassing than the skirt), and a couple of T-shirts that would have seriously bared Maxie's midriff and just covered mine. There was also plenty of silver jewelry and various accoutrements, each guaranteed to make me feel horrified and self-conscious until I could get home and into what I laughingly referred to as my "wardrobe."

Once the pain of the assessments and fittings had passed, we went to Kitty's ridiculously neat sewing room. Honestly, I believe that if a single thread was misplaced, Kitty would have burned the entire house down and started again. The woman was *neat*. She began the undoubtedly arduous task of making Maxie's style fit my body, and I sat in a cushy chair next to the window.

"What's all this about, anyway?" Kitty asked. She had not questioned the idea of doing as Maxie had asked, and had seemed wholly uninterested in the need behind it until now.

I had hoped to get out of the house without discussing it, because I wasn't sure what kind of reaction I'd get, but there was no reason to lie. "Well, I suppose you've heard about what happened to Bob Benicio," I began.

Kitty's face closed. She kept working on the clothing, but her voice was no longer expressive and warm as it had been just a moment before. "That swine," she said.

It had a familiar ring.

"Did you know him well?" I asked.

"I only met him once or twice, and those friends of his." She rolled her eyes. "I usually liked Maxie's friends, but not those . . . Except Luther. I always felt there was a gentle soul in that boy."

"I heard he came to see you a few days ago," I said, recalling Luther's story.

"Yes. He didn't know . . . about Maxie. And he seemed really devastated by the news. I wished I could have told him she was still, well, around. But of course I couldn't."

"I know the feeling," I agreed.

"Luther was the one I wished Maxie had taken up with, out of that crowd." Kitty scowled. Really. "Not the one she did," she added.

"I take it you were no fan of Big Bob's," I said.

"You could say that," Kitty said, "if you wanted to be polite. The fact is, I hated him with all my heart."

Hate? I could see that she would have thought Big Bob inappropriate for her daughter, that she would have been seriously angry with the way Maxie said Big Bob had treated her. But hate? That didn't seem to be Kitty's style. "Really?" I said.

"Really," Kitty acknowledged, her mouth now small and pinched. I was surprised she could force sound out through it in its current configuration. "Did you know he hit Maxie? Gave her a giant bruise on the right side of her jaw? Did she tell you that, or did she leave out that little detail?"

"No, she told me about it," I told her, in the unusual position of defending Maxie to her mother. "But she still had feelings for him, I guess. And when she heard how he died . . ." My voice trailed off.

"I don't care how he died," Kitty spat out. "All I can tell you is that I'm glad he's dead. If I'd had the kind of nerve I wish I had, I would have killed him myself."

Eleven

"She actually said she wished she'd killed Big Bob?" Luther Mason asked. "She was that mad at him?"

We were driving in my Volvo wagon because I don't sit on the back of a motorcycle (especially in *this* get-up), holding on for dear life against a guy, unless I at least get dinner and maybe some flowers first. I'm an old-fashioned kind of girl, I guess. It was still hot and humid, and the Volvo had amazingly not grown an air conditioner, so we both had our windows wide open, pretending that was going to do some good.

"Well, you saw her a few days ago. How did she react when you mentioned Big Bob?"

"I *didn't* mention Big Bob," Luther told me. "I knew how she used to feel about him, and I figured she knew he was dead because it had been in all the papers. But I get your point. She really didn't like him."

"She didn't *mean* she would kill him," I said, defending Maxie's mother. "Big Bob hit her daughter, and that was all

Kitty needed to know." The thought of it, frankly, was pretty powerful in my mind's eye as well. Melissa was only ten, but if any future boyfriend of hers ever thought he could get away with something like that . . .

Let's just say I understood where Kitty was coming from.

"It only happened once," Luther said.

"That's one more time than it should," I told him, and we were quiet for a while.

There wasn't much traffic on this part of Route 35, but it was, after all, New Jersey, and it was the shore during the summer, so there was still *some* traffic. There always is. I was always dismayed at the proliferation of fast-food places and ATM machines along this route these days. When I was growing up, much of this area was still underdeveloped, at least by Jersey standards. Now you couldn't swing a baseball bat without hitting a drive-through.

After about ten minutes, Luther broke the silence. "Are you sure this is what you want to do tonight?"

I gave some thought to the minuscule black leather skirt and somewhat, um, restrictive T-shirt I had on, and said, "Why, is the Moscow Ballet in town? Because I sure am dressed for that."

Luther grinned and shook his head. "You look . . . fine. I just don't want you going in there thinking that you're entering enemy territory. These are people just like you and me, and they're here to meet and have a good time. That's all. This is not the Hells Angels with the Rolling Stones at Altamont."

"Wow, you're schooled in rock history—I'm impressed," I said, and the big surprise was that I meant it.

"I'm just saying, these people didn't just touch down from Mars. They're not hostile to you, and you shouldn't be hostile to them. It's just that a good number of us like to ride motorcycles. That's the only difference."

"I'll try to stay on my best behavior," I said.

Following Luther's directions, I pulled into the parking lot at the Sprocket, made up to look as much like a log cabin as possible. There were plenty of motorcycles in the parking lot, but pickup trucks were well represented, too, and there were some older cars and a few newer ones in attendance. Nothing from Lexus, Mercedes-Benz or BMW, so my Volvo wagon didn't feel especially intimidated as I maneuvered it into a parking space and turned off the engine. I took a deep breath.

"One last chance to back out," Luther reminded me. He took a good look at my outfit. "We could go to a really dark restaurant instead."

"No. If I'm going to find out what happened to Big Bob, I have to gain some trust among the people who knew him. These are the people who knew him, right?"

The grin returned. "Yeah. That's who these people are."

The Sprocket was divided into two large rooms: In the main bar, where there were tables and some TVs, all tuned to sporting events (mostly NASCAR races), there was loud music playing. A small stage was set on one side, but no band was playing at the moment; the music was piped in through massive speakers hung from the ceiling.

There was a corridor, which had doors to the restrooms (marked "Guys" and "Not Guys"), and that linked to a second, smaller room bearing a sign that read "Gear Box," in which there were two pool tables, a few actual working pinball machines, and a bowling machine (the kind where you rolled a little puck over mechanical sensors that determined which of the pins—really lightweight plastic faces in the shape of bowling pins—were "knocked down").

The people, I noted, were dressed mostly in jeans (some cutoff jeans on the women) and T-shirts, none of which bore slogans. Mine (Maxie's, on loan) had lettering that read "Oh yeah?"

There were no World War I helmets, no chain mail belts (besides the one I was wearing) and no toothpicks in mouths. Maybe Luther had a point when he'd suggested I was thinking of bikers as an alien race.

After a quick tour of the place, during which at least six

people shouted hello to Luther and at least as many eyed me up and down as if trying to figure out how I'd slipped past security, we came to rest at the main bar, where I asked Luther to order for me, as long as it was beer. He—surprisingly—went with a ginger ale, saying that he might have to drive home if I got drunk. Which I found both kind of sweet and kind of insulting.

We had been standing there perhaps twenty seconds when one of the men who had waved to Luther from across the room approached us and nodded his head at me in greeting. He was one of the older bikers in the room, probably in his late fifties, with gray hair and a face that had clearly been out in the sun for a good portion of its adult life. He said his name was Rocco Palenty, which sounded to me like a name a nineteen-forties screenwriter would make up for a prizefighter or a racetrack tout. It fit him.

"Didn't realize you were doing business with the working girls these days," Rocco told Luther, with what could only be described as a twinkle in his eye.

"Easy," Luther warned him. "She's a friend of Maxie's. Helped her with that house she was fixing up. Remember? Big Bob told us what Maxie was doing just before he disappeared?" That was the story I'd told Luther—that I hadn't just happened into the house, but that I'd known Maxie and was helping her with the improvements on the house, then bought it after she was killed.

Rocco's face immediately became serious, and he lowered his head. "My apologies," he said to me. "I was just joking with Luther. I should have realized; that's the kind of thing Maxie used to wear when she first showed up here."

I began to feel a Maxie trap spring around me. "When she *first showed up*?" I asked.

Luther nodded thoughtfully. "Yeah, that's true. When Maxie first started coming around, even before she was with Big Bob, she wore that kind of outfit. You know, that's what she thought bikers were like. It didn't take her very long to realize she was dealing with a Hollywood stereotype, and she looked pretty normal after a little while. So I guess you're a lot like Maxie."

Grrrrr . . .

But that didn't mean I couldn't dig for a little ammunition while I was here. "What was Maxie like in those days?" I asked Luther and Rocco.

Luther looked at me a little strangely. "Didn't you know her then? It wasn't long before she died."

"Well, I get the feeling she was one way when I knew her and another when she was with you guys and Big Bob. Tell me—it's really all I have left of her." I would have thrown in a poignant catch in my voice, but the music was too loud for it to have been detected.

Rocco actually scratched his head in thought. "You know, she was kind of funny in the beginning, acting like it was some sort of strange culture and she was . . . What's that woman's name ran around with the Samoans all that time?"

"Margaret Mead," Luther volunteered.

"That's right." Rocco pointed a finger at him to acknowledge it. "But you know, having come out of design school only a few years before, Maxie just didn't have this kind of lifestyle in her head yet."

Wait a second. "Maxie went to design school? Like, college?" It had never occurred to me. Maxie seemed like the polar opposite of a person who would actually have continued her education after high school.

The slit-eyed scrutiny I got made me realize I wasn't exactly convincing in the role of Maxie's friend, but it would have been difficult—if not impossible—to explain to these two that I'd only gotten to know her after she'd been murdered. I wasn't sure I could explain it to myself. Telling them I'd only known her a short time should have been covering my lapses, but I wasn't selling it well.

"Maxie never talked about school, or anything from her past," I said, heading off their inevitable questions. "She didn't seem to want to talk about anything except the house she was fixing up. It was so sad when she didn't get to finish it." Sad especially since it would have meant so much less work for me when I bought the place. But I could talk intelligently about the house.

I figured the best thing to do was to deflect their questions about my relationship with Maxie and concentrate on the reason I'd come to the Sprocket in the first place. "Do you really think Big Bob was going to try to get back together with Maxie before he died?" I asked Rocco.

He shrugged. "I only knew Big Bob from riding with him," he answered. "We didn't talk that much. Little Bob would probably know."

"Little Bob?"

"Yeah," Luther said, smiling a little embarrassedly. "Little Bob and Big Bob used to pal around together a lot." He motioned to the bartender, who walked over. "Hey Lou, is Little Bob around tonight?"

Lou nodded. "Saw him in the Gear Box just a couple minutes ago."

"I think we should introduce Alison here to Little Bob," Luther told Rocco.

Rocco smiled. "Wouldn't miss it," he said.

I wasn't crazy for the way they were grinning at me, but I didn't think anything especially worrisome would happen under Luther's watch, so I followed them into the Gear Box. The sound system was less insistent in here, so my ears stopped ringing a little. Once we were inside, looking at the five or six patrons playing pool and the one man on the pinball machine, I spotted the guy who must have been Little Bob. And I came to understand the grins.

Little Bob must have been seven feet tall and resembled, more than anything else, the Chrysler Building. He was playing the bowling game, and he had to practically bend at the waist just to reach the face of the table.

"Robert!" Luther called from the doorway, and Little Bob stood up to his full height and waved his hand. For a second, I thought he was wearing a catcher's mitt, and then I realized that was just Little Bob's hand. "Come on over."

"Luther," the grizzly bear rumbled in return. Little Bob's voice was so deep that I was amazed the floor didn't quiver when he spoke. "I'll be right there. I got a perfect game going."

Rocco and Luther couldn't help it—they were watching my face for a reaction to their very, *very* large friend.

"Okay, I get it," I said. "Big Bob was little, and Little Bob is big. Stop looking at me like I'm going to burst into flames."

"Maybe it's just enjoyable to look at you," Luther said, and a moment passed where we exchanged a look. I wasn't sure what it meant, but it wasn't unpleasant.

"Or maybe it's funny because Little Bob is so big," Rocco jumped in. Yeah, that was a possibility, too.

The apparently bottomless depth of this hilarious fact was mercifully left unmined because the subject of our awe trundled over in our direction, holding a pint mug of beer. It looked like a shot glass in his paw. "Who's your lady friend, Luther?" the basso rumbled.

"This is Alison, a friend of Maxie's," Luther explained. "She's here because she read about Big Bob in the paper." Luther and I had agreed to tell the guys that much, because he didn't want them to know he had hired me—they'd equate a private investigator with the police, and the cops weren't tops on most bikers' fan club lists.

The tremendous person in front of me looked like he might cry. "Oh, it was a shame what happened to him," he rumbled. "I figured he'd just ridden out of Jersey, you know, to California or Montana or someplace. He was always talking about doing something like that. Never occurred to me he was right there in the ground at Seaside Heights."

"What do you think happened?" I asked. Maybe one of these guys could provide some insight.

Little Bob blinked, as if trying to understand some hidden meaning in my question. "Somebody hit him real hard in the back of the head," he said.

"I know, but who would do that? *Why* would somebody do that?"

Rocco and Little Bob made the exact same face, flattening out their bottom lips in expressions of total bafflement. "Beats the pine tar out of me," Rocco said. "I never even heard about Big Bob so much as having a loud argument with anybody."

I looked around the room; there were only a few people back here. "Would anyone else here know Big Bob? Any ideas where we could find someone who might have talked to him right before he vanished?"

Luther gave the room a look, and shook his head. "Nobody in here, and not that many out in the main bar," he said. "It's been a couple of years, and this isn't the most grounded bunch ever. Bikers by nature tend to move around a bit."

"Makes sense," I said.

Luther nodded. "The only other person I can think of who was around at that time was Wilson Meyers. You remember Wilson?" he asked Little Bob.

The huge statue of a man pondered the question a moment, and I started to get a sense of where Rodin got the idea for *The Thinker*. "Little guy? Curly hair?" he asked.

Luther and Rocco laughed. "Everybody's a little guy to you, Robert," Luther told him after they contained themselves. "Wilson's probably about five ten. But yeah, that's him. He was part of the club used to ride with Big Bob and the rest of us. But I don't remember the last time I saw Wilson."

"Come to think of it," Little Bob said, "it was probably around the time Big Bob disappeared."

The other two thought about that, and nodded.

Twelve

"So that guy at dinner last night—that was your husband?"
Luther sat back in the passenger seat of my wagon and pushed
his baseball cap over his eyes to show (1) his weariness and (2)
his nonchalance. I wasn't buying either one. Luther had agreed
I could drive based on the fact that I'd had exactly one beer
and he was "dog tired." So I wouldn't need his services as a
designated driver. Besides, it was my car.

"Ex-husband," I said. "Why do you ask?"

"How long you been divorced?" he said without opening
his (so nonchalant) eyes.

"Have you ever noticed that you tend to answer questions
with other questions?" I said.

"Do I?"

"We've been divorced about two years," I said. There was
no sense being coy about it; he'd just ask me more questions.
"And before you ask, yeah, he cheated on me. Anything else
you want to know?"

Luther smiled just a little and opened his eyes just a slit. "You seemed fairly cozy for a divorced couple. You guys getting back together?"

"Cozy? What's cozy?"

"*Now* who's answering a question with a question?" I didn't respond, so Luther chuckled and went on. "Cozy, like you were a nice little family, you and him and your daughter. He put his arm around you at one point."

"Yes, and because my daughter was in the room, I very politely didn't gnaw it off to discourage such behavior in the future. What are you getting at, Luther?"

"Have you been dating since the divorce?"

"A couple of times." Okay, three, but I wasn't being precise at the moment. "Why?"

His voice softened a bit. "I just wanted to make sure I wasn't muscling in on another man's territory," he said.

Well, *that* was an interesting statement, on several levels. "Let's take this point by point," I began. "Are you asking me out? On a date?"

"Yeah." If Luther had been chewing on a long blade of grass, he couldn't have been a more perfect picture of a farm-boy gentleman. (Is that even a term?)

"Then ask me out. Don't ask me if my ex-husband will approve. I don't care if he approves; he's my *ex*-husband. I get to choose; he doesn't." And while we're at it, equal pay for equal work, and other sisterhood principles. Hail to thee, Gloria Steinem.

Luther sat up straighter in the seat and pushed his baseball cap back to a normal height on his head. "Alison, would you go out on my bike with me Wednesday?" he asked.

"Well, that's better. I'd be happy . . . What?"

"Thought I'd take you out for a ride," Luther said, grinning just enough that I knew he was enjoying my sudden discomfort. "Let you see what this whole alien 'biker' thing is all about. Turn you into a real biker chick, maybe." I shot him a look, then looked back at the road. "Or not."

I had never been on a motorcycle in my life. I was, what's the word? Chicken. That was it. I was a big, feathery chicken afraid of driving somewhere without the rest of the car around me. I was a wimp, a wuss, a scaredy-cat, a marshmallow— feel free to stop me anytime.

"A ride on the hog, huh?" I said. Had I spit out the window, I still wouldn't have been able to project the kind of toughness I was pretending to have. "Sounds like fun."

"So you'll go?" I wasn't sure if Luther's surprise was a good or bad thing.

"Sure." Now, if I could just stop my teeth from chattering in fear . . .

"Great. I'll get us a picnic lunch." He smiled and went back to slouching on the seat and pretending to be asleep.

A picnic lunch with a biker. Since I'd bought that guest-house, absolutely nothing in my life had gone the way I'd expected.

"It's not much to go on," Paul said. "Another biker stopped coming to the bar at around the same time Big Bob disappeared? That's pretty thin."

We were in the attic the next morning, and my friend (and Jeannie's husband) Tony Mandorisi was there helping me figure out a key problem of my renovation: access. I could build Melissa a wonderful haven, but if she couldn't get inside it without a boost from the Flying Wallendas, it wasn't going to do her much good.

Paul was watching the proceedings with a degree of disinterest—when there was a case to be solved, he was almost totally single-minded—while Tony sized up the space and made his "thinking" face. Tony was aware Paul was in the room, but he couldn't see or hear the ghost. I'd reassured him that Maxie wasn't present—frankly, Tony's a little scared of her, so I saw no reason to inform him that she was actually perhaps four feet behind him, lying on her back a foot or two from the ceiling and ignoring him completely.

"Okay, so it's thin," I said. Tony looked up, realized I wasn't talking to him, and started pacing around the attic, looking for a logical place to put a staircase. "But it's what I've been able to do in a short period of time when I was also running a full guesthouse and looking into . . . other things." I gave Paul a significant look, and he nodded.

Maxie looked at me, then at him, and twitched her mouth. "What do you mean, 'other things'?" she asked. "What other things?"

"Nothing that you need concern yourself about," Paul told her. I felt it was better not to talk directly to Maxie, because I needed Tony to concentrate on the task at hand, and not his unfounded—if understandable—fear of the female dead person in the room.

"I'm not talking to you after that outfit you arranged for me to wear," I whispered so that Tony wouldn't hear. "Did that note to your mom say to give me the most embarrassing clothes you owned? They told me you didn't really wear stuff like that except for the first time you went there."

"What?" Tony asked.

Maxie stifled a giggle.

"Anyway," I continued my conversation with Paul as if the exchange with Maxie had not taken place, "I'll see if I can find out more when Luther takes me for a ride on his hog on Wednesday." I watched Maxie for a reaction, and got the one I wanted—she looked astonished.

"*What*?" she shrieked. "You're going out on a date with Luther? On his bike?"

Paul sputtered a bit as well, and for that matter, so did Tony. "You're afraid of small cars, and you're getting on a motorcycle?" Tony asked, chuckling to himself.

"You barely know this man," Paul protested. He gets testy when I show interest in a man who's, you know, breathing.

"I'll be fine," I told the three of them. It would have been nice if I'd believed it, but I think I made it sound convincing, anyway. "It'll be an opportunity to find out more about what happened to Big Bob."

"I don't see how," Paul said, pursing his lips. That meant he was back into thinking mode. If it had been a *really* difficult problem, he'd have stroked his goatee. "Luther is the person who came to us." Paul likes to think we're an operating detective agency—in fact, Luther had come to *me*. "I think you've gotten all the information out of him that you're going to get."

"Well, what do you think my first move should be, then?" I asked.

"The way I see it, the only real chance for access without taking half the house apart and costing you tens of thousands of dollars is a spiral staircase based down in your bedroom, right below here," Tony said. "It won't involve any outside construction and it won't involve incapacitating a lower bedroom that you need for guests."

"You still don't have any facts about the murder," Paul butted in as soon as there was a gap in the conversation. Okay, so I'd really been asking him the question, but still. "You haven't spoken to the police and found out what they know yet."

"I talked to Lieutenant McElone," I told him.

"Why?" Tony asked. "The police don't issue building permits in this town."

"I'm talking to Paul," I said. "Wait. I'm thinking about the staircase thing."

"And Lieutenant McElone's involvement in this case is . . . ?" Paul asked.

He had me. "Okay, nothing. The murder's being investigated by the Seaside Heights cops and the county prosecutor's major-crimes division."

Paul nodded. "So you have to talk to them."

I rotated my eyes. "I guess so," I intoned. I hate talking to cops I don't know. I'm not crazy about talking to McElone, but at least she's predictable.

"So what about the spiral staircase?" Tony asked when I hadn't spoken for enough time.

"I don't know," I said. "It's not that I'd mind Melissa having to go through my bedroom on her way to her room, but . . ."

"But at some point in the future, it *could* become a problem to have Melissa going through your bedroom on her way to her room, no?" Tony said. He was nodding.

"Not to mention, we wouldn't be able to get any furniture up there with just a narrow spiral staircase," I added.

"We got the sheetrock up here," Tony pointed out.

"Yeah, and we needed a scaffold and four workmen to do it, not to mention that was before the window glass went in, and I had a great big gaping hole to pass it all through."

"This is so *boring*!" Maxie whined, and she vanished up through the ceiling to pout on the roof. Normally, she would have found such talk fascinating. The thought of my riding on the back of Luther's bike must have been too much for her.

"Yeah, I'm going to have to think about this one," Tony said. "Are you totally against keeping the pull-down stairs, maybe widening them some and making them more stable?"

"I'm not totally against it, but it's not my favorite idea, either," I told him.

Paul coughed, which had to be an attention-getting device, since it was pretty much impossible for him to get sick. "About those *other things* you've been looking into . . ." he began.

"I'm working on it," I insisted.

"So am I," Tony said. He walked over to the pull-down stairs in question, and started gingerly down them. "I'll be in touch." He waved in a direction completely opposite from Paul's hovering position. "Bye, Paul," Tony said.

Paul actually waved back.

"Are you sure you don't want any help finding Julia?" he asked after Tony's steps could no longer be heard on the stairs.

"I'm doing this myself," I told him. "Don't worry."

Paul made sure he had my gaze, and said quietly, "It's important to me, Alison. I need to know if she's all right."

"I know it's important to you," I told him. "That's why I need to do it myself."

Paul nodded significantly. I headed for the stairs down to the second floor. And as I walked, I wondered if I really did want to find Julia MacKenzie.

I was halfway down the stairs when my cell phone buzzed, Now, if someone is calling me, my cell phone rings. If someone is sending me a text message, it buzzes. This is the system set up by Melissa, because I am incapable of figuring out how to make technology do things. I hand it to my ten-year-old daughter, and she takes care of it in less than a minute. It's efficient, but infuriating.

I realize it's stupid, but I always get a little jolt when the phone buzzes. I never get text messages, and the sound makes me think an emergency has arisen. So I gasped a little at the buzz, then calmed myself and looked for the incoming caller's name.

There wasn't one. It was from a number I'd never seen before. *Great. Someone's texting me nuisance sales calls now. The march of technology—new ways to annoy people.* But on the off chance it was something necessary, I clicked through to the message.

It read, "Big Bob is dead. Stop asking questions, or it can happen to you."

Thirteen

I recall something about a frantic call to Lieutenant McElone, who asked for the incoming number, punched up some buttons on her computer (I could hear the clacking) and told me the message had come from a prepaid disposable cell phone and couldn't be traced to an owner, but the good news was that "if you get another one from that number, we might be able to GPS it to whoever's using it."

"That's the good news?" I asked. "What's the bad news?"

"He's probably thrown it out and gotten a new one by now."

I'd been threatened on cases before (okay, one case, when I was investigating Paul's and Maxie's murders) and had not developed an immunity to abject terror in the process. So I ran back upstairs and told the ghosts what had happened.

Paul, at first, insisted I quit the Big Bob case immediately. "It's not worth it," he said. "We've agreed you wouldn't take a case that involved this kind of risk."

Maxie lifted a broom to swing at him, but Paul simply vanished and reappeared across the room.

"This happened the day after you met with the bikers at the Sprocket," Paul pointed out, not missing a beat. "It can't be a coincidence that the threat came so soon after you showed up last night asking questions about Maxie and Big Bob. I'm guessing it was someone in the bar."

"I'm guessing I don't want to live in terror," I countered. "I'm not interested in dying—no offense."

"None taken," Paul said politely.

"So you understand why I think I should drop it."

"Drop it?" Maxie glared at me. "You promised me!" Melissa had given up that tactic when she was eight.

"Well," Paul said after a pause, "it might not be necessary to stop asking questions. I'd give it time before I decided."

"Hold on just a second," I said, "Are you the same dead guy who said I should give it up a minute ago? What changed your mind?"

"Look. Don't do anything on the Big Bob case today. Just go see the police in Seaside Heights and tell them what you know. Then leave. That's not asking questions, and it shouldn't get you in trouble. But it *will* get the information to the police there, and maybe that will mean a better level of protection for you."

Not doing anything—other than passing along information—was definitely my easiest choice, so I took Paul's advice and decided to call the cops in Seaside Heights. A Detective Ferry deigned to see me later that day. I told the ghosts not to mention the threatening text to Melissa or Mom under any circumstances, and moved on to the investigation that wasn't currently threatening my life.

The address for Julia MacKenzie I'd gotten from my pal Megan Sharp at Monmouth University was a charming little two-family Colonial in Gilford Park. It sat on the most nondescript street in town, about four blocks from the beach, with the obligatory porch—all the houses down here have one—and an adult man's bicycle leaning against the side wall.

The problem was, neither of the mailboxes bore the name

"MacKenzie," and although she could have gotten married in the past two years, the prospect of Paul's ex-love being here was less than optimal. But Paul always said that you follow up on every lead if you want to be a good investigator, so that was precisely what I intended to do.

I rang the bell marked "E. Francisco" first, but got no answer. The one marked "Lamont" was for the upstairs apartment, and when I rang the bell, instead of a person coming to the door, I heard someone call out from above my head, "Somebody there?"

I had to step back from the door to look up, and used my hand to shield my eyes from the sun, which was directly behind the house. There was a woman standing on a parapet, a deck surrounding the upper apartment, and she was calling down to me.

"Hi," I called up. "I'm looking for a Julia MacKenzie." *Do you have one*?

The woman shook her head. "Don't know anyone by that name here," she said. "You sure you have the right address?"

Before I could answer, I heard a child shout, "Ma!" behind the woman, and she turned.

"I'll be right there!" she yelled. "Take off your bathing suit and get in the shower!"

"I think she used to live here," I shouted up to the woman. "Do you mind if I come up?"

I'm sure she didn't mean to, but the woman upstairs moaned when I asked. "I really can't come down to unlock the door right now," she said. "My four-year-old's in the shower." She turned away again and shouted, "And use soap this time!"

Although I certainly understood her plight, screaming up at her wasn't getting me anywhere. I tried one more time. "How long have you been living here?" I asked.

"We're just renting for the week," the woman replied. "Vacation. We're out of here tomorrow night." She sounded more exhausted than any person on vacation I had ever heard.

"Who's the owner of the house?" I tried. "Maybe they'd have some records of the person I'm looking for."

"The guy downstairs owns the place," she answered. "Esteban Francisco. But he doesn't come back until around five."

I nodded. "Okay, thanks. Have a nice rest of your vacation," I called as I turned to walk back to the car.

"Uh-huh," I heard the woman say as she headed inside. "Shampoo, Jason! Shampoo!" Parenting—it's not just a job; it's an adventure.

I wrote out a note with my contact information and my question about Julia MacKenzie for Mr. Francisco on a pad of paper I keep in the glove compartment of the Volvo. I also folded a business card—"Kerby Investigations"—into the note. Then I walked back to the house, slipped it under his door (amid youthful cries of "It wasn't me!" from above), and got back into my pizza oven of a car to ride to Seaside Heights.

It was less than a ten-minute drive, but I had a little time to think. Since Julia MacKenzie apparently no longer lived in the Gilford Park house, where could I look next? The Monmouth University records had only given that address, and there was no telephone number listed. As with most such problems involving any investigation I found myself roped into, I asked myself the key question:

What would Paul do?

I knew from studying that, ordinarily, the key in a missing-persons investigation like this one, where the only contact was the university, would be to hang around there and ask people if they knew Julia MacKenzie: Sooner or later, you hoped, the law of averages would play in your favor. But Julia had been taking classes mostly at night and online, Paul had said. That meant fewer contacts with other people. Still, the records I'd copied had showed a few of the classes she'd taken, and maybe talking to the professors would make a difference. Even the online ones would know, at least, how well she'd done on her course work. That wouldn't tell me where she was, but it might lead to some better understanding of her personality and her mindset, which *could* lead me to her. Maybe.

The other place to go was CableCom, in Freehold, Julia's last-known employer. That was a longer drive, but maybe an initial inquiry on the phone would be useful. If I could find her supervisor or some coworkers, I might get more information. I'd ask Paul if they'd had any mutual friends; I couldn't believe I hadn't thought to do that yet.

And after living with the idea of the scary text message for a few hours, I decided not to be intimidated by some unseen jerk whose only demonstrable talent so far was that he could type with his thumbs. I was made of sterner stuff than this! I'd press on with the plan, and then cower in my bedroom under the covers tonight. That seemed reasonable.

By the time my thought process had gotten that far, I'd already reached Seaside Heights and was pulling into the parking lot at the municipal complex. Which gives you a general idea of how short that drive really was.

Once inside, it was not a difficult task to find Detective Martin Ferry, who had been assigned (or as the cops put it, "caught") the investigation into Big Bob Benicio's death. Getting Detective Ferry to talk, on the other hand, was not going to be as simple as falling off a log, assuming one was silly enough to climb onto a log in the first place.

"I don't care if you're Philip Marlowe; I don't have to talk to you about an ongoing investigation if I don't want to," the charming detective said after twenty minutes of negotiation over whether I could actually enter his office and speak to him. "There's no law that says I have to give out information to private detectives."

"There's no law that says Dunkin' Donuts has to sell bagels, and yet they all do," I pointed out. "What's it going to hurt if I try to help your investigation along?" It wasn't just that Ferry, an average-height man with a prodigious stomach, intimidated me. It was more that I'd called ahead and made an appointment, and *still* he was acting like I'd barged in unannounced and insisted I was a better detective than he was. On the contrary, I was convinced that I wasn't a better detective than *anybody*.

"I'll tell you what it's going to hurt," he said, sitting down in a squeaky chair behind his desk and half sneering at me. "You're going to bother witnesses I need to talk to, and that will make them less willing to talk to me. You're going to expect things like ME reports and filed police documents that you have no right to see. You're going to muddy the waters with suspects and drop pieces of information that I don't want dropped. I've worked with PIs before, and I've been burned too many times. Go away."

I stared at him a moment. "It's because I'm a woman, isn't it?"

Ferry heaved a sigh and put his head in his hands. "No, it's not because you're a woman," he said. "I have no problem with women. My old partner was a woman, and we got along just fine. My problem is that you're not a cop, and anybody who's not a cop is just going to get in the way on this kind of investigation."

It's the standard police argument—nobody but a cop knows anything about asking people questions or examining a crime scene. And in my case, of course, he had a point. But I'd promised Maxie I'd do what I could, and Luther was an actual client, so I couldn't let it go at the standard police argument. Although the text from my secret tormentor was a compelling argument to do so. I decided to press on.

"Detective, I understand your position," I began. "But I can tread very lightly. I'll only speak to witnesses you've already interviewed, if you like. I have insight from another angle, a more personal one, than you do, so I can look into who Big Bob was and why he might have ended up with a heavy object coming down hard on his head. Why not give me a chance to help you? I'll be happy to share whatever information I find out, and you can take it from there. I'm not interested in making the bust; in fact, I prefer that you do it. But if you let me, maybe I can make a difference that helps you. What do you say?"

"Big Bob?" Ferry asked. "The victim was known as Big Bob? He wasn't that big."

Oy. He didn't even know that? Wasn't that one of the most basic pieces of information in this case, other than the fact that a male human had died of a cranial injury?

"Yes, that was his nickname," I told him, not pointing out that he'd missed a basic fact.

He looked at his computer screen. "But he was only five eight," he said.

"Ironic, isn't it?"

"Have you been talking to people I haven't?" Ferry asked. "You said about sharing what you know."

"'Quid pro quo, doctor,'" I replied.

"Quid pro . . . what?" Ferry asked.

"It's from *The Silence of the Lambs*," I pointed out.

"Uh-huh."

"It means, I give, you give," I explained. "I'll share if you share. Tell me what the ME's report said and show me the crime scene, tell me who you've talked to, and I'll tell you what I know. What do you say?"

You could see the wheels spinning in Ferry's head. He really didn't want to cooperate with me, but he knew I had some pieces of information that he'd missed so far. Cops are competitive; they want to be the one to break the case. What he was doing now was figuring the minimum he could give away to get the maximum return.

"Okay," Ferry said finally. "You go first."

"I give you one thing, you give me one thing," I countered.

"Fine. You go first," he repeated.

"I already gave you Big Bob's nickname."

"That's nothing," he protested. "How does that help me solve the case?"

"Not my problem. It's a piece of information. You want more, you give me something."

"Nice talking to you, Kerby."

"Okay." I told him about the threatening text, gave him the incoming number and purposely did not tell him McElone had already checked it out, so that he could check it out and find out exactly what I already knew. He wrote down the information and said he'd check on it after we were through.

"That's my quid," I said. "Now you pro quo."

Ferry nodded, but he didn't smile. "All right. The ME said *Big Bob* died of severe trauma to the back of the head, and by the look of it, just one blow, a tremendous, hard blow. Still metal particles in the skull. Best guess is that the victim got hit with a steel tool, like a wrench or a hammer. Now. Give me something worth continuing."

This was going to be something of a conundrum, since I didn't have very much. But I could vamp with the best of them, or at least, the top 30 percent of them. "Big Bob was married briefly to a woman named Maxie Malone."

Ferry was taking notes on a legal pad. "Maxie?"

"Short for Maxine. They got married in Vegas about two and a half years ago. Sort of a joke. Got it annulled even before they came home. But people tell me that Big Bob was planning on seeking out his ex-wife right before he died. Maybe to try to reconcile with her. Maybe not. Nobody heard from him again after that."

"This ex-wife—she available for interview?"

Well, sort of. I shook my head. "She's dead," I told him. "She was poisoned in a real-estate scandal in Harbor Haven about six months after Big Bob ended up with a heavy-metal headache." I liked speaking Tough Cop. Maybe I could get the Rosetta Stone software for it, and make it my second language.

Ferry looked up, suddenly interested. "She got murdered, too?" he asked. "Sounds like they could be related."

I told him the story of Maxie's and Paul's murders, and why it was extremely unlikely they had anything to do with what happened to Big Bob. "Now, that's a lot of information I just gave you, detective," I said. "I expect a lot in return."

He stood up and reached for his sport coat, a light one for summer weather. "All right, Kerby," he said. "Let's go see where Big Bob died."

Fourteen

It wasn't where you would have thought.

I had pictured the area where Bob Benicio's remains had been discovered to be somewhere away from the ocean, in an isolated area where no one would have seen the killer digging the grave, and where the tide would not have had a chance to reveal Big Bob for more than two years. Without any specific information, I'd been picturing it somewhere near one of the abandoned properties on the beach, away from people and their prying eyes.

The actual site was none of those things.

Detective Martin Ferry drove us over. It was a stifling July day, but, luckily, the car was air-conditioned. He drove a Crown Victoria, the model once known as an "unmarked car" before the police figured out what everyone else already knew—nobody except police departments ever bought a Crown Vic. They were eventually discontinued by the Ford Motor Company as a consumer-line vehicle for exactly that reason. On the New Jersey Turnpike, where the official speed limit is twenty-five miles above the legal speed limit, everyone slows down to the Jersey version of a "crawl"—only ten miles above the limit—when a Crown Vic is spotted in the left lane, invariably doing at least ninety.

Ferry had taken us through the chain separating the street from the beach by asking a young officer nearby to unlock the barrier for us, then drove directly down onto the crowded beach. We didn't get far enough onto the beach to make tourists scramble for their lives, which was considerate of the detective, I thought.

Then, Ferry made a hard left and drove us down almost to the edge of the boardwalk's underpinnings. For a second, I wondered if he was going to stop at all, or just ram us into the pilings. But he made sure we had a foot or two to spare.

I followed him out of the car, and Ferry led me to a spot a good hundred and fifty yards under the boardwalk. Song lyrics aside, I could not almost taste the hot dogs and french fries sold directly above my head.

"It was just about here," Ferry told me, indicating a section of the sand between two pylons. A couple of caterpillar earthmovers were parked nearby. "If the county hadn't decided to do some excavating for some crazy environmental project, we probably never would have found him. Your pal Big Bob was a good eight feet down."

"This is a weird place to bury a body," I said. "The tide comes up here twice a day. He'd have to be that far down just to avoid being washed up in a matter of days."

Ferry nodded. "And that's just the beginning of the stupidity of burying him here. It's a public beach, so anybody could have been here. There's no real access unless you happen to know a cop with a key, or you're driving a dune buggy."

"Or a motorcycle," I thought out loud. "Big Bob was a biker, after all."

"Yeah. Or a motorcycle. But a motorcycle bearing a dead body, not to mention the kind of excavation equipment to put a man that far down into the ground, wouldn't make it down the hill. It would take at least two people to get all that stuff down here."

I considered that. "Could have been two people bringing him down." I said.

Ferry did a sort of half nod, half skeptical lean of the head. "Or he could have forced Big Bob to dig his own grave."

I shivered, and it was over 90 degrees, even in the shade of the boardwalk.

The best thing was to try to get away from the emotion of the situation, not think of Big Bob as a person (easy, since I had never met him) and concentrate on the mechanics of the problem. That way I could manage to overlook the yellow crime scene tape still sticking to some parts of the wooden beams beneath the boardwalk.

"I understand there was no missing-persons report at the time," I began, "but even after two years, shouldn't there be a county team investigating a murder? Isn't that considered a major crime, or is it a low priority because Big Bob was a biker?"

Ferry curled his lip in derision. "You're the second person who's suggested that to me," he said, "and I'm frankly getting insulted. I don't care if the guy was a member of the Hitler Youth. Somebody killed him, and I need to find out who."

"Sorry," I said. "Who was the first?"

"The first what? First murderer? Cain, if you read the Bible."

It was my turn to curl my lip. "The first person who said you might be less interested in a biker's murder," I said.

"This other biker guy who came in, uninvited, right after it showed up in the paper that we had identified the remains. Wanted to know what was going on with the investigation, were we following up. Said he figured we wouldn't care because the victim was a biker."

"Let me guess," I suggested, closing my eyes. "He was a tall, soft-spoken guy with a mustache, and his name is Luther Mason."

Ferry's eyes widened just a little, and then he regained his patented snarl. "So you know Mr. Mason, do you?"

Luther hadn't actually asked me to keep his identity a secret, so I said, "He's my client."

"And you think that the county isn't trying to solve this because the guy rode a hog?" Ferry shot back. "That I'm the B Team?"

"Hey, somebody missed his meds. Calm down," I said. You see enough movies, you learn some cop speak. "I'm not saying you're not good enough. I'm saying *I'm* not good enough, but I'll give you anything I can get if you share some information."

"Uh-huh." He'd decided to go with "petulant four-year-old." It's a choice.

I thought I'd get back to the facts and see if I could get Ferry back into a sharing sort of mood. "It would take hours to dig a hole big enough and deep enough," I said. "Why risk being seen for that long?"

"I could understand it if this had happened in January or February, when there's nobody around," Ferry agreed, seeming to have snapped out of his snit. "Do you know the exact date Benicio vanished?"

I had asked Luther and Little Bob, and neither of them could come up with a precise answer. I told Ferry that, adding, "They both agreed it was probably in the spring, around April maybe." Then, I remembered something else they'd told me, and asked Ferry if there had been a missing-persons inquiry filed on Wilson Meyers.

He didn't know, but said he'd check when he returned to his office. "If Benicio was killed in March or April, there would have been some people around, but not nearly as many as during the summer," he said. "If it happened at night, it's possible they weren't seen. But this one still doesn't make any sense."

"Is there any way of knowing how far the body had been dragged or transported before it was buried?" I asked Ferry.

He got a funny look on his face and shook his head. "ME

says there were no indications on the bones that the body was dragged or forced here, but after two years, that's a shot in the dark, really. It's impossible to know for sure after this amount of decomposition, but there were no bone bruises or breaks, nothing that would seem to indicate Benicio had been badly treated on his way here."

"What does that tell us?" I asked.

Ferry snapped awake from the puzzled feeling he'd been giving off a moment before, and smirked at me. "I don't know what it tells *you*," he said, "but it tells *me* that Big Bob Benicio was alive when he came down to the beach."

The drive back to the municipal complex was quieter than the drive to the beach had been. I know I was thinking about what Ferry had shown me and what we'd discussed, and I assumed he was doing the same.

The thought of a man being led to the spot where he'd be buried and possibly forced to dig his own grave—especially one that deep—shook me pretty solidly. But I found that instead of scaring me off, the concept was making me angry and increasing my resolve: Now I wanted to find out what happened to Big Bob so that the police could deal with the twisted mind behind it.

From the look on his face, Detective Ferry might have been thinking the very same thing. Or he might have been wondering what kind of chance the Mets had this year. His face was showing nothing.

Once we got to Ferry's parking space in the lot and I opened the door of the Crown Vic to let the heat smack me in the face once again, Ferry squinted over at me (I guess sunglasses are for wimps) and asked, "So, Kerby, you still want in on this investigation?"

I could match him last name for last name. "You know what, Ferry? I still do. And I still promise to share what I find out with you. Can I count on you to do the same?"

"Absolutely not. But if I decide there might be some advantage in talking to you, I'll reach out. How's that?"

He didn't wait for an answer but got out and walked briskly—given the wilting heat—to the police department entrance without looking back.

The fact is, that's about as much cooperation as you can expect from most cops, so I considered the visit a success. I didn't have much more pointing me to a suspect in Big Bob's murder, but I did know a little bit more than I had when I'd gotten into the car this morning, and that was something.

So I was reaching for some encouragement. So sue me.

Driving home, I prioritized the remaining tasks before me. First up, I had to decide on the next step in the Julia MacKenzie search without help from Paul. The address in Gilford Park had turned out to be a dead end; the phone number had been disconnected. McElone wasn't about to let me see police telephone records.

Good. That meant I'd have to be devious. I didn't know yet *how* I'd be devious, but I liked the idea of it.

At the same time, it would be necessary to look into Big Bob's doings just before he disappeared. Luther could help me with some of that on the dreaded (and I mean that literally) motorcycle ride tomorrow. Assuming I survived it.

But a search for Wilson Meyers seemed just as important. Now that Ferry knew about Wilson, he might begin an investigation, but it was just as likely the county would decide to start digging up the beach, especially the area under the Seaside Heights boardwalk, in a search for Wilson's assumedly just-as-decomposed body. That was a bad thought on a number of fronts, not the least of which was that it wouldn't help figure out what had happened to Big Bob. Dead, Wilson would be no help to anybody.

And last but not least on my agenda: telling my ex-husband he had until the following Tuesday to get out of my house. That would be enjoyable, certainly, but tricky, since I couldn't let Melissa think I was kicking her father to the curb. But the fact was, with new guests arriving eight days from now, the only other place for Steven to sleep would be in my bed. And *that* was certainly not going to happen.

All of this was completely forgotten when I got home to find Maxie having a screaming fight with her mother.

I could hear it from the backyard, where I parked the Volvo, and it only got louder once I walked through the kitchen door. Some of the pots and pans (sadly underused) hanging over the center island were swinging back and forth. And I knew that although I could hear both Maxie's and Kitty Malone's voices, the guests in the house were getting only Kitty's side of the argument. And since Kitty couldn't actually see or hear Maxie, the fact that they were managing to *have* an argument was something of a wonder in itself.

Rushing through the kitchen to the den, I pushed open the swinging door and almost hit poor Francie Westen in the face as I did. Francie, looking absolutely rattled, was wringing her hands and biting her lips.

"I know I signed up for a haunted-house vacation, but this is just unpleasant!" she cried as I apologized for almost clocking her with the door and proceeded toward the library, the room where Kitty and Maxie usually had their visits, and from where the sound was emanating now.

"You just hated him from the beginning, and you weren't ever going to change your mind!" Maxie bellowed. "You never liked any of the guys I brought home!" Then there was a long pause. Maxie must have been writing out her end of the dustup.

Halfway to the library, Don Petrone slowed my frenzied progress with a huge grin on his face. "If I'd known we were getting an extra ghost show today, I would have set up my camcorder," he said. "Can you post a schedule from now on?"

"I'll see about it, Don," I told him. "Excuse me, won't you? I'd prefer to cut this off before something gets broken. Or someone."

"He abused you," Kitty shouted. "He hit you for no reason. I was supposed to embrace a man who did that?"

"You hated him long before that," I heard Maxie tell her. "You never gave him a chance." And again, the pause.

I didn't hear any crashes or dishes being broken, so I thanked my luck that this appeared to be strictly a verbal confrontation at the moment. I blazed past Don, still enjoying himself immensely, and noted Albert at the door to the library. I didn't give him a chance to say anything to me, brushing by and into the library. I would have closed the door, but in a fit of stupidity while I was redesigning the house, I'd removed the library door to make it look larger and so that people would always have access to books at any time of the day or night. Another in a series of decisions I had come to regret.

The argument might have been all talk now, but that clearly had not always been the case. The room, though hardly a shambles, was certainly disheveled. Maxie had knocked books off shelves on every wall, and many of them were lying on the floor, spines cracked, pages crumpled. I'd bought every one of them used, but it was the principle of the thing.

"Okay, break it up," I said as I entered the library. "Everybody to their corners."

They both turned to look at me for a moment, then resumed their positions, facing off against each other, although Kitty was facing the wrong way, since she couldn't actually tell where Maxie was.

"He stole your money, and he lied to you," Kitty continued, as if I hadn't entered the room and called for a halt in hostilities.

"He was my husband!" Maxie shouted back as she tapped out those exact words, in all capital letters, on the laptop—*my* laptop—she'd placed on a side table in Kitty's line of sight.

Kitty read it, and snorted her reply. "Husband. For a long weekend? That's not a marriage. It's barely a one-night stand."

Both Malone women had told me on separate occasions that they'd had a somewhat contentious relationship when Maxie was alive. But all I'd ever seen was a mother and daughter who were thrilled to have been reunited after a horrendous incident, and they'd never so much as frowned in each other's direction before while I was there to see it.

"I wasn't kidding," I said, not loudly enough to be considered shouting, but loudly enough to be heard over the din. "There are guests here, and they're watching. This. Ends. Now."

Maxie, disregarding me, started to tap the laptop's keys again, and I closed the cover as she typed. She gave me a positively rabid look, but I picked up the notebook and tucked it under my arm. She reached for it, but I danced out of the way, and Maxie went past me and through an armchair.

"There'll be no more arguing now," I said. Turning to Maxie, I added, "And if you keep up this attitude, young lady, your Internet privileges will be revoked. Is that clear?"

"On that old dinosaur?" Maxie sneered. "I'm surprised I'm not getting messages from 1998."

Kitty, meanwhile, seemed to be composing herself, looking conscious now of me and the couple in the doorway (Francie had joined her husband), who were watching with either delight or anxiety. Or both. It was hard to tell. "I'm sorry, Alison," Kitty said. "I got a little carried away with myself."

"I take it the topic of conversation was Big Bob Benicio," I said.

"You tell her—" Maxie began.

I cut her off. "I'll decide what messages get passed back to your mother," I told her. "So you keep a civil tongue in your head, because *I* respect her." Sometimes having Maxie in the house gives me a glimpse into what life would be like if I'd had a second daughter. One less mature than my ten-year-old.

"You always side with her," Maxie pouted. See what I mean?

I ignored her. "I appreciate your anger," I told Kitty, "but this was years ago, and Maxie is, well, beyond pain these days. Isn't it past the point of argument?"

Kitty appeared determined to show me that Maxie came by her stubborn petulance naturally. "Some things transcend time, Alison," she said. "I don't hate people. I try to see the good in everyone. But that man violated every possible notion of decency, and he made an enemy of me for life."

"Apparently even longer than that," I pointed out. "He's dead."

Kitty nodded. "True," she agreed. "But if there's one thing I'm learning, it's that dying doesn't make people change their personalities." She searched the ceiling for a sign of her daughter, as if she could tell whether or not Maxie was there.

Maxie took the bait. "Big Bob wasn't perfect, but he saw me for who I was, and not who he wanted me to be," she told her mother, and I chose to forward that message along. I did not see the point in adding, "Unlike *some people*," as Maxie did.

"He let you be who it was easiest for you to be," Kitty countered. "You never had to try. And when you did try, when you wanted to buy this house and begin a career in home design and real estate, he was nowhere to be found."

"I hadn't seen him in almost a year!" Maxie countered. "You saw to that."

"All right, that's fair," her mother said. "But he borrowed money from you when you were together, and he never paid it back."

Maxie fingered the cameo around her neck. "*You* didn't help me buy the house," she said to her mother, ignoring the acknowledgment she'd just gotten that Big Bob couldn't have helped. "You didn't talk to me for months when I signed the mortgage."

Kitty shook her head sadly. "No, but I made sure to sell it to someone who cared when I had to execute your will," she said in a whisper.

They stood there (well, Maxie floated, but it was the same principle) for a full minute. I didn't have any idea what either was thinking, but I knew this argument wasn't ever going to be over. There was no way to resolve it. Maxie was dead, but still in communication with her mother. Big Bob was just as gone—maybe more, because Paul hadn't been able to raise him on the Ghosternet. There couldn't be a resolution, because life doesn't end on a schedule. It ends in the middle, every time.

Finally, Maxie broke through her melancholic stupor. "It doesn't matter anymore," she said through me to Kitty. "You never wanted to give Big Bob a break, and now you don't have to. You have things exactly the way you want them."

I doubt she meant that the way it sounded. Sometimes Maxie forgets—or refuses to accept—the fact that she is dead. But she didn't bother to rephrase her statement, and I failed, in my role of interpreter, to edit it for her.

"Is that what you think?" Kitty gasped. "Is that really what you think? You think I don't wake up every morning in a good mood, and then remember that you're not here anymore? You think it doesn't bother me that you'll never get to finish anything you started, that all your promise was wasted? That you'll never be able to have a daughter you love as much as I love you? Is that what you think?"

She had built herself up to an obvious state of agitation, and Maxie hovered in the air staring at her mother. She either wouldn't or couldn't answer.

"If that's what you think, Maxie, I believe I won't be coming back for a while. You can say what you want, but I've done everything that I thought I could for you. And as for your 'Big Bob,' well, for my money, he deserved everything he got, and more."

With that, Kitty turned on her heel and marched out of the library. Francie and Albert stood by at each side of the door, like a military guard.

Maxie's lips pulled into her mouth and she whimpered a bit, then vanished entirely, something she rarely does. Usually she huffs out of a room through a wall or another person just for effect. But now, she just evaporated.

"You put on some show," Francie said after a moment. "The flying books? How did you do that?"

I didn't have time to respond, because my ex-husband

appeared in the doorway behind her. He pointed toward the front door, where assumedly Kitty was currently leaving.

"I don't know who that was," he said, "but you could hear her all over the house, and it sure sounded like she was confessing to something."

Fifteen

Dinner that night was sort of a distracted affair.

Steven insisted on taking Melissa and me to a restaurant while the guests were out getting their dinners. This necessitated us eating on the early side, since Don Petrone and the two sisters especially were early-bird-special enthusiasts, and I wanted to be sure we were back for the evening, in case someone in the house needed something from the hostess (that's me).

So we trekked out at an ungodly hour to Trees, a new restaurant in Harbor Haven meant to appeal to the upscale crowd without the whole "money" thing that put off the rest of us. In keeping with its name, Trees made sure to pile on the ambiance: There were pictures of trees on the wallpaper, the menus, the plates, the window shades and the ceiling tiles, and there were actual twenty-foot palm trees growing in the restaurant, requiring ceilings so high that the noise level in the place approached that of the third tier at Yankee Stadium during a playoff game. Each tree in each framed picture on each tree-adorned wall was identified by genus and species. The wait-staff was required, we discovered, to point out various trees in the decor and explain their significance. We had been treated to a dissertation on the mighty larch when ordering appetizers and drinks, and now I was bracing myself for the moment when the server (whose name was Eric, and he'd be taking care of us tonight) would reappear to discuss the California redwood while taking our dinner orders.

Trees, despite its name, was not a vegetarian restaurant and was in fact named for its owner, Richard Tree. The spelling of the name of the restaurant was based on the apparent new rule in the English language that apostrophes should be used only when they are not needed, and never used when they are. It's a new linguistic age.

Mentally, I gave the whole enterprise six months, and wondered to where the palms might be transplanted when the lease ran out.

"Does Phyllis really think I'm ready to start delivering the *Chronicle*?" Melissa was asking when a leaf blew across my plate. I had to make her repeat what she'd asked because of the high volume (see above re: high ceilings).

"I don't care if Phyllis thinks so or no. *I* don't think you're ready yet to be riding your bike all around Harbor Haven at five in the morning, so you're not doing it," I replied. This issue was a nonstarter with me. Besides, I was trying to figure out why Kitty Malone had been so uncharacteristically hostile regarding her deceased ex-son-in-law. Was it the one incident from years ago? That was enough for many, surely, but Kitty's personality was usually so easygoing that it was hard to reconcile that kind of polar-opposite reaction.

"Oh, I don't know," Steven butted in. "Melissa's an awfully mature ten-year-old. Don't you think—"

"No." If The Swine thought he was going to ingratiate himself with me by trying to play "good parent" to my "prison guard," he was sadly mistaken.

"It's okay, Daddy," Liss told her father. "I don't care that much." My daughter, the peacemaker.

"Okay, baby," he answered. Honestly, their mutual admiration was enough to nauseate you. Well, me, anyway.

"The two of you are going to have to cut this out," I said.

Both jaws dropped, as if rehearsed. "Cut what out?" they each said, almost simultaneously.

"This perfect-family act you're putting on to convince me that things should go back to the way they used to be," I answered. I looked at my daughter. "Liss, honey, you have to understand. Daddy and I are divorced. That's final. We're not going to get back together, and it's not just my decision, but that's the way it's being made to look. I'm sorry, baby, but things are going to stay the way they've been once Daddy goes back to California."

Melissa and Steven looked at each other; his expression was smug, and hers was slightly surprised. "You haven't told her?" Melissa asked her father.

My voice dropped an octave. "Haven't told me *what*?" I asked.

"I'm not going back to L.A.," Steven said after giving Melissa another look. "I want to come back here and live in Harbor Haven."

Oh, boy.

"You're not serious," I said. It was clear he *was* serious, but I was hoping to give him an easy way out. The last thing I needed was The Swine in my neighborhood, doing his charming thing and turning my daughter into his campaign manager. Not to mention, it had become very tiring trying to keep him from noticing that quite often Melissa, my mother and I were looking at dead people he couldn't see, and it would only get worse if he stayed long-term.

"I've been doing a lot of thinking," Steven said. "You were right about a lot of the things you said about me. I did lose my way somewhere along the line. I discovered how to make money and forgot that there's more to it than that. I started out wanting to use the financial system to help people who needed it, and I ended up screwing those people—cover your ears, Melissa—out of their savings."

"I'm not six," my daughter interjected.

"So what's your plan?" I asked. With Steven, there was always a plan.

His face lit up; this was always the part he'd enjoyed the best—selling his dreams. "Remember how I was going to create a fund for people with very little money to invest? How I was going to build that into something they could use as a nest egg or a retirement fund, or for college tuition?"

"I remember," I assured him. If I didn't remember, we might not have gotten divorced. Oh wait, there'd been Amee. Yeah, we'd still be divorced.

"Well, that plan might have worked in another economy. Now, people are going to be afraid to invest their money in stocks or mutual funds. So I'm going to create my own fund, find investors who'll put up the money, and guarantee an interest rate above prime for investments of as little as ten dollars a month." He grinned at me, clearly convinced he had laid out the blueprint for the most brilliant design since the Sistine Chapel.

"Okay," I said after it was clear he was finished talking. "Could you repeat that in Lithuanian? Because I think I might understand it better if you did."

Steven smiled. "Sorry about the jargon," he said. "Let me see if I can explain."

"Dad's going to be like a bank," Melissa said. "He's going to put up money for poor people, let them invest really small amounts, and make sure that no matter what, they'll get more money back when they're done. The more they put in, the more they'll get out, but they'll never lose anything."

Now *that* I understood. "So it's a Ponzi scheme," I said.

Melissa rolled her eyes, and Steven smiled his "you just don't get it" smile. "No it's *not* a Ponzi scheme," he said. "The money we pay out doesn't come from the contributors. I'll have outside investors who will get their piece of the profits as well. It hinges on me knowing how to invest wisely."

I thought about how he was leveraged out on three credit cards that I knew of yet still bought a karaoke machine to use for one night. "Uh-huh," I said.

"You're not convinced," Steven said.

"I'm not deciding now," I told him, and then saw Eric, the server, who had been approaching our table, put his pad back in his pocket. I tried to flag him down, but he was off to the kitchen for another table's order.

Both Steven and Melissa looked so glum that I needed a way to perk up the gathering. So I fell back on one of the things that my ex-husband was always best at—he loved to give advice, mostly to me.

"Steven, suppose there was someone you were trying to find and the usual avenues weren't helping," I said. "Her phone number is disconnected, and she's not living at the last address you have available. What do you do?"

Immediately, Steven brightened up. He got a sly smile on his face and asked, "Is this a private eye thing?"

"I'm a private investigator, Steven. Get over it. Now, do you want to help me or make fun of me?"

Immediately, he took on a serious expression. Had to show support in front of Melissa, especially. And making himself look smart was possibly his most abundant asset. "This is a business matter?" he asked. I nodded. Sure, it was a business matter. Paul couldn't pay me money for my services, but we had a business arrangement. Sort of. Close enough.

My ex made a show of thinking about the complex problem with which I had entrusted him. He looked down at his unopened menu and nodded slightly. He probably had his lips pursed, too, but I couldn't see from my angle. That is his classic "thinking" face, so I can only assume he'd gone full-tilt with it.

Melissa watched her father with a terrific concentration. He was, even after a few days, still something of a new experience for her again, and she wasn't yet used to all of his moods and what I considered his "tricks." She was a smart ten-year-old, but a ten-year-old nonetheless.

Steven raised his head, having received the wisdom he sought from on high. "If it's someone who's not paying a previous invoice, your best bet is to get in touch with a collection agency," he said. "They have access to records that you can't, like credit-card receipts and things like that."

That would be what The Swine would come up with—a collection agency. First of all, neither Julia MacKenzie nor Wilson Meyers owed me any money. Besides, I'd have to pay a collection agency a fee, and that wasn't going to fit my budget even when there was a full contingent of guests in my house. And what could a collection agency do, anyway? Find old credit-card receipts, utility bills, addresses, cell-phone numbers . . . Hey, wait a minute.

"Actually," I told Steven, "that's exactly what I should do."

Eric appeared at my left shoulder. "Everybody ready?" he asked.

Sixteen

I was startled to see a small boy, perhaps seven years old, walking by himself out of the building as I entered the nondescript office complex in Eatontown Wednesday morning. It wasn't until I was almost upon him that I realized he was dressed in nineteen-twenties' fashion, and that he was transparent.

That seemed terribly sad, but the boy didn't look the least bit unhappy, and was in fact moving with a little skip in his step. He went directly into the arms of a smiling woman in her mid-sixties, whom I heard him address as "Granny." I guess after almost a hundred years, you can get used to pretty much anything. The woman took the boy's hand, and they floated up above the diner across the street and into the morning sky.

This ghost-seeing thing could be creepy or beautiful, and often was both at the same time.

I made my way to the second floor of the building and down a hallway without noticing any other see-through individuals. On door 213 was a sign reading "AAAAAAble Collection Service." I aaaaaadmired the determination of the owners to be first in the Yellow Pages listing for collection agencies, and wondered whether that made any difference in this digital age. I opened the door and walked inside.

The office consisted of two cubicles and a reception desk. There was no one at the reception desk.

"Can someone help me?" I called into the small office.

"I can," a man's voice came from inside one of the cubicles. "Come on around."

I walked around the reception desk and the false wall that had been erected behind it, toward the sound of the man's voice. And sitting at a desk with nothing more than a telephone, a computer, and a dusty plastic fern, was a small, balding man of about fifty, wearing a sport coat so loud he had to shout to be heard over it.

"What can I do for you?" the man asked. A small engraved sign on his desk identified him as Timothy Feldner. He gestured toward a steel-and-cloth chair to one side of his desk, and I sat down.

I identified myself and told him about my guesthouse business, and then being careful with my words, said, "I'm trying to track someone down who might owe some money, and I figured this was the place to ask about something like that." Hey, I didn't know that Julia and Wilson *didn't* owe anyone money. So it wasn't a lie, Melissa.

"That's what we do," Feldner exhaled. Every word out of his mouth sounded like it had been forced out through a bellows. Everything he did seemed to take enormous effort. He looked like a basset hound, only sadder. Chasing after delinquent payers must have been a remarkably demoralizing job. "What's the person's name?" he asked.

"It's actually two people," I told him. "The first is a woman named Julia MacKenzie, who lived in Gilford Park a little over two years ago. I checked her previous address. And her phone number from then has been disconnected."

Feldner pondered that a moment and asked, "You got a birth date?" I gave him the one Paul had told me, and he dutifully punched the keyboard for a while, positioning his screen so that I couldn't see it—don't give away the merchandise for nothing, after all. He shook his head. "Nah. I don't have anything with that date. Possible she was lying about her age?"

"Not by too much," I told him. Probably not, anyway. What if Paul was a lousy judge of women's ages?

"Okay," Feldner said, "Tell you what. I'll get on it, and we'll get you back your money." He reached into his desk and pulled out a piece of paper already on a clipboard that had a pen attached to it with a rubber band. "Fill out this form, and we'll call you in a few days."

It's not that I hadn't anticipated that response, but I'd been hoping to avoid it. I took the clipboard, but didn't start filling out the form. Instead, I gave Feldner my best smile, the one I hadn't used in a while but was hoping to have saved for a more enjoyable occasion, like after I got off Luther's motorcycle later today, assuming I was still alive.

"I'm really in a hurry on this," I said, my voice dropping to what I'd hoped would be a purr but what sounded more like a seriously sore throat in need of chicken soup *stat*. "Isn't there a way we can speed this process up a little?"

Feldner wasn't buying the voice or the smile. "Lady, it's summer, and our business is slow," he said. "We're only open four days a week, and, frankly, it's mostly to do paperwork. We don't get a lot of walk-in business. So level with me: You're not really interested in this as a collections matter at all, are you? You lost track of this Julia person, and you don't know where to find her, so you want me to push a few buttons and furnish you with an address, right?"

Busted. I dropped the smile and moved into a grimace. "A phone number would do," I suggested.

"We don't work like that. Find yourself a private investigator." Feldner took the clipboard from my hand and put it back in his desk drawer.

"I *am* a private investigator," I told him. I took the license out of my tote bag and showed it to him. "I have a client who wants to find Julia MacKenzie, and the cops won't help me out. I don't have a source in the records bureau. You can take five lousy minutes and punch up her information, can't you? I'll make it worth your while." I pulled a twenty-dollar bill from my wallet and held it between my fingers.

He wheezed out a laugh. "Twenty bucks?" He coughed. "You want me to risk losing my license for *twenty bucks*? You must be really desperate. Not to mention cheap."

"I'm both those things," I assured him, then thought about it. "I don't know that *cheap* is the word I would use . . ."

"Sorry, lady," he said. "I'm not able to help you."

"It's for a really good cause," I tried.

"I gave at the office."

I stood up, defeated. "I really don't know what else to do," I said. I'm not even sure I was speaking to Feldner.

"So now you're doing pathetic?" he said. "You think I don't see pathetic every day and hear pathetic on the phone about once an hour? That's the best you can do?"

I put my hand on my hip and faced him. "I don't have money," I told him. "I'm really not interested in offering you sex."

"You're not my type anyway."

"Yeah, thanks. I really don't have a huge arsenal of tactics to try out," I said, a little more forcefully than I'd anticipated. "You got any ideas?"

"Tell me what's so special. How come you've got to find this Julia person?" Feldner, for all his bluster, really seemed to want to find a reason to help me. "And this time, do us both a favor and tell the truth. I've heard a million lies, and I can smell them through the phone now."

The truth? Fine. "Okay," I said. "I have two ghosts in my house. One of them was about to propose to Julia MacKenzie when he was murdered, and now he wants me to go find her and give her his ring."

He sat there for a long time, his eyes shifting from my face to his phone—maybe he was thinking about calling the cops to have me removed—and back again. Then he sat back in his chair and exhaled again. "I thought I'd heard them all," he said. He put on his glasses. "Give me the twenty."

"What?"

"The twenty bucks. Hand it over."

So I did. Feldner took the bill without looking at it and stuffed it into his shirt pocket. "Now you're a client," he said. "I'll look into this and call you later today. We close at four; it'll be before then. How's that? If anybody asks, I have no way of knowing that you're anything but a creditor searching for a delinquent payer. Got that?"

I nodded. "There's one more person I want to find," I started.

He looked over his half-glasses at me. "For twenty bucks?" he said. "You're on your own for that one." He handed me back the clipboard. "Fill out the form."

I filled out the form.

"There's nothing to it," Luther Mason said. "Just hold onto me and relax."

Personally, I didn't see how that was going to be a relaxing activity, but then, I'd never ridden on a motorcycle before.

There had been just a little tension when Luther rode up to the guesthouse to pick me up. Steven, having been alerted to the situation by his spy (who at one time had been my daughter), made sure to be in the front room at noon just "by coincidence." He glowered at me when I came downstairs in a pair of jeans, my high school windbreaker and a pair of boots.

"Long sleeves and long pants in this heat?" he asked.

"If it gets too hot, I'll take off the jacket," I answered.

"I don't want to hear about what you're going to take off," he snapped.

I stopped in my tracks at the door. "Excuse me?" I said.

"You heard me."

I turned to face him. "Just in case you need a reminder," I told The Swine, "we're not married anymore. So I can see anyone I want and do pretty much anything I like. Are we clear?"

He looked like I'd hit him in the face with a wet washcloth. "I'm not accusing you of . . . anything, Alison," he said.

"That's right, you're not. So get a look on your face that says you've accepted what I've told you, and I'll see you when I get back in a few hours. Okay?"

He changed his disapproving grimace into a disappointed grimace, which I guessed he considered an improvement, and I walked out the front door, where I could hear the motorcycle idling. Motorcycles, even when not in gear, are not quiet.

And, in this case, not even road-ready at the moment. Luther was making some adjustments on two front-wheel bolts with a pair of pliers, which made me put my hand to my mouth.

"Big motorcycle mechanic doesn't have the right tool for the job?" I teased when I got close enough.

"These aren't standard bolts," he answered with a wry grin. "None of the standard wrenches work. Do your homework before you make fun of someone."

Duly chastised, I admitted to knowing nothing about motorcycles and being just a tiny bit apprehensive. I might have mentioned something about throwing up. Luther grinned some more, which was appealing, and said he'd "be gentle." Which was wiseass, and not that appealing.

Luther first instructed me on how to shift my weight when he did, making it easier for him to turn and keep balanced. He then handed me a helmet and insisted I put it on, fitting the straps to my head. "We don't move so much as down the driveway without a helmet," he said.

I bit back my accumulated anxiety and got on the seat after Luther was already on the bike. Now I was supposed to grab him around the waist from behind and hold on tightly. But apparently, I wasn't doing that well enough.

"You've got to hold me tighter than that," Luther yelled over the engine rumble. He adjusted my hands on his midsection, and pulled so that my arms reached further around him. "Like this."

Before I could shout back that I wasn't entirely sure his concern was really for my safety, we were off. And I immediately gripped him like a boa constrictor, too terrified to put together actual words.

Luther knew better than to take roads with a great deal of traffic or the major highways, where all we would see would be other vehicles and the only smells we would experience would be various kinds of exhaust fumes. Instead, he headed for the back roads near the beach and headed south.

The boardwalks were incredibly crowded today. Even a weekday in July with no rain on the New Jersey Shore meant enormous hordes of people flocking toward our most famous natural resource. Aside from Bruce Springsteen.

But Luther, as a longtime rider in this area, knew how to get near the shore without using the main drag. We could see the beach, and he got closer in the areas without a boardwalk or public swimming, where there were fewer people.

It did get a little freaky when I saw a biker riding in the lane next to us turn toward me and tip his helmet. It wasn't his friendliness that bugged me; it was when I realized he was transparent that I got a touch unnerved.

I'd like to tell you the ride was exhilarating, and in a way, it was. The wind in your face really does make you feel free and part of the scene around you, not locked in a separate reality like you are in a car, although I could have done without the bugs hitting my visor every minute or so. I was aware of everything going on around me, and I felt like I was as close to flying as I'll probably ever get.

Aside from that, I was absolutely petrified with fear.

Luther had told me to tap him on the shoulder if I needed to stop for any reason, probably concerned that I might feel sick to my stomach at some point, in which case he'd want to be anywhere but directly in front of me. I didn't feel ill, but I still didn't see how I could keep a tight hold on Luther's waist and tap him on the shoulder at the same time. If I'd had a third arm, believe me I'd have been using it to hold onto him tighter.

Hello. My name is Alison, and I'm a major coward.

Eventually, Luther must have realized I'd had about as much as I could take for a first time out, and he steered toward the entrance to Island Beach State Park.

We finally got off the motorcycle—I doubted I'd ever feel right calling it "a hog," no matter how natural it sounded when Luther said it—near a campsite where the campers had clearly gone to swim in the bay, giving us a somewhat secluded area. All I knew was that it felt great to be standing up and taking off my helmet, even if my legs were a tiny bit shaky. Like a tumbleweed in a tornado.

Luther took off his helmet and gave me a grin. "So," he said. "What'd you think?"

I knew exactly what I wanted to say—I'd been rehearsing it the whole ride. "It was really exhilarating," I told him. "It made me feel alive and free. Please don't make me ever do it again."

Luther laughed. "I'm afraid I'm going to have to," he said. "There's no other way to get you back home."

"There's no bus?"

"Afraid not," Luther said.

"Well okay, but just that one time."

And that's when he kissed me.

I enjoyed the moment for just a moment—and he was quite a good kisser and the mustache was interesting—and then pulled away.

Right now, my life was very complicated. I had an ex-husband in my house, not to mention two ghosts and even more guests, all of whom were clamoring for my attention. It's not that Luther had taken me by surprise; you have to really be distracted not to see a kiss coming at you. But the swing of emotions from fear to relief to suddenly being held close was a little startling. And I realized I barely knew Luther; we'd met only a few days earlier. Aside from the job-related trip to a biker bar, this was the first time we'd been alone together since our first meeting, at Veg Out.

And frankly, I felt a little like a line was being crossed without my expressed consent.

Luther gave me a confused look. "Too soon?" he asked. "Or did I miss a signal?"

I hadn't had time to sort through my feelings yet, so I said, "Maybe both. I'm not sure, but I know I'm not ready."

Luther nodded, absorbing the information. "Fair enough," he said. "You let me know when you are."

"Sorry if I gave you the wrong impression," I said.

"Don't be. I can handle it. I'm a big boy. That's what my therapist says, anyway."

Luther was constantly surprising me. "You see a therapist?" I asked.

He grinned on the left side of his mouth. "Bikers can't have issues that need to be addressed?" he said.

"That wasn't what I was thinking," I told him. Although it sort of had been. I decided to change the subject. "So how'd you get off work at the bike shop on a weekday to come here with me?" I asked.

"Well, it's possible I didn't tell you the whole truth about working at the bike shop," Luther said, grinning on both sides now.

"You don't really have a job?" I asked.

"No, it's more in the area of my not so much working at the bike shop as I own the bike shop."

I nodded. "Ah. So that makes it easier to get off work when you want to."

He laughed. "Yeah, my boss is really understanding about that sort of thing."

"I'll bet. How'd you come to own the bike shop?"

Luther looked shy, almost, like a little boy who was worried about sounding too boastful. "I worked hard for a long time and saved my money. Then I came into a little more when my mom passed on, and I had just enough to buy it out from the old owner, who liked me and wanted to retire. I've been running the place for a couple of years now, and I have to tell you, it's been the best time of my life."

We sat on the grass and Luther produced what he called a "picnic lunch." It was in a white paper bag in a carrying compartment on the side of the bike, and consisted of a roast beef sandwich on rye for me (he'd called ahead for my order) and a green salad in a plastic container for him, both of which he said he'd gotten at New Deli, a sandwich store in Harbor Haven.

He also brought out a small bottle of wine with one glass—Luther said he didn't drink when he rode—and a bottle of diet soda. He poured for me, we clinked glass to bottle, and partook of our elegant repast, which took roughly seven minutes to finish.

"Who do you think killed Big Bob?" I asked Luther as we sat there. I took off the long-sleeved jacket; it was well into the nineties.

"Is that why you came with me today?" he asked. "To pump me for information?"

"I'm not asking for information," I said. "I'm asking for your opinion."

"You're dodging the question."

"I know."

Luther lay back and looked at the sky through his sunglasses. "I honestly don't know who could have been that mad at Big Bob," he told me after a while. "Maybe he and Wilson got into something and that's why Wilson took off. Wilson is sort of . . . impulsive."

"Violent?" I asked.

"Nothing serious, but I saw him take a swing at a guy once

or twice. He and Big Bob got into a fight about a bike once. A
broken beer bottle was waved around, but nobody was seriously hurt."

"That sounds impulsive, all right. Was Big Bob violent?"

Luther shrugged. "I didn't think so, but it's possible I didn't
know him as well as I thought. Maybe Big Bob was involved
in something I didn't know about, drugs or something.
But . . ." His voice trailed off.

"But what?" Sure, I liked Luther, but the truth was, I *had*
come out today to try and sort out the Big Bob thing, at least
to have a direction in which to go. That was part of it, anyway.
And Luther seemed to be thinking of something that might
suggest a direction.

"There was a thing with Little Bob, not long before Big
Bob stopped being around," Luther said. "I was never really
sure what it was about. But there was this one night that they
got into an argument at the Sprocket, and they pretty much
had to tear Little's hands off of Big's throat. You know, sometimes Little Bob doesn't remember how big and strong he
really is."

"So you think Little Bob might be a suspect?" I asked. It
was simultaneously easy and difficult to imagine; the man
sounded so gentle but looked so capable of doing serious damage.

Luther shook his head. "I can't even think it. Little Bob is
such a sweet guy most of the time. And I think the argument
was about Big Bob's ex, which just wouldn't have made sense,
even then."

That stunned me. "They were fighting about Maxie?" I
asked.

"I'm not sure. Her name sure came up a lot that night; that's
all I know. I asked Big Bob about it later, and he said it was
just a misunderstanding and that they had both had too much
to drink. But the way he said it made me think he might be
lying."

"Did you ask Little Bob?" I said.

"Tell you the truth, I wasn't in much of a hurry to see Little Bob get that mad again," Luther answered. "I haven't ever mentioned it, and after Big Bob vanished, it just didn't seem that important. I had no idea he was dead."

There was one more person from the Sprocket to ask about. "What about Rocco?" I said. "Any dark moments I need to know about him?"

"I don't know Rocco that well, just sort of a bar kind of thing," Luther said. "I don't ride with him. He's older, you know. I'll see if I can find anything out."

We sat for a while longer without talking. I don't know what was on Luther's mind, but I had finished the small bottle of wine and was feeling just a tiny bit tipsy, trying to sort out what I'd just heard and decide what I could do with my new information.

"We should get back," Luther said a short while later.

I was so preoccupied that I didn't even get antsy about climbing onto the back of Luther's motorcycle again. Before I had time to think about it, my helmet was on and we were off, heading north. Luther took a more direct route this time, and we were back at the guesthouse in less than an hour. Despite my reservation about being on the bike—not to mention the awkward kiss—I had enjoyed the picnic, and told him so when we reached my front door.

As I handed Luther back the helmet, Melissa came running out of the house, looking as close to panicked as I've ever seen my preternaturally composed daughter appear.

"You've got to come inside!" she huffed. Then she looked at Luther, seemed to remember the rules about what we can and can't say in front of the uninitiated, and said, "A friend of ours needs help."

That couldn't be good. I looked at Luther. "Go on inside," he said. "I'll call you."

He got himself back onto the bike, and I headed for the house with Melissa. "What's up?" I asked as soon as I heard the bike's engine start up.

"Maxie's going crazy," my daughter told me.

"That's it? Maxie goes crazy twice a week."

"Phyllis Coates called," Melissa told me. "She said she couldn't get you on your cell."

"I couldn't hear it, I guess. What did Phyllis want?"

We made it to the front room, where Maxie was literally circling the ceiling. She went around and around up by the crown molding with such speed that she seemed to be one incredibly elongated ghost stretching 360 degrees around the room.

Melissa gave me a significant look. "The Seaside Heights police have arrested Maxie's mom," she said.

My stomach, still in recovery from the transportation I'd been subjected to this afternoon, sank down to somewhere around my knees.

"What for?" I asked, but I was sure I didn't want to hear the answer.

"For murdering Big Bob," Melissa said.

I was right; I didn't want to hear the answer.

Seventeen

"I don't recall agreeing to alert you when we had a suspect." Detective Martin Ferry of the Seaside Heights Police Department was walking to the chair behind his desk in the dismally lit squad room and turned back to give me the benefit of his smug grin. It was not having the desired effect. Or perhaps it was—if Ferry's desire was to piss me off.

"Look at my face, Detective," I said. "Do I appear amused in any way? You've got the wrong suspect behind bars."

Ferry sat down in his squeaky chair behind his standard-issue government desk, and his face turned sour. "And you know that because you have tangible evidence proving Katherine O'Malley Malone did not kill Robert Benicio?" he asked.

"I know the suspect," I said, ignoring that I hadn't even known Kitty's real name was Katherine. I mean, it figured, but I'd never considered it before. "Technically speaking, I bought my house from her. But even if she wanted to kill Big

Bob, she couldn't possibly have done it. She's not big or strong enough."

"My former partner would argue with you about that," Ferry admonished. "She believed that women could be just as big, strong, and stupid as men. She thought a woman could play major-league baseball, if she wanted to." He waited, as if expecting me to laugh uproariously at the very notion.

"We just don't want to show up the boys and make them cry," I deadpanned. "So, what makes you think Kitty Malone could even have considered killing her ex-son-in-law?"

"What reason would I have to tell you the evidence we have against a woman you consider a friend?" he asked, with a growl on his face.

It was a good question. I'd been relying on the idea that Ferry was going to act like a person and not a cop, but it wasn't seeming especially likely. "Well, how about the fact that I could inform the press that you're holding a woman in her fifties on no evidence? A woman who has devoted her life to helping local children with language disabilities?"

He waved a hand in indifference. "The arrest will be on a police PR release within minutes," he said. "Do you think we want to hide the fact that we caught a murderer?"

"How about the fact that you haven't found the other missing biker?" I asked. "Wilson Meyers might just as well have killed Big Bob—in fact, it's more likely that he did it than Kitty. Is that going to be in your press release?"

If I could appeal to Ferry's ego, he was more likely to tell me something he didn't want to say. That was my theory, anyway.

"Wilson Meyers didn't kill Robert Benicio," he said with an air of certainty.

"I think he did." Challenge what a man like Ferry knows, and he'll tell you exactly how he knows it.

"Unlike Mrs. Malone, Wilson Meyers didn't have a reason to kill Benicio," he began. How did he know? Ferry had no idea where Wilson was, let alone what his motives might have been. "Wilson Meyers was not heard recently saying that he was glad that Benicio was dead." I started to protest, and Ferry held up a finger. "*And*," he emphasized, "Wilson Meyers did not have the murder weapon stored in his basement."

Wait. What?

"You're telling me that Kitty Malone had—"

"A large adjustable wrench whose metal matched the shavings that were found still lodged in Robert Benicio's skull, yes," Ferry answered. "A search warrant issued by a judge—which wasn't even necessary because Malone played the innocent, let us in and didn't object—turned up the murder weapon in a toolbox in her basement. The tests are conclusive. It's the same metal."

That sent me into a momentary trance. If Kitty had the murder weapon in her house, and she'd said on more than one occasion that she had been mad enough to kill Big Bob, could she really have hit him on the head with a wrench hard enough to murder him?

"How is that possible, to match the metal from a wrench?" I asked. "Aren't almost all wrenches made from steel or something like it?"

Ferry nodded. "But the shavings matched in age and manufacturer as well as type of metal. It's not as conclusive as the striations on a bullet casing, but it'll hold up in court. That wrench is the murder weapon."

That sounded as plausible as a giant rabbit handing out brightly colored hard-boiled eggs, but I knew I wasn't convincing Ferry, so I moved on. "What led you to Kitty to begin with?" I asked.

"I heard that she was making noises about how she was glad Benicio was dead and how she'd have been happy to do it herself."

"Yeah, because all brilliant criminals run around screaming to the high heavens about how they should be considered a suspect. Amazing, Holmes!" I said.

"Not every criminal is brilliant," Ferry answered. "And a lot of them are so proud of getting away with a crime that they'll tell anybody who walks in and sits on the next barstool."

I was probably better off not talking to him about Kitty anymore right now. "Can I see her?" I asked. "I promise I haven't baked a file into a cake or anything."

Ferry made a "droll" face and stood up. "You can see her," he said. "But it's not going to do either of you any good." Cops love to say stuff like that; it makes them sound tough and authoritative. I let him have his smugness as long as he'd take me to Kitty. If I showed up at home without having seen her, it was possible Maxie would find that adjustable wrench and come after me with it. She was, let's say, a little high-strung.

He led me down one corridor to a second, which led to a door, behind which were three holding cells. The only one occupied was Kitty's. A uniformed officer with a sidearm sat behind a desk opposite the cell.

"She'll be arraigned in the morning and then moved to county lockup," Ferry said, making sure Kitty could hear us. That was below the belt, and I mentally took the detective off my Christmas card list. That would teach him.

"County?" I asked. "You don't think she'll be out on bail in the morning?"

"On a murder? She's not going to make the bail the judge will set. Your friend's going to be in jail for a long time." He grinned.

"You're a regular ray of sunshine, Detective," I said. "Now could you leave us humans alone to talk?"

Ferry scrunched up his face into a grimace and left without another word, which was a number of words too late, but better than nothing. The officer behind the desk, whose nameplate read "Montrose," set a chair down next to the bars and then retreated to his post.

"I'm not listening to your conversation," he said. Officer Montrose couldn't have been more than twenty-two years old, and looked like he should start shaving any day now.

"Thank you," Kitty said, and I sat down. "Does Maxie know?" she asked before I could say hello.

"How do you think I got here?" I asked. "Maxie heard when a reporter called my house and left a voice mail."

"Is she all right?" Kitty asked. In context, it didn't seem odd that a woman would ask if her daughter was handling things well, despite said daughter having been dead for nearly two years.

"She's a little . . . antsy," I said. "She's worried about you. What happened?"

"I honestly don't know," Kitty told me. "I was doing some painting when the doorbell rang. Seaside Heights police, and they wanted to come in and talk, they said. Could they look around the house, they said. I didn't see any reason why not; I hadn't done anything. Then that detective started asking me about Bob Benicio, and I got a little snarky, I guess."

Oh, boy. "What did you say to him, Kitty?" I asked.

She looked away, pretending to examine the cell, which was not especially noteworthy as cells go. There were walls and a cot. That was about it. This was not the kind of place a prisoner stayed long. "I might have mentioned that I wasn't sorry that man was dead," she said softly.

"You were talking to a cop, Kitty," I reminded her.

"I know." She still wouldn't look back at me, no doubt out of embarrassment. "It's just that I get so mad whenever his name comes up."

I leaned a little closer to the bars. "What is it about that, Kitty?" I asked. "I realize that he hurt Maxie and that is absolutely inexcusable, but your reaction for just one incident seems a little extreme. What's going on?"

Kitty hung her head a little, then took a deep breath and looked at me. "The first time Maxie's father, Phil, hit me, I thought it was because he'd been drinking," she said. "The next time, I figured it was my fault, because I'd been on his case about something. Isn't that funny? I can't even remember what it was. But then there was a third time, and a fourth. After the fifth time, I had a broken rib. And the next day, I packed Maxie up when he was at work, and we moved here from Chicago."

"You never saw him again?" I asked, in a voice that I hoped was gentle.

Kitty shook her head. "He never even looked for us, and I was glad," she answered. "I heard he died sometime in the late nineties. Had another wife by then, another kid. I don't know if he . . . abused them, too. I always thought I should reach out to his widow, but I never did, and I'm ashamed of that."

"I don't think you need to be ashamed," I told her. "You did what you had to do to protect your daughter." I really hated myself for it, but then I asked, "Did you do that again two years ago?"

Kitty stared at me a moment with a blank expression on her face. Then her eyes widened. "Are you asking me if I killed Big Bob?" she asked me.

I cringed, because that might have been loud enough for the officer at the desk to hear. He showed no sign of it, working on a computer screen. "I had to ask," I said to Kitty. "The cops seem so sure."

"I understand," she said in a more normal tone. "No, for the record, I didn't murder my daughter's ex-husband. I was mad enough, but it's just not in my nature. I can't figure out why they think I did."

As quickly as possible, I outlined what Ferry had told me about the reports of threats from Kitty and the adjustable wrench in her toolbox that appeared to be the murder weapon.

"I don't even think I own an adjustable wrench that big," Kitty said. "I don't remember buying one."

"Ferry will say you're lying. He thinks he's got you solid," I told her. "Have you spoken to a lawyer yet?"

Kitty shook her head. "One's supposedly on his way. I called the real-estate lawyer who handled the sale of Maxie's house—you remember, of course—and he got in touch with a friend who does . . ." She cringed a little. "He does criminal work. When the door opened, I thought you were him."

"What's his name?" I asked. "Maybe I can help."

"Alex Hayward," Kitty said. "And I don't know how much help you can be, dear."

"Why not?"

"Well, somebody had to tell people I had said I would have killed Big Bob myself, and the only person I said that to was you," Kitty told me.

Eighteen

"You put my mother behind bars?" I had decided not to tell Maxie about Kitty's comment, but when she'd asked about my visit with her mother, it had come spilling out. Maxie, having missed the afternoon spook show (according to Paul and Melissa), was hovering over my bed, onto which I had flung myself in exhaustion, although it was not even dinnertime yet.

"I didn't actually put her behind bars," I said. Well, *somebody* had to defend me, and since it was just Maxie, Paul and me in the room, there were few appropriate candidates. "I'm relatively sure I didn't even mention her name in Detective Ferry's presence before she was arrested. It doesn't make sense."

"She didn't tell anybody else! You did something to get her thrown in jail!" Maxie's clothing changed, possibly without her knowledge, from an orange top and khakis to a black T-shirt with no slogan (the first time I think I'd seen that on her) and black leather pants. Her hair spiked out. It was like having an argument with a see-through Pat Benatar.

I couldn't see a way to calm her down, and Paul, who might have been helpful if he'd been listening, seemed distracted. His head was down, almost parallel to the floor. In fact, he was hovering almost horizontally, like a man floating facedown on a raft in a swimming pool.

"What can we do to help Kitty?" I asked him in an attempt to rouse him out of whatever reverie this was, but he just mumbled something and kept floating. It was a little disconcerting, to tell you the truth.

"Paul!" Maxie yelled. Say what you want about Maxie, she could get a man's attention. Even a dead man's.

Paul looked at her. "What?" he asked.

"You're the resident private dick. What do we do to help my mom?"

I supposed that crack was supposed to be insulting—I do, after all, have a private-investigator's license—but I was aware that I was a fraud, so she wasn't saying anything I didn't already know. I was far more concerned about Kitty.

"Clearly," Paul answered, "the best thing to do is to prove that she didn't kill Big Bob."

"Thanks for the news bulletin, Blitzer," Maxie said. "How do we go about doing that?"

"Find out who did." Paul was being as much help as a pack of tissues in a hurricane.

"Once again, that's really helpful, Captain Obvious," I said. "Can you give me some direction here? Where do I take the Big Bob investigation now? The murder weapon was in Kitty's house. If she didn't kill him, how is that possible?"

Paul seemed to wake up a little. "Well, the first thing you'll have to do is figure out why Detective Ferry wants to make it look like Mrs. Malone might have killed Big Bob. I mean," and he gave me a significant look, "*metal shavings*? In a skull? Left by a wrench? I'm not even sure that's physically possible, but it's ridiculously unlikely. The detective is trying to sell you a load of goods, Alison, and you're buying it because you feel guilty."

As charged, I thought. "So beyond pointing out that I'm stupid, what do you think our course of action should be?" I asked.

"You're going to have to get into the house and look around that basement," Paul said. "It sounds to me like someone wanted it to look like Mrs. Malone is the killer. That means they had to break into the basement without her knowing and plant the wrench. If you find out how they did it, Alison, that might lead us to who."

"Besides that, what?" I asked.

Maxie, whose clothing had changed once again, this time to a pair of blue jeans and a T-shirt that read "Future Home of Bob's Dry Cleaners," seemed to have calmed down, or what passed for calm with Maxie. She was directly over my head, possibly in an effort to intimidate me. It was working.

Paul did his goatee stroke, his best Sherlockian move. "You need to establish a list of possible suspects," he said. "If Mrs. Malone didn't kill Big Bob, and we're assuming she didn't—"

"Damn right," Maxie said.

"Then we have to determine who had a motive, the opportunity, and the ability to do so. What do we have so far, Alison?" He turned to me with those piercing blue eyes, the only parts of his body that seemed solid most of the time.

"We have Little Bob, who apparently had some kind of argument with Big Bob just before he vanished." I turned to Maxie. "They were apparently arguing about you. Any ideas?"

She pursed her lips. "None. Little Bob never said anything to me."

I went back to counting suspects. "We have Wilson Meyers, who vanished right before Big Bob died. Did you know him, Maxie?"

Maxie made a wavering motion with her hand: *Sort of yes, sort of no.* "I'd seen him a couple of times. I mean, I didn't hang around with this crowd very long, just a couple of months. But Wilson was sort of the sidekick, you know? A mouse. You only knew he was there when somebody else talked to him. Not invisible, but sort of in the baseboards, looking for crumbs. And then once in a while he'd blow up over something. I think he was using."

"Swell," I told her. "A violent drug user. We need to find Wilson, don't we, Paul?"

He was looking out the window. "What?"

"Wilson Meyers," I reminded him, and he seemed to focus again.

"I don't know if that helps or not," Paul grumbled. "Besides Wilson and Little Bob, we have the other biker, Rocco Palenty, who doesn't have a motive, so far as I can tell. It's possible— and I'm sorry, Maxie, but I just said 'possible'—that Big Bob was involved in something bad, and the people he worked with had a grudge."

Maxie nodded slowly. "It's possible. I hadn't seen him for a while before all this happened. I don't know what was going on."

"What about Luther?" Paul asked me.

"Luther?" I repeated. "Luther's our client. He asked for the investigation, and he doesn't have a motive." Besides, he was a pretty good kisser.

Maxie shook her head. "Not Luther," she said. "He loved Big Bob."

"I agree in theory," Paul said. "But aside from Kitty, whom I'm dismissing on principle, I'm not eliminating any suspects until I have proof that they *didn't* murder Big Bob. I'm only saying don't assume anything."

I'd come up here to rest and escape, I remembered. Melissa and Steven were just home from the movies, I saw out my window (that man was relentless in his quest to be the fun parent), and she'd be full of questions. He'd be full of something else. "I'm going downstairs," I said. "If there's another way I can mess up today, feel free to call me."

And just as I said "call me," my cell phone rang. The caller ID indicated I was being contacted by "FIND DEADBEATS," so I came close to not answering until I realized who was calling. I hit the button.

"Ms. Kerby, this is Tim Feldner at Able Collection Service."

"Shouldn't that be 'AAAAAAble Collection Service,' Tim?" I wasn't really in a state of mind to be polite. If my mother were here, she'd be appalled but contain her horror and tell herself that I, being perfect, must have a very good reason for acting so rudely. I did, but it wasn't Feldner's fault.

"That's very amusing," he answered atonally. "Yeah, I've never heard *that* one before. I have information about your Julia MacKenzie. Do you want it, or not?"

I glanced up at Paul, who had flipped over onto his back and was letting his arms hang down, as if he was lying on a beam. When Maxie, who was pouting in the corner, wasn't around, I would try to find out what exactly was sapping Paul of his— pardon the expression—spirit.

"Yeah, I want it," I told Feldner. "Fire away." That sounded very PI-like, I thought.

"It isn't much," he answered, and I thought I heard something scratching, like he was rubbing his pencil on his head. It was better not to picture this stuff. "I found the records of her living in Gilford Park, and her job in Freehold. After that, there is a speeding ticket in Harbor Haven—she went fifty-three in a thirty-five-mile zone—and continued employment at CableCom until the beginning of this year. Then, nothing."

I hadn't even heard anything worth taking a note on yet. "What do you mean, nothing?" I asked.

"I mean, nothing," Feldner said. "The rent checks stop at the place in Gilford Park. The bank account at Wells Fargo is closed. Even the speeding ticket was paid last November, and no further violations are recorded. No checking account, no residence established, no employment registered, no legal name change, and, weirdest of all, no credit-card bills. She doesn't actually have a credit history. Who is this woman—Mata Hari?"

Once again, I looked at Paul, considering what I could ask him about his lost love. He was lying on his back and had not actually blinked in about two minutes. He seemed to be a hopeless case, or at least so upset about my lack of progress that pushing him any harder might be dangerous, or at best cruel.

"I don't know," I told Feldner. "Something's certainly not right about it."

"You're damn straight," the collection man answered. "I'm glad I'm not really looking for this woman. Either she's actually vanished off the face of the earth or she very seriously doesn't want to be found."

This day just kept getting better and better. I decided to go downstairs. The people down there either loved me, paid me, or were my ex-husband. And they were all alive. A real advantage.

It was too hot to cook, as if I would anyway, and too hot to eat anything that was, you know, hot. So, over sub sandwiches that evening, I asked Melissa whether she'd be happier going to day camp for the month of August. "Cleaning up around here and hanging with all the seniors and your mother must get really boring after a while," I suggested.

My daughter looked at me as if I had suggested sending her to Abu Ghraib on vacation. "What are you talking about?" she asked. "I don't want to go to day camp. None of my friends are going, and besides, I like it here with my parents." She was savvy enough not to overemphasize that last word—a crafty one, my daughter.

"Well, after Monday, it's just going to be you and me with the guests in the house again," I told her. "Dad's going to find another place to stay."

"What?" Melissa said, heading in the direction of full wail. "Dad's leaving?"

Steven, about four inches into his foot-long everything sub, twitched his eye and shook his head. "I'm sorry—what did you just say?" he asked.

"I have more guests booked," I explained. "I'm going to need the room you're staying in now. You'll have to find a hotel or something." *I* was savvy enough not to overemphasize the "or something," too. With any luck at all, he'd take this as an opportunity to head back to California and patch things up with the Silicone Queen.

"Thanks for the advance warning," he snapped.

Oops. Had I forgotten to mention this to him before? Monday was, after all, five whole days away. "I'm sorry about the short notice," I told him, trying to save face. "I honestly thought I'd mentioned it before."

My ex sighed. "Maybe you did," he said. "You know how I get when I'm working on a project. And this idea of small investors getting a piece of the pie is exactly the kind of thing that occupies my mind." He took a hefty bite of his sub, chewed aggressively, then had almost swallowed everything in his mouth when he said, "Isn't there some arrangement we can make here?"

He couldn't be asking what it sounded like he was asking. "Like what?" I prodded.

"Well," Steven looked at Melissa, then seemed to choose his words carefully. "Maybe we could share."

Okay, so he *could* be asking what it sounded like he was asking. Even Melissa raised her eyebrows at that suggestion.

"I don't think that's a good idea," I said calmly.

"Dad could stay in my room," Liss suggested. "I could sleep on the floor, or in your room until we have another vacancy." She'd learned how to talk like a real innkeeper since we'd started getting paying guests.

Steven, regaining his diplomatic face, shook his head. "No, Mom's right, Lissie," he said. "I need to find a hotel for a while, and then maybe an apartment here in town." He made sure to maintain eye contact with me when he added, "I think I'll be here in Harbor Haven for a while."

Lucy Simone stuck her head in from the den, just opening the swinging door enough to be seen. "Excuse me?" she called. "May I come in for a moment?"

I stood up, always anxious to help a guest. "Sure, Lucy," I said. "What can I do for you?"

Lucy walked into the kitchen and pretended to "notice" Steven at the table. Her mouth might've wanted to talk to me, but Melissa and I were irrelevant to her eyes. "I just wanted to clarify—about that laptop computer flying by the library? I think I saw it again just now heading up the stairs to the second floor, but it was going really fast, so I can't be sure." I'd alerted Melissa to my lie about the laptop, but the fact that she was sitting next to me here in the kitchen was going to really damage my ability to use it in this case.

I had also spoken to each of the Senior Plus guests—as I always do—about not mentioning any ghostly happenings around the house to anyone outside of their own tour. The tour company *wants* spooky things to happen, but I'm not crazy about the reputation the guesthouse has around Harbor Haven, or the added burden on Melissa for being "Ghost Girl," which frankly is more of a worry to me than it seems to be to my daughter.

But this was an eyewitness incident; no matter what I'd said to Maxie, she did sometimes need the computer (often at my request), and there was very little she could do to conceal my old, bulky laptop other than putting on a small tent as clothing. Maybe I would ask her about that when she was in a better mood. But there was nothing to be done about it now; I'd have to try and defuse the situation as quickly as possible.

"I doubt that's what you really were seeing . . ." I began, but Lucy wasn't looking at me. She'd never taken her eyes off Steven.

He stood, taking advantage of the attention. "I think I can help you," he said to Lucy, gesturing toward the door. "You say you saw something fly by the door? Can you show me where?"

Lucy giggled. No, seriously.

Steven led her out the door, and as it swung back and forth, I could hear Lucy say, "It was the freakiest thing!" as Steven laughed his charming laugh.

I wondered what he'd tell her, since I didn't think he knew about the ghosts. Unless . . .

"Liss," I asked my daughter, "have you said anything to Dad about Paul and Maxie?"

Melissa looked up from her turkey sub with a slightly alarmed expression. "No!" she said with great force. "I know I'm not supposed to. But if Dad's going to live here . . ."

"Dad's *not* going to live here," I told her. "Get that out of your head. I'm very happy that you and he are getting along so well, and that you're able to spend time together this summer, but no. I'm not letting him come back, we're not getting married again, and he's not living in this house, ever. Is that clear?"

No one can look at you with pity better than a ten-year-old girl. And among ten-year-old girls, mine is considered the gold standard at this activity. Other ten-year-old girls come to her for "looking at your parents with pity" lessons. This wasn't necessarily the pinnacle of her work in the area, but it was certainly in her top ten attempts.

"I meant, if he's going to live here in Harbor Haven," Melissa said.

"Oh." If I had felt any smaller, I could have squeezed between two boards in the kitchen floor and vanished.

"Anyway, if he is going to live here, he's going to hear the rumors about the house," Melissa continued, as if I hadn't just been reduced to a quivering mass of stupidity. "What are we going to tell him then?"

"Let's see if that time comes first," I said. "But for right now, let's just ignore the fact that Paul and Maxie are here when Dad's around, okay? And you've been doing a really good job of keeping him out of the house when the spook shows are on, so let's keep that going. Think you can do that?"

"Sure," Melissa said. "He goes pretty much wherever I suggest."

I remembered what that was like, and hoped that The

Swine wouldn't disappoint his daughter the way he had his wife. "Okay," I said. "Now, do you have any idea what's been bothering Paul?"

She widened her eyes in recognition. "No!" she said. "I thought you would know. He's been floating around like a bath toy all day." Once again I gave my daughter credit for being more perceptive than I am. "I know he asked you to do something for him. Do you think it's about that?"

"Maybe," I said. Before she could ask, I added, "He wants me to find somebody for him, someone he knew when he was alive. And it's been harder to do than I expected. I hope he's not getting like this because I'm letting him down." My roast-beef sub was suddenly less appetizing than a minute ago—was I being arrogant in trying to find Julia without Paul's help, and causing him the ghost equivalent of pain in the process?

"So you're trying to help Luther and Maxie find out who killed her ex-husband, and you're trying to find an old friend of Paul's?" Melissa asked. "Isn't that a lot to do all at once?"

I nodded. "I'm worried I can't do it all myself."

Melissa tilted her head in an expression that said, "Well . . . ?" Then she said, "You know what you do whenever you feel over-whelmed. Who do you always call?"

Jeannie.

I sighed. "Not sure I can do that this time. It's a ghost thing."

My daughter smiled with her wise-beyond-her-years de-meanor. "You'll find a way," she said. "Or Jeannie will figure a way that it's not a ghost thing. She's really good at that."

Steven pushed the swinging door open and walked back into the kitchen, grinning. "I think I actually convinced her there was a real person carrying a laptop whom she didn't see because of the way the light hit the computer casing," he said, sitting down and picking up his sandwich. "There are days I believe I can talk anybody into anything." He took a big bite and chewed thoughtfully. After he managed to clear his mouth again, he looked at me and asked, "Now, what was that all about?"

Luckily, I'd had time to think. "There's no point in trying to keep it from you, Steven," I said with my best sincere voice. "You can't have been in town even a few days and not heard the rumors about this house."

The Swine does many attitudes well, but coy is not one of them. "Rumors?" he asked. Melissa stifled a laugh.

I nodded with great solemnity. "I hadn't been back here long enough when I bought the house, or I might have held off," I said. "But it's relatively common knowledge around Harbor Haven that this place is haunted."

Melissa's eyes showed no change, but she scratched her nose, which is something she does when she's nervous. She was clearly wondering if I was going to let Steven in on the truth about Paul and Maxie.

My ex laughed. "Haunted?" he said. "People really believe in haunted houses?"

I saw an opening, a way to make things easier, even in spite of what I'd said to Liss only a few minutes before. "Can you believe it? But then I discovered that there are people who *want* to take a vacation in a haunted house, so I've been playing it up to some of the guests." I told him about the Senior Plus Tours, excluding the fact that the ghosts involved were actual ghosts. No sense telling The Swine *everything*. He hadn't done so for me, after all. "So we do some spook shows twice a day now—all fake, of course, with flying objects and stuff—but that's just for the Senior Plus guests," I explained. "Lucy's not part of the tour, so she isn't in on the gag. And I guess something happened in front of her that wasn't supposed to."

Steven's face had gone from amused to enthralled as I'd told him my sordid tale, and now he was positively jubilant in his demeanor. "That's *amazing*, Alison!" he gushed. "You took a business challenge and turned it into an asset. I'm so proud of you!" Really, his pride in me made me feel so *vindicated* (that's sarcasm, ladies and gentlemen)! He walked over and embraced me, which I endured without reciprocation. I just let him hug me, smiled neutrally, and took a bite of my sub. "Did I also hear that a TV show shot here a few months ago?" he asked. "Was that about the 'ghosts,' too?"

That comment about the TV show was kind of out of nowhere, and my suspicious nature tickled the back of my throat. "No, that was just an accident," I said. "The house they were going to use burned down, so they stayed here for a few weeks. It was no big deal."

Steven had a way of looking at me that made me think he didn't believe me. But he shrugged it off and asked, "How can I help?"

Help? When we were married, he'd never so much as volunteered to help me with the dinner dishes, so this question had caught me sort of off guard. "Help," I said, thinking. "Well, one of the more difficult things is seeing to it that Lucy is out of the house when we're putting on one of the spectral spectaculars. And she seems to find you fascinating. Think you could keep her occupied for a short period twice a day?"

The Swine smiled, then a thought seemed to occur to him, and he looked at our daughter. "That's what you've been doing with me, isn't it, you little minx?" he asked her.

Melissa grinned and looked away from him. Perhaps she was a little minx, after all. "I guess so," she drawled at him.

Steven gave her a big hug and laughed. "It's okay, honey," he said. "You were helping Mom. You did the right thing." Then he turned to me. "All right, Alison," he said, although I could tell he wanted to say "Ally." "I'll help out with Lucy."

"Thank you," I told my ex-husband. I never thought I'd say that to him ever again. This was threatening to become an actual touching moment, so naturally Maxie stuck her head through the ceiling, wearing an expression I wouldn't have expected on her: concern.

"Something's going on with Paul," she said. "You'd better come upstairs."

Nineteen

"It's *nothing*," Paul insisted. "I'm all right."

"You don't look all right," I told him.

Getting away from Steven without a plausible explanation had been a little tricky. I was lucky that way, because making an excuse for me to leave and getting Melissa to keep her father occupied solved two problems at the same time: It got me out of the kitchen to attend to Paul, and it kept Melissa from seeing what I was seeing, which would have upset her.

"I'm fine," Paul reiterated.

It was hard to accept his assurance on the subject. "You're upside down," I told him.

"No kidding," Maxie said. "Like he didn't know he was upside down."

Paul was, in fact, completely inverted. In my house, that's not entirely odd. The difference this time was that it seemed he had gotten that way unintentionally.

"I've been upside down before," Paul pointed out. "I float. I'm a ghost, right?"

"Yeah," I agreed. "But then, you could straighten up when you wanted to. Let's see you do that now."

Hanging from the newly installed ceiling in the attic, face about three feet off the floor, Paul looked like a muscular, goateed, English Canadian bat. He scowled and flared his nostrils a little. "Fine," he said. But when he tried to straighten up, he could bend at the waist and move himself side to side but could not become normally vertical. It looked like he was doing those abs crunches where you hang from your feet (as seen on TV).

"Okay," he said, huffing and puffing a bit. "Maybe I can't straighten up. But that's no big deal. I can get along just fine the way I am now."

"Doesn't all the ectoplasm rush to your head?" I asked.

"Okay," Maxie said. "So you're going to spend the rest of whatever floating ar nd like you're hanging by your feet from a hook?"

"Do you have any suggestions?" Paul demanded.

It was up to me to mediate this dispute, and to bring some sanity to the proceedings. Laugh if you want to. "Paul, do you think you might be sick or something?"

"He's already dead," Maxie noted. "How much worse can he get?"

Paul and I ignored her. "The last time I saw you, you were floating horizontally, like you were in a swimming pool," I said. "You didn't seem very happy then. Was this starting to happen to you already?"

Paul was silent for a moment, and I wasn't sure whether he was pondering the question or simply wasn't interested in answering it. Eventually he said, "I don't know. I can't say I've been feeling strangely, because I don't really feel all that much. But something has been wrong."

I needed to get Maxie out of the room. "Would you mind going downstairs and telling Melissa that Paul's okay? I'm sure she was worried." Maxie and Melissa have an interesting relationship, in that they actually like each other. You can't always choose your child's friends.

Maxie, glad to have reason to talk to Melissa—and warned to do so discreetly if Steven or Lucy was in the room—zipped through the attic floor and vanished. I looked Paul up and down, toe to head.

"Is this about Julia?" I asked him. "Is she weighing on your mind so heavily that it's giving your head more gravity?"

"I really don't think so," he answered. "But what have you found out?"

I can be extremely stubborn when I have decided on something. "I'll let you know when I find out something for sure," I assured Paul. "But don't ask me about every step of the way, because that's just going to worry you and slow me down."

"Worry me? Is there something for me to be worried about?"

"See what I mean?" I asked.

"All right, so finding Julia is weighing on my mind," he admitted. "But I honestly don't think that's enough to turn me upside down."

I was already craning my neck to look at him; this was going to prove to be a problem. "Is there anything I can do? Something Maxie can research?" I asked. Maxie does the online research for our investigations when necessary. She has unusually keen computer skills, especially for someone who's dead. But the occasional floating laptop computer was the price one had to pay for such talents.

"Believe me, Alison, if I could think of something that might fix this, I wouldn't hold back," Paul told me. "Ask Maxie to . . ."

No need to wait; Maxie appeared through the floorboards once again. "I'm here," she said. "Ask me what?"

"Where is she?" Paul asked, trying to twist himself around. "Ah, there. Maxie, I'd appreciate it if you could . . . What are you looking at?"

She was staring at him rather oddly. "Can you raise up?" she asked. "Your feet are in my face."

Paul levitated higher, going face to face with Maxie, but still inverted. "That better?" Assured by Maxie's nod that it was, he went on as if nothing had happened. "I'd appreciate it if you could get on the Internet and see if there are any reports of people like us who were inverted. Report back to me; I doubt I'll be traveling much out of the attic until I can figure this out."

I felt like a heel, but I had to ask, "What about the spook shows? The guests already saw a performance with *only one of you*." I looked at Maxie.

"My mother is in *jail*!" she responded.

Paul's voice took on a dryness that was unusual for him. "I'll see what I can do," he said. "Maxie . . ."

"I'm on it," Maxie assured him. She disappeared into the floor, presumably to go to one of her hiding places and start in on her assignment. I noticed that she hadn't addressed her frustration with me, and had spoken to Paul whenever she could avoid speaking to me. Ghosts can be so self-centered.

"And you?" Paul asked me.

"I'm going to sing a little karaoke and go to bed," I told him. "Any requests?"

"Yes. Keep the volume low."

"Julia MacKenzie worked here for about a year." Bud Pandell, the human-resources manager at CableCom, was a balding, red-faced man who breathed through his mouth and wore a white short-sleeved polyester-blend shirt. "She never got written up for shoddy performance or insubordination." Wow—did companies really still use words like *insubordination*? "And that's really about all that I know. I'm sorry I can't tell you more."

"Why did she leave?" I asked. If she'd moved out of the

area, that might give me a direction to follow. "Any record of that?"

It had taken a little fast talking to get into the CableCom offices to speak to Pandell this morning. I'd told the receptionist I was from a government agency (no initials, but the work was "classified above your clearance level") that was considering Ms. MacKenzie for a somewhat sensitive position and wanted to vet her through some information from past employers. Pandell, once notified by the receptionist, had appeared to escort me into his office in less than a minute.

Pandell looked through the folder marked "MacKenzie, Julia," and ran his finger down one particular page. "According to her file, she had just gotten her master's degree, and I guessed she was either going for a doctorate or looking for a job in the field she'd studied."

"And what was that field?" I asked.

"Psychology," he answered. "CableCom actually contributed to her education."

"Don't you sort of frown on employees leaving right after you finish paying for them to go to college?" I asked.

"It's not our favorite thing," he admitted.

"Did she leave an address where she might be found when she left?"

Pandell looked at me. "Who are you with really?" he asked.

"What does that mean?"

"It means you're not with a government agency, Ms. Kerby. You're not asking human-resources questions, and you're not interested in classified information. You're trying to find Julia MacKenzie, not vet her for anything. So I'll ask you again— who are you with really?"

There was no point in attempting to play my original role. "I'm a private investigator," I said. "I've been hired to try to find Ms. MacKenzie, but I promise you, it's not for any purpose that will cause her trouble."

Pandell looked at me for a long time, and it seemed like he

was deciding something. He ran his hand through what hair he had left and twitched his mouth for a while. Then, apparently having made his evaluation of me, he leaned forward with a great degree of confidentiality.

"You're looking for Julia?" he whispered, and the way he said "Julia" sent a warning shiver up my spine. This wasn't a human-resources response.

I nodded, but didn't venture saying anything.

"Have you made any progress?" Pandell asked hopefully. "Do you know where she might be?"

"Not yet," I managed. "That's why I came here to ask you."

"But you're a detective," he said. "You'll find her eventually."

This conversation was veering into weird territory with dizzying speed. "I intend to," I said. "But I can't guarantee anything."

"This client of yours," Pandell went on, not acknowledging what I'd just said. "Is it her parents or someone like that?"

"I really can't say," I told him. *No, it's her almost-fiancé who happens to be dead.* "I keep my clients confidential." When it suits me.

"Can I be your client?" he asked, suddenly seeming like an overeager terrier whose owner had just come home from work. "Can you search for her and tell me when you've found her?"

"Did she steal from the company or something?" I asked. Why would the HR guy from her job want to track down an employee who'd resigned? And wouldn't he be in a better position to do it?

Pandell shook his head vigorously. "Oh no," he said. "It's nothing like that."

"Then, what's it something like?"

He bit his lips and looked toward the window. "It's personal," he said. "She just left without saying anything."

This had an eerie feel to it. "You mean, she didn't say why she was resigning from CableCom?" I could hope.

"No. I mean she didn't say anything to *me*." Pandell reestablished eye contact and sat up straighter in his chair. "We . . . dated for a while."

After I recovered enough to speak, I asked Bud Pandell about his relationship with Julia MacKenzie. The dates coincided with the time she was also seeing Paul exclusively (Paul had believed). And that, no matter what scenario I could fabricate in my head, wasn't good.

He said he'd asked Julia out a number of times before she'd agreed to a date, and that even when they were as involved as they'd ever get, she was never his "girlfriend." They hadn't discussed exclusivity, but based on the way he talked, she'd certainly never told him about Paul.

Eventually, having squeezed as much information out of the little man as I could, I sympathetically told him I was unable to contract with two clients for one investigation—I did not mention that the other client, being deceased, was not paying me anything except a two-a-day spook show to keep my guesthouse going—and promised, when I located Julia, to "tell her Bud said to call."

Okay, so maybe that wasn't going to be tops on my list of messages for Ms. MacKenzie when I found her, but if it came up during the conversation, I'd be sure to pass it along.

Twenty

My mind was spinning as I drove to the Sprocket to talk to Little Bob and Rocco Palenty about Big Bob again. This time I thought I could let them know I was looking for Wilson Meyers as well (if by "looking" one meant "trying to figure out how to look"), and see if they had any ideas about where he might be. I'd asked Luther if he wanted to come along, but he'd been strangely aloof on the phone—maybe a reaction to our awkward kiss—and said he had to work. Men.

It hadn't ever occurred to me that Rocco and Little Bob wouldn't be at the bar in the middle of the afternoon, and luckily, it hadn't occurred to them, either. I found Little Bob back at the bowling machine, and Rocco, mug of beer in hand, cheering him on.

Rocco stopped encouraging Little Bob for a moment to say hello, and, after eyeing me uncomfortably (for me) up and down, to comment, "I see this is what you really look like. Sorta liked the little black skirt, myself."

"Sorry about that, Rocco."

Little Bob didn't look over—he was trying to convert a difficult spare—but he also offered greetings and a beer. I opted for a diet soda, then told the two men why I'd come to the bar today, and after Little Bob's game ("Only a two twenty-three") was completed, we sat down to discuss any possible leads I'd missed on Big Bob Benicio or Wilson Meyers.

Rocco did some head scratching to show off how hard he was thinking, but after a little while, he said, "I just can't come up with anything. Big Bob didn't seem any different around that time than he'd been before. He wasn't worried or anything. I don't know what the deal was."

"That's not exactly right," Little Bob jumped in. "Big Bob *was* antsy for a couple of days before he disappeared. I don't know why, but I do remember he was moody and just sitting around staring into his drink for two or three days."

I turned toward Rocco. "And you didn't see any of this?"

Rocco shook his head. "Nope. But then, my memory could be a little off. You know, I drink a bit." He winked, probably thinking it made him look impish. It really didn't.

"Did you ask him what the problem was?"

"Tried," Little Bob said. "He jumped right down my throat, told me to go away and leave him alone. So I did."

This was leading a grand total of nowhere. "I hear that you and Big Bob got into a fight right before he vanished," I told Little Bob. "What happened?"

Little Bob looked sheepish, like a small boy who'd been caught with his hand in the cookie jar for the seventeenth time this morning. "We did have a little dustup," he admitted, hanging his head (or just looking down to make eye contact with me). "But it was at least a month before Big Bob went away."

"What was it about?" I asked, remembering that Luther had said the fight was over Maxie, or maybe not.

"Tell the truth, it was about Maxie," Little Bob told me. "I knew they had got a divorce, or an annulment, or something, and I asked Big Bob would it be okay if I asked Maxie out to a movie or something. And he got real mad."

"You wanted to go out with Maxie?" I needed a minute to wrap my brain around the concept.

Little Bob nodded. "I had a little crush on her, you know. But Big Bob started yelling at me that Maxie deserved better than us, you know. Said she should find herself some college guy or something. Said her mom was right about us, that we were nothing but criminals and drug addicts."

Rocco suddenly looked as if someone had hit him in the face with a garbage-can lid and flattened his features. He made a sound like a horse does with his lips and rubbed his hand over his unshaven chin. "Her mom said that?" he asked.

You'd think he'd be more upset that his friend Big Bob had categorized him as a criminal and a drug addict, but that didn't seem to faze either of the guys.

"I dunno," Little Bob told him. "I wasn't there. That's just what Big Bob told me."

But I was focusing on another part of Big Bob's alleged rant. Maybe I could get one of them to react. "He said you were criminals and drug addicts? Did Big Bob have a substance-abuse problem?"

Rocco grinned. "Not unless beer is a substance," he said. He took a nice long swig on his own to provide the visual.

Well, actually, it is, but that's not the point. "Did Big Bob drink too much? So that it was getting to be a problem? Or was he into anything else, anything illegal?" I asked Little Bob, having come to the conclusion that talking to Rocco was not going to be incredibly helpful.

"Oh, I don't think so," Little Bob replied, chewing his lips a little in a sign that he was thinking. "I never heard about anything like that. Big Bob was always either working at the grill, riding his bike or here drinking with us. He didn't have time to be a drug addict, too."

Maybe it wasn't going to be incredibly helpful talking to either one of these guys.

I decided to shift gears (no pun intended). "What about Wilson Meyers?" I asked. Wilson was my last chance. "What can you tell me about him?"

"Wilson was basically a weasel," Rocco said. "I don't think he had a real job. He'd just pick up work, delivering packages for people, sometimes doing little odds and ends around a house. He wasn't a real good carpenter, but he could paint okay. During the off-season I think he might have worked at the bike shop sometimes when Luther was just the manager, but Luther never kept him long because Wilson would only show up for work on time about once a week. Half the time he was in jail after getting into a fight or sleeping something off."

That was something, anyway. I'd have to ask Luther about Wilson again the next time I saw him, if he ever called me again. Boy, don't react to one little kiss the way they want, and men get all funny around you. I might have to suck it up and call him myself; officially, he was still my client after all.

"Wilson didn't have a crush on Maxie, too, did he?" Maybe this whole thing was a product of the twisted power Maxie had on men. Though the thought absolutely baffled me.

"I don't think so," Little Bob piped up. "He never said nothing about it. I think he was just lazy."

"What did you think when he vanished around the same time as Big Bob?" I asked them.

"Tell the truth, I didn't even notice that Wilson was gone until Luther mentioned his name the other night," Rocco answered. "He just wasn't that memorable a guy. I didn't like him."

"I figured he and Big Bob went someplace together," Little Bob said. "I hope that's not what happened."

I nodded, then picked up my tote bag, thanked them for the soda, and started heading for the door. Little Bob asked me where I was going.

"I have to try and get Maxie's mother out of jail," I said.

* * *

"The judge didn't deny bail," Alex Hayward, Kitty's attorney, said. "He just set it so high that there was no chance of Kitty making even the 10 percent cash equivalent. He saw it was a murder, even one that took place two years ago, and he decided Kitty was a flight risk."

Alex, who was decidedly not a man as Kitty had suspected, leaned forward and placed her elbows on her very nicely appointed desk in her very nicely appointed office in the very nicely appointed building in which her firm, Morris, Hayward, Esteban and Weisel, occupied the entire very nicely appointed ninth floor. "It doesn't make sense. If Kitty were a flight risk, she would have taken off two years ago," Alex went on. "But the guidelines mention a million dollars as the proper bail for a homicide, and he didn't even consider the circumstances. The prosecutor asked for no bail at all, and with what the judge did, he might just as well have granted that." The mid-afternoon sun was hitting the blinds just right, so her face looked especially concerned.

"I don't understand," I told her. "Why would anybody think Kitty was a flight risk? Why do they think she killed Big Bob?"

"Well, the murder weapon in her house didn't help her case much," Alex answered with a raised eyebrow.

"What did the judge say about the metal shavings in Big Bob's head?" I asked, just to see if anyone else had fallen for that line of Ferry's.

"Metal shavings?" Alex asked. "Nobody said anything about metal shavings. I don't even think that's possible." *Okay, so I'm the only idiot.* "But I'm told that the police heard about some *comments* that Kitty made in regard to the victim that aren't going to play really well in court," Alex added.

"I'm tired of these insinuations," I said. "I didn't tell the police *anything* about what Kitty said to me."

Alex stood up and stretched her neck, bending it from side to side like an athlete preparing for the big game. I half expected her to drop to the ground and start grabbing the soles of her feet for a calf stretch. "Well, somebody did," she said. "Finding out who that was might give us a lead. I'm going to put an investigator on it today, and I hope you understand that I'm not going to be hiring you."

No, you want someone who knows what she's doing. "I completely understand," I said. "But I'm not going to stop looking into this. I already have a client who's asked me to find out who killed Big Bob."

Alex nodded. "Since I have you here, I'd like to pick your brain a little. What motivation would Kitty have to kill Bob Benicio? He and Maxie had already annulled their marriage; the records are clear that they were married four days in total. What difference would Bob have made to Kitty months later?"

"I'm not going to mention any names, but I am told by people who knew Big Bob that he was thinking about reconciling with Maxie, and if that news had gotten back to Kitty—although I have no idea how that would have happened—she might have gotten upset. But the idea that she would have killed Big Bob for *any* reason is ridiculous." I looked away, trying to think the problem through. As I did, I noticed the spirit of an old man watching me intently, as if trying to figure out who I was and why I was there. I realized his face matched that of a younger version I'd seen in a photograph in the lobby marked "Our Founder." I'd practiced not reacting, but that one was hard. I was proud of myself.

Enough of that. Any way I looked at it, there was no sense in the idea that Kitty had murdered Big Bob. And it was even more ridiculous that the police had arrested Kitty and the prosecutor insisted on unreachable bail based on the evidence they'd found. Yeah, the weapon was in Kitty's house, but as far as I was concerned, that pointed more toward someone setting her up than to her being a devious killer who had stuck the wrench back into her toolbox rather than simply burying it next to the body, where it would never be able to tie her to the crime.

Besides, how hard could Kitty Malone really have hit Big Bob with that wrench? She was hardly a firebrand of physical energy. Wouldn't the medical examiner have concluded that the murderer had to be someone much stronger than Kitty?

I expressed all those thoughts to Alex, who took careful notes and nodded as I spoke. "I agree with you," she said, still leaning over her desk and writing on (what else?) a yellow legal pad. "There's something we're missing, and I have no idea what it might be, but I'm willing to bet it's the key to this situation."

"So there's no way to get Kitty out of jail now? She's stuck in the county prison?" Maxie was not going to be pleased with the news I was bringing home, and for once, I wouldn't be able to blame her for a bad mood.

"It's possible, I suppose, if you know someone with very deep pockets," Alex said. "It's a million dollars or 10 percent from a bail bondsman, so a hundred grand."

"Not that deep," I answered. The wealthiest person I knew was The Swine, and he was living in my house on credit cards.

"Then I'm afraid there isn't much we can do, short of finding out what really happened." Alex sat back down behind her desk, heavily. The stretching clearly had not helped, since she still seemed to have the weight of the world on her shoulders.

"That's what we'll have to do, then," I said.

Under normal circumstances, that would have motivated me enough. But when I got to my car in the parking lot, my cell phone buzzed again, and this time, the thrill of fear I got was justified—there was another text message from a different number I hadn't seen before.

"I warned you," it read.

And I knew, for the life of me (literally), that I should have been terrified. I knew I should call Luther immediately and tell him I was off the case, then pick up Melissa and move to Utah, where we wouldn't be found again. I was aware of all that. I had every right and every reason to be feeling absolute dread.

But the fact of the matter was, this time the wild texter had just pissed me off. It was time to stop asking questions and start doing something to answer them.

Twenty-one

"I've never broken into a house before," Jeannie said. "Do you think I'm the first pregnant woman who's done this?"

"The first one today, maybe," I replied. We stood outside Kitty Malone's cute little Cape Cod the next morning as I searched under the third stone in the walkway just to the left of the mailbox post, just as Maxie had advised. "And we're not breaking in," I insisted. "We're going to use a key, and we have permission from the owner." Sort of. I'm sure Kitty wouldn't have minded if she'd known, but technically it was her deceased daughter who had indeed endorsed the idea with the comment that it was "about time you did something helpful."

I'd told Paul about the second text, but not Maxie. I had called McElone with the new incoming number, but not Ferry. I was making choices, mostly about who I liked better than someone else.

"You're taking the fun out of this for me," Jeannie answered.

"Sorry. I—there it is!" I found the front-door key, a little

grimy but completely usable, and cleaned it off with my hands.
"Let's go."

"That's gross," Jeannie said, I'm assuming about the key.
"You don't have a moist wipe or something?"

"Get over it." We walked—that is, I walked and Jeannie
sort of waddled—up to the front door of the house. I admired,
as I had the other few times I'd been here, how well Kitty
decorated and kept the place alive with plants, some of which
were looking a touch peaked at the moment, since their care-
taker had been gone for more than a day. I picked up a watering can Kitty had left on the porch, filled it from a spigot on
the side of the house and did some watering.

"All ready to go in and snoop around now, Ms. Stewart?"
Jeannie asked. "Or may I call you Martha?"

"Has anyone ever encouraged you to go into stand-up com-
edy?" I asked her as I unlocked the front door.

"As a matter of fact—" she began.

"They were wrong." I made sure to wipe my feet on the
mat before entering, and indicated to Jeannie that she should
do the same. It was like going to my grandmother's house
when I was little.

I looked around. There was, of course, not a thing out of
place. But then, that was weird—there *should* have been stuff
out of place. "The cops didn't toss her house?" I said to Jeannie. "How'd they find the wrench if they weren't searching
everywhere?"

"Maybe she cleaned up after they found it," Jeannie said.

"In handcuffs?"

"Leave me alone. I'm pregnant."

I felt strange even walking around in the house without
Kitty there, but we walked slowly through the living room
into the dining room, and back toward the kitchen. Nothing
appeared to have been touched.

"I don't get it," I said.

"The only thing that makes sense is if they knew what they
were looking for, and where to look for it," Jeannie suggested.

The full force of that took a moment to hit me, but when it did, I stopped walking. "Somebody dimed Kitty out?" I asked. "You think someone tipped off the cops about where they could find the wrench that killed Big Bob?"

"Hey, nice lingo, Bogart! Forgive me, I didn't go to private eye school like some of us," Jeannie said. That was what I'd told her I had done, when in fact I'd gotten lessons from the exist-in sleuth in my house. It was just easier to tell Jeannie about the "Private U Detective School."

"No, I think you're right."

She grinned, and then said she had to use the bathroom, which was something she did about every eight minutes these days. They say women would never have more than one child if they could remember what being pregnant and giving birth were really like. I think that's nonsense; some women would still have twins. I, personally, recalled Melissa's strong legs kicking me from inside and the "miracle of birth" well enough to be thrilled with what I had and want no more. If you catch my drift.

With Jeannie out of the room, I could call Melissa and ask her to get Paul's reaction to what I was finding out. I spoke quietly so Jeannie wouldn't hear me, even though she was two rooms away. The woman has ears like a bat. But an attractive bat. And not having to have the "you really don't have ghosts in your house" conversation with her again was worth dropping my voice to a gasp temporarily.

Liss got up to the attic, where Paul was still doing his "Dracula during the day" impression, and put the phone up next to where his ear would be if he were really there. Luckily, his ear was a lot closer to the floor now than it would have been normally, so she could reach much more easily.

"They didn't toss her house?" he asked once I'd given him the *Reader's Digest* version of what we'd found (or, more specifically, had not found). "That doesn't make any sense at all, unless—"

"Unless they knew where to look, right? Someone's trying to set Kitty up for Big Bob's murder, aren't they?"

I could almost see Paul stroke his goatee in thought. "That seems like the most logical reasoning," he said. "You should get in touch with her attorney again when you're finished searching the house and see if you can get the message to Kitty in county lockup."

"I hate thinking of her there," I told him. "It must be so scary."

"You're working toward getting her out," Paul answered. "Focus on that."

"You're pretty smart for a guy who can't keep his head off the floor."

"My life is just upside down these days," he said; then he thought about what he'd said and added, "My so-called life."

"I'm going to check the basement," I said. "What should I look for?"

There was another goatee-stroking moment. "Any evidence that someone broke in down there," he said. "Clearly, the weapon was planted in the basement, and Kitty probably didn't knowingly let the murderer into her basement, so we have to assume that someone broke in and planted the wrench."

"Okay," I said. "Thanks for the help. I'll—"

I snapped the phone shut as I heard Jeannie open the bathroom door. By the time she walked out, I had already slid it back into the hip pocket of my jeans. "Were you talking to somebody?" Jeannie asked. "I thought I heard your voice."

"Just talking to one of my ghosts," I told her. It wouldn't make any difference now, and sometimes I like to push her, just to see how she'll rationalize it when I tell her the truth. "Getting advice on the investigation."

"Oh, good," she said, smiling her "you're just so funny" smile. "What did the ghost say we should do?"

"Check the basement."

"Big deal. *I* could have said that. Huh! Ghosts." She started toward the door to the basement stairway, and I beat her there.

"I'm faster than you," I teased her. Jeannie stuck out her tongue at me. We have a very mature relationship.

We started down the basement steps. "Hey, how come you can't just ask Big Bob's ghost who killed him?"

There was no point in trying to explain the "some ghosts do, some ghosts don't" policy. "He was hit from behind," I told her. "He didn't see who it was."

Jeannie giggled. "You kill me."

"I almost never want to."

The basement, as in most of the older full-time homes near the shore, was small and relatively dark. Kitty had not had it finished, so the walls were still bare concrete and the ceiling consisted of bare beams. But Kitty had organized the space more than efficiently; it had been done artfully. The basement, neater than my underused kitchen, was a sight to behold.

Clothing was kept on garment racks (on wheels, for easy transportation), each article in a plastic garment bag, clear, to better identify them yet keep them protected from the damp. Down the shore, we do damp like nobody's business.

Relics from another age, like vinyl records, VHS tapes, scrapbooks and photograph albums, were kept in plastic bins with lids, each bin marked very specifically ("Maxie pix 1985" was the one I'd most like to have looked at). Nothing was random, nothing was stored on the basement floor, but on pallets, and nothing—*nothing*—was out of place.

"They didn't toss down here, either," I said.

"Somebody gave really good directions, don't you think?" Jeannie said.

I looked at the outer walls. If there had been a break-in, it came from outside ("Well, *duh*," I heard Melissa say in my head). "Can you reach the windows?" I asked Jeannie.

"When I was *unencumbered*, maybe," she answered. "Not so much now. Why?"

"I want to see if there are scratch marks where somebody broke in carefully."

"Well, wouldn't the marks be on the outside?" Jeannie asked.

Wise guy. "Yes, but there might be something in here, too. We're here, so let's look. We can look outside later."

We spent the next ten minutes trying to raise ourselves (more specifically, myself; I wasn't risking Jeannie on an egg crate) to the level of the basement windows. Finally, standing on an egg crate placed on an ottoman, I could stand at eye level with the windowsill. Of course, there was no mark here, and only five more windows to check from this precarious perch.

"Do you want me to go outside and look?" Jeannie asked.

"No, I want you in here to call nine-one-one when I fall and break an important bone or two," I told her. "Look around the basement. Find the toolbox where they found the wrench."

Jeannie started to move around the basement, index finger curled and touching her upper lip, the International Sign of Jeannie Thinking. It wasn't going to take long; the room was wonderfully organized, so there weren't many little nooks into which something could have been secreted.

"The cops didn't have to disturb anything down here, either," she said, thinking out loud. I didn't answer. "So it had to be out in plain sight."

"Do you think they took the whole toolbox?" I asked, setting up under the second window.

"Why do that? It seems like someone was practically putting up neon signs with arrows that said, 'Here's the murder weapon.' It's not like they think someone killed him with a roll of electrical tape." Jeannie had a point.

"No, but they didn't know it was a wrench, did they?" I stood up on my wobbly contraption again, testing it carefully before putting my full weight on the inverted egg crate. Why hadn't it occurred to me to look for a ladder in this basement? There had to be one. "I mean, they knew it was a heavy metal object. Could have been anything."

"We're dealing with cops who had been really carefully led here," Jeannie said. "I think they knew exactly what they were looking for, and found it in the first two minutes of looking."

"So how come you haven't found the toolbox yet?" I asked.

"Just check the damn windows."

I looked at the frame of each window around the basement, and found no scrapes, no missing paint, no broken glass, nothing that would indicate a break-in. It was one of the few times in my life I've been disappointed to see that things were in perfect order. Come to think of it, it was one of the few times in my life I've *seen* things in perfect order. My life tends to be slightly messier than Kitty's.

Except Kitty was in jail. Had to keep that in mind, and go on looking.

Jeannie was somewhat luckier in her search. She simply opened the door on a storage cabinet, and found a small metal toolbox with three pull-out drawers. I climbed down off my shaky perch to examine it with her.

"Should we wear gloves, or something?" Jeannie asked. "There are some gardening gloves over there." She pointed toward a small bucket that Kitty clearly used in the garden, with a tiny spade and a pair of gloves inside it, looking clean enough to eat with.

"We're not committing a crime," I reminded her. "If the cops had wanted to confiscate this stuff, it would be gone now."

The toolbox was, as I now expected, very well organized. Kitty didn't own a lot of tools, but the screwdrivers were all kept in one spot, the one hammer in another, the tapes (electrical, masking, painter's) together, paint brushes, roller sleeves . . .

. . . and wrenches.

There wasn't a wrench set, like the one my considerably more massive toolbox (on wheels, with nine drawers and two doors) in the guesthouse contained. There were exactly three wrenches: a three-sixteenths, a small adjustable and a larger, maybe six-inch, adjustable wrench.

"What's wrong with this picture?" I asked Jeannie. "Your husband's a contractor. Why is this wrong?"

She looked at me. "I don't know. I work for an insurance company. If you want me to call Tony and ask him . . ." She reached for her cell phone.

I shook my head. "No. Here's the problem; she already had two adjustable wrenches, both sized for the kind of problems a homeowner would encounter. The one that the cops took out of here had to be much, *much* larger to do lethal damage to Big Bob's skull."

Jeannie picked up on my vibe. "So . . . why would she need a wrench that big? Why would she have had it in the first place?"

"And, more than that," I said, "where would she have put it in this toolbox? The wrench area is much too small to accommodate it."

Jeannie pointed at one of the small storage areas on the bottom. "It would fit in there," she suggested.

"Yeah, but this is Kitty we're talking about. This is her toolbox. I've never seen such a neat, organized toolbox in my life. If that's where the wrenches went, that would be where *all* the wrenches went, or she'd move them all to keep them together."

She thought about that and nodded slowly. "This is an even more obvious plant than we thought." She stopped, thought and shook her head. "Those cops are really dumb."

I pulled my cell phone out of my pocket. "That's the thing," I said. "I really don't think they are." I dialed Alex Hayward's number.

Twenty-two

Alex promised to look into what I was saying, and informed me that Kitty Malone had not yet been moved to the county jail. She said the prosecutor and the Seaside Heights police wouldn't give her a satisfactory explanation for her client's continued stay at the small holding facility down the shore, but she wasn't complaining about not moving Kitty into a larger, scarier jail. She said she'd call me the next day.

Maxie was not exactly buoyed by the news that her mom was still in a small barred room, and although I hadn't exactly expected a ticker-tape parade in my honor, I had hoped that the fact that Kitty was still in a Seaside Heights cell and not the county lockup would be considered something approximating "good news."

Not so much.

"Why couldn't you get her out of jail?" she wailed at me the instant I walked through the front door. Maxie had apparently been eavesdropping on a phone call I'd made to Melissa on the way back from dropping Jeannie at her house in Laval-lette. "My mom didn't kill Big Bob! What's she still doing behind bars?"

"Not now," I singsonged to her as I walked through the living room, where Mrs. Spassky was watching the flat-screen TV the *Down the Shore* production crew had left hanging from one of my hundred-year-old crossbeams. "I have to talk to Paul."

"Captain Inversion is up in the attic, being all girly about how nobody should see him like this," Maxie scoffed. "Like somebody besides us could see him. What's he going to do for you?"

"Not me; it's what he's going to do for Kitty," I said in a conversational voice.

"Oh," Mrs. Spassky said, looking around on the floor. "Do you have a cat?"

"No, Mrs. Spassky. Just a ghost."

She nodded and went back to CNN. Apparently, a Hollywood starlet had entered rehab for the third time, and the news anchor had the gall to look as if she was surprised.

Francie Westen, fanning herself despite the completely effective air-conditioning in the room, stopped me on my way toward the backyard, which I could see through the French doors at the rear of the den. Steven was out there talking to Lucy Simone, and Melissa was nowhere in sight despite it being late enough in the day that her chambermaid duties would certainly have been fulfilled by now. She was on her own, which made me start thinking of my ex as The Swine again. "The brochure mentioned direct contact with the spirits in the house," Francie said with a confrontational tone. "I'm leaving in a few days, and so far, all I've seen is stuff flying around the house. When do I get to talk to a ghost?"

"You're talking to one now, lady," Maxie said. I gave her a very quick disapproving look, and she twisted her mouth into a sneer and vanished into the ceiling.

We had experimented with the idea of a "séance" in the house when the first guests had arrived a few months before, and the results were, let's say, something I'd rather not have replicated. But part of the Senior Plus deal was that the guests who wanted a conference with those beyond the grave would have the opportunity. I had cut back, therefore, on the spooky accoutrements involved with the "séance" and scheduled a few daytime sit-downs during which I would field questions for Paul and Maxie. It was sort of like *The View*, but with dead people.

"We'll be doing that tomorrow at nine thirty, Francie," I told her. "Have your questions ready."

But Francie continued to frown. "I was hoping for something a little more . . . personal," she said.

That stopped me, even as Lucy was laughing at something "witty" The Swine had said to her. "In what way?" I asked Francie. This was sounding just a bit kinky.

"Like a one-on-one discussion. Something I could tell the folks back home about. 'I got to talk to a ghost,' you know. That sort of thing."

I wasn't sure I was getting this. "Well, you *will* get to talk to a ghost," I said. "Tomorrow, at nine thirty."

"No, I'll get to talk to *you*," Francie countered. "How do I know there's a ghost present? How do I know you're not making up any answers you want?"

Oh. That. "Not to worry, Francie. I guarantee you, there's no way you'll walk out of that room thinking you didn't talk to a ghost. Trust me."

Francie puckered up her lips, like she didn't want to trust me at all. "Okay," she said, drawing the word out a few feet. "But remember—"

"I know. A personal experience." I nodded. I'd gotten this before. Some guests didn't just want to see ghosts; they wanted the ghosts to think that they, the guests, were the most fascinating people on the planet. It's sort of interesting to watch.

I managed to break free from Francie and walk out through

the French doors into the backyard. The Swine and Lucy were standing at one end of the yard, closest to the slope that led down to the beach. They were facing the ocean, and my ex-husband swept his arm in a gesture of . . . something. I wasn't that close yet.

When I got closer, I could hear him saying, "They'll all be able to better their financial future, with only a tiny investment, really the price of a cup of coffee a day."

"Not that many lower-income people spend four bucks on a latte every day," I said, from behind him. They both turned to face me, and The Swine lowered his arm, as he was finished envisioning things. "If they did," I continued, "they'd have fourteen hundred and sixty dollars a year. Do you think poor people can afford to invest fourteen hundred and sixty dollars a year?"

"Alison," he said, as if he was surprised it was me. "Of course I don't expect low-income people to invest that kind of money. It was just an expression."

"I have another expression for you," I said. "Where's our daughter?" Then I looked toward Lucy. "Hi, Lucy." She was a guest, after all.

"Hi, Alison." Lucy was quick on the pickup.

"Wendy called and asked if Melissa wanted to go with her to shop for . . . something, and then your mother said she'd pick her up at Wendy's and bring back some dinner," The Swine answered. "They should be back in a half hour or so. Why? Is something wrong?"

"Of course not. May I speak with you for a minute?" I gestured toward the house. "You don't mind, do you, Lucy?"

"Mind what?" Smart as a whip, that one.

Steven walked inside with me to the kitchen, where the air-conditioning isn't quite as efficient, but still better than the sweltering July heat. I put my hand on my hip and shook my head in the general direction of my ex-husband.

"I asked you to see to it that Lucy was out of the house during the spook shows," I told him. "I didn't ask you to adopt her."

"What's this about?" he demanded. "You can't be jealous, can you?"

"I'm not jealous; I'm annoyed. You got rid of your own daughter so you could dazzle Princess Jasmine with your financial prowess."

The Swine looked at me sideways, like I would make more sense if he could use just his good eye. He spoke slowly and lowered his voice for emphasis on how controlled he was being.

"Wendy's mother called," he said. "She asked if Melissa could go with them to the mall, and then Melissa asked your mother to pick her up so they could get something for dinner. Melissa wanted to go. She asked me if it was all right, and I said yes. Now. Which part of that indicates that I was trying to get rid of my daughter?"

Have you ever been so frustrated in an argument that you couldn't speak because you *knew* you were right, but you couldn't *prove* it? I had seen this movie before, and I knew how it ended. But everything Steven said made perfect sense in context, and there was absolutely no counterargument I could make that would make a difference.

So, in a triumph of maturity and emotional stability, I stormed out of the kitchen and ran up all the stairs to the attic.

There, I encountered the inverted ghost of a rookie private detective and the right-side-up spirit of a perpetually twenty-eight-year-old interior designer, who took one look at me, bared her teeth and flew up onto the roof through the attic ceiling, making a noise like a disgruntled preteen denied tickets to a Justin Bieber concert. Paul, who had been facing away from me, rotated on his head to see who had entered the room.

"So," I said. "How has *your* day been?"

"Same old, same old," he answered.

Paul got into sleuth mode when I mentioned Kitty Malone and the Big Bob case, and listened as I updated him on the situation. I did not fill him in on the Julia MacKenzie search, because that one seemed destined to end badly. He understood my ground rules on my attempts to find Julia, and did not ask about my progress. As if there had been some.

When I was finished recounting the day's events (adding that we had found no *obvious* signs of a break-in at Kitty's house, even outside the basement windows), and Paul had stroked his beard to a fine froth, he chewed his bottom lip a bit and said, "Interesting that there were no signs of a break-in outside. How did the wrench get into Mrs. Malone's basement, then?"

"If I could answer even one question about this case, I'd feel like I had a good day," I told him.

"But I think you've analyzed it impeccably, Alison," Paul told me. "It sounds very much like the police were being led to that discovery by someone who wanted to frame Mrs. Malone, and for some reason, they're choosing not to see that."

"Luther kept saying the cops aren't interested in one biker killing another one," I told him. "I guess they figure they've found a nice easy solution, and they're not looking a gift horse in the mouth."

Paul frowned. Upside down, it still didn't look like a smile, no matter what my mother had told me when I was six. "It's not like bikers are gang members anymore, really. Most never were. I really don't want to believe that the police are acting with that level of cynicism. There has to be another explanation."

"They decided to show Kitty some hospitality because they think she'll review their jail for Zagat?"

He ignored that, which shows what a wise man he is. Was. Anyway, he said, "If the police aren't going to be any help, we will have to proceed on our own. It's dangerous to assume without enough facts, but the only motivation I can imagine for someone to want Kitty to be arrested as the murderer is—"

"To get the real murderer off the hook," I said, nodding. "But the question becomes, Is the person doing the framing the killer or someone who just wants the killer to go free?"

"A very good question," Paul agreed. "We might be able to make an investigator out of you after all." He smiled.

"For a guy who's upside down, you can be pretty nervy," I told him. "What are we going to do about that, by the way?"

"Since we don't know what caused it, I really can't say how we can cure it," Paul answered, the smile having left his face. "Unfortunately, we can't just call Dr. Bombay and get the supernatural pill that will solve the whole problem."

The *Bewitched* reference made me think of cures. "What has Maxie turned up on her Internet research?" I asked him. "She's so mad at me about her mom that I'm pretty sure she wouldn't tell me now if I asked."

"You two need to work out your problem," he said. Personally, I believed that any animosity between Maxie and me would evaporate once Kitty was out of jail. If she didn't get out, well—I didn't want to think about the problems that would cause for us all. "She told me she'd only done some preliminary research, but so far, she hasn't found another case like mine."

"Swell." Maxie, despite her constant grumbling about being stuck with "desk work," was a very good online researcher. If she couldn't find any references on heels-over-head ghosts, it was extremely possible there weren't any, and we were on our own in trying to get Paul floating on his own two feet again.

"But she did say that there were references, on some very obscure websites, of people like us who could not gain equilibrium just before they moved on to a different plane of existence," Paul said.

That was a large statement, and it took a moment to sink in. Paul and Maxie, having become ghosts not long after they were murdered, seemed to be on the first, or lowest, level of postlife experience, as it would no doubt be described in brochures, assuming such things existed. Although Paul was always careful to remind me that he had been given "no handbook" on how to be a ghost, we had seen a spirit move on to the next level months before, and it had seemed like a positive experience for him.

"You mean you might be changing?" I asked him.

"Life is constant change," Paul said. "There's no reason death can't be the same thing, I guess. I know this feels different than before, but I can't really describe how that is."

"But the only time I saw this happen to somebody, it happened pretty fast," I said. "This has been more than a day already, and maybe longer." I found myself arguing against the idea, and I wasn't immediately sure why I wanted to.

"I'm not saying that's what it is," he answered. "Even Maxie said it was just the first try at researching this."

I mused on that for a while, and stood up, causing Paul to rise higher in the air to maintain eye contact. "Well, assuming you don't move on to Nirvana before tomorrow, you're still going to be around for the ghost meet-and-greet, right?"

He smiled. "Yes. I won't be visible to anyone but you and Melissa, so my . . . affliction won't alarm anyone."

"So, what do I do about Kitty and Big Bob?" I asked him.

"I think the key to this whole question could well be Wilson Meyers," Paul mused. "His disappearing at the same time as Big Bob is too big a coincidence not to be related. He must know something. We're going to have to track him down."

"Any ideas on how?"

"Sit down, Alison," Paul said. "I'm going to teach you how to find a missing person."

Just what I'd wanted to learn.

And that's when it hit me: I knew exactly why it bothered me that Paul might be evolving into the next kind of ghost. The one and only time I'd seen it happen was to a ghost we'd just gotten to know, and he'd been ecstatic as he moved on to the next level.

But then he was gone, and we'd never seen him again.

Twenty-three

"I don't get it," said Detective Lieutenant Anita McElone. "I pay my taxes. I donate to charity. I'm nice to small furry animals and I volunteer at the local soup kitchen. So why exactly am I being punished? This is the second time you've come in to bother me this week. Is that fair?"

McElone was sitting behind her desk with a fresh iced coffee and a bran muffin. But having been blatantly insulted, I felt it best not to throw gasoline on the fire by noting to McElone that there were worse things that could happen to cops, even if they were being a royal pain.

"I'm not here to torment you. I left Jeannie at home," I pointed out. "I'm just looking for some help with two missing persons. One of them is actually even missing."

McElone took an aggressive bite out of the muffin, chewed carefully and swallowed. She would never speak with food in her mouth. "You want me to help you find two missing people, and only one of them is missing? That just makes the other one a person."

"Well, she's not *legally* missing; it's just that I can't find her," I explained. Maybe I should have brought Jeannie, after all. It had worked in the past.

"Does it occur to you—as a 'private investigator'—that asking the police to do all your work for you borders on fraud? I mean, if all you do for your clients is ask me to do something they could ask for themselves, what are you being paid for?" McElone did not move to punch anything in on her keyboard, which probably made sense, since I hadn't mentioned Wilson Meyers or Julia MacKenzie yet.

"I'm not asking you to do *all* my work, and I don't appreciate the air quotes around 'private investigator,'" I told her. "If I had your access to motor-vehicle records and rap sheets, I'd be able to do this myself, but I don't, so I can't. Are you going to help me, or do I have to call in the big guns?"

The lieutenant's eyes widened, but I think the expression was meant to be taken ironically. "You're not going to bring your mother in to intimidate me again, are you?" she asked. That had worked in the past, too, but not as well. I didn't take the bait, so she waved her hand toward me. "Okay, let's see the name of your missing person. The nonmissing one we'll discuss later."

I thought that was partially unfair, but any help is better than no help, so I handed her the paper on which I'd printed out (okay, Maxie had printed out) Wilson Meyers's known information, which was essentially his name. I had no address, no driver's-license number, no telephone number, no Social Security. I was lucky I knew his first name was "Wilson."

"Why are you looking for this guy?" McElone asked me.

"He was a friend of Big Bob Benicio, and he disappeared at just about the same time," I told her.

She furrowed her brow. "I thought they already caught somebody for that murder in Seaside Heights," she said.

"They did. The wrong person."

McElone looked at me quickly, to see if I was kidding, and clearly saw that I was not. "How sure are you of your facts?" she wanted to know.

"Sure enough to look into Wilson Meyers. The truth is, anybody who wanted the right solution to the crime, and not the easiest, would be searching for Wilson." I went on to explain how obviously Kitty Malone was being framed, and McElone listened carefully and did not interrupt as I detailed my evidence. She was annoying, but she's a good cop.

"I don't know," she said when I was finished. "I know a few people in the Seaside Heights department, and they're not the type to coast like that. Something else must be going on."

I saw an opening. "Then help me prove it," I said. "Help me find Wilson Meyers."

She curled her lower lip a bit at the obvious saleswomanship, but tapped away at her keyboard for a minute or two. "I'm getting a few things on your friend Wilson," she said. "Get out your notepad."

Instead, I produced a small digital tape recorder I use when I'm out "in the field," as Paul says, so he can hear everything someone says to me when I report back to him later. McElone took no notice.

"First, he had a couple of priors on his record even before Benicio got himself killed," she began. "Minor possession, two for breaking and entering. Burglary. Nothing big, but there were . . . seven of them all together. But after the approximate date of Benicio's murder, there's nothing."

I nodded. "And no new address, no phone number, nothing like that, right?"

"That's right."

I looked to the ceiling in frustration. If the police department's resources couldn't raise anything on Wilson, it was looking more and more possible that he was dead or had vanished so well I'd never be able to find him myself. What was I going to—

"Except . . ." McElone said.

My neck practically spasmed as I got her back in my sights. "Except what?" I asked.

"This is weird," McElone said. So I waited.

Nothing.

"What's weird?" I asked.

"There's nothing on Wilson Meyers."

"That's not so weird," I pointed out.

"Maybe not, but I just got a hit on someone named Meyer Wilson." McElone looked at me with a cocked eyebrow.

What? "That's too big a coincidence to be a coincidence, isn't it?" I asked.

"Maybe, maybe not."

"How old is our Mr. Wilson? Does he fit the description?"

McElone looked at the screen, but wouldn't turn it to let me see. "Right age, but he's a little smaller than your description of Wilson Meyers, and the one in the previous data. So I guess it's not him. Except . . ."

"*Again* 'except'?"

"The description comes from the driver's-license data," she said. "They don't weigh or measure you at the Motor Vehicle Commission. They take the information you fill in on the form. So he could have lied about his height and weight. And he seems to have moved into Pennsylvania about fifteen minutes after Wilson Meyers stopped hanging around the New Jersey Shore."

"Why is there a hit on Meyer Wilson?" I asked. "Drugs?"

McElone shook her head. "Speeding ticket." She punched some keys. "Yours was a motorcycle guy, right?"

"Yeah," I answered. "Loved his bike, the guys tell me. Why?"

"Well, in Norristown, Pennsylvania, he was driving a Ford Focus."

A Ford Focus. Wilson Meyers, former scary biker. That didn't seem to add up. "How fast was he going?" I asked.

McElone checked her screen and put on reading-glasses to make sure she was reading it right. "Twenty-nine in a twenty-five-mile zone," she said.

I was doing my very best not to repeat everything she said just to give myself time to absorb it, so instead I said, "That seems a little out of character."

She nodded. "Yeah, and a little aggressive on the part of the officer who ticketed him."

"There had to be a driver's license when they gave him the ticket. Does it show an address?" I asked. That would be too much to hope for, wouldn't it?

"Yes," McElone answered. "The address is in Levittown, Pennsylvania." She read it off to me and gave me the phone number listed to the address. There was no cell phone number.

"What do you think the odds are he really lives there?" I asked.

"It depends," McElone answered.

"On what?"

"On whether that's really Wilson Meyers."

That was something it appeared I'd have to find out.

I tried to interest her in the matter of Julia MacKenzie, but McElone pointed out that there was nothing in that case even remotely smacking of illegality. "She might be a tramp, but if she's not charging for it, there isn't a thing we can do," was her exact quote.

I thanked her, a little grudgingly, and left.

Levittown, Pennsylvania, would have to wait—that was close to an hour-and-a-half drive away—so with no new ideas, I decided to revisit the site of a past triumph.

Okay, the site of a place where I hadn't failed entirely.

My pal Megan Sharp grimaced—yes, actually grimaced—when she saw me approaching. But, consummate pro that she was, she handed a manila envelope to the distinguished-looking fiftyish gentleman ahead of me in line and waited for him to turn toward the door before almost shouting out, "No more stuff about Julia MacKenzie!" before I even had a chance to ask. The gentleman flinched, I thought, at the volume of Megan's voice.

"Megan," I said, in my most soothing voice, as the man left the office, "I just need a little bit more information. Seriously. I won't bother you again after this."

She glanced up in the direction of the security video camera, which now appeared to be connected. Or maybe they always were. "I've already broken enough rules helping you," she said. "I was *seen* in the break room when I wasn't supposed to be on break! I got yelled at—and it could have been worse! So go away." Then her training got the best of her, and she added, "Please."

I smiled at her sympathetically. "I'm sorry if I got you into trouble," I said. "Is there something I can do to fix it? Someone I can talk to for you?"

"*No*," she moaned. "The only thing you can do is leave. That would be really helpful."

"You know I can't do that," I said. "I'm right on the verge of finding her, Megan, and just one more little piece of information would probably do the trick. All I need to see is the roster of other students in her last term's schedule, just the classes she actually attended in person, and . . ."

Megan Sharp clenched her teeth so hard I thought they'd shatter, but she managed to push through them one word, "No." Then she didn't say anything else.

I leaned over the counter, elbows down and chin on my hands. "Megan, have you ever done something for a guy . . ."

"Get. Out," she said.

"No, listen. Just one semester's roster . . ."

"Now!" She was almost vibrating with tension, and watching the video camera. For emphasis, she pointed dramatically toward the door, like the evil landlord in a melodrama from 1912.

So I left. Without the records, I couldn't contact anyone who might have been in one of Julia's classes, and who might still be in touch with her. I had a grand total of no leads. No help for Maxie on who killed her ex. I had promised to help Paul find *his* ex, and here I was, absolutely stuck with no ideas and an upside-down client.

No progress on the *Ex-Files*. Sorry.

Not to mention, I was definitely removing Megan Sharp's name from my "willing resource" file.

I walked down the hallway of the student-records office and out the front door of the building, and was hit in the face with the heat and humidity that we do so well in New Jersey in July. It's funny how quickly you forget what it feels like when you're in air-conditioning for two minutes.

I had almost reached the parking lot when I heard a voice behind me say, "Excuse me. Miss?"

I almost didn't turn around, because on a college campus, even during the summer, there are plenty of people around who could be called "Miss" ahead of me. But the voice was close enough that I knew it was speaking to me, so I stopped and turned.

The distinguished-looking gentleman who had been ahead of me in the student-records line stood there, dressed too warmly for the day, in a sport coat and dark slacks, but thankfully no necktie. He was, as one might expect, sweating pretty heavily, and might actually have run to catch up with me, because he was panting just a little bit, too.

"Can I help you?" I asked.

"Did I hear correctly, that you were trying to find student records for a Julia MacKenzie?" the man asked. His gray hair was cropped fairly close, and he had a goatee that looked like Paul's would if it had been completely white.

I took a step back, though the guy looked harmless enough. "That's right," I told him. "Do you know her?"

The man nodded. "I was her professor for Advanced Sociological Practices," he said. "My name is Douglas Kunkel."

Finally, a break in finding Julia MacKenzie! "Professor Kunkel!" I said, perhaps a little too enthusiastically—this time, *he* backed up a step. "So nice to meet you!"

"It's Doug," he said. "And you are?"

I told him who I was, and even showed him my PI license, possibly just to impress the guy because I was so happy he had come to me. I shook his hand at least three times. He started to look as if having sought me out might have been the biggest mistake he'd made this decade.

"So what can you tell me about Julia?" I asked after I was done gushing. "Do you know how I can find her?"

He exhaled. "I'm sorry. I was about to ask you that very question. Ms. MacKenzie vanished even before she received her final grades, and did not attend the commencement ceremony. I have not heard from her since, and I had become somewhat concerned. Frankly, I was hoping *you* might know where she is today."

Damn. "I'm afraid I don't, Doug," I told him. "I'm trying to track her down, but I'll tell you, she didn't leave much of a trail." Any information I could get from him would be more than I had now. "Was she a good student?"

He tilted his head from side to side. "Good, but not great," he said. "I think she might have been less interested in the subject matter than she should have been. I always got the impression that it was more about having the degree than gaining the knowledge for Ms. MacKenzie. She was concerned about her grades, but never asked a question about the material."

I was getting a picture of Paul's so-called almost-fiancée that didn't seem to match the one Paul had offered. "Did she have any friends in class? People she'd show up with or talk to? Anything like that?"

The professor shook his head. "She always sat in the back, by herself," he said. "But perhaps I can get those records you were looking for. A member of the faculty might be able to access them if it was considered necessary. Give me your business card, and I will get in touch if I find anything that might be useful."

I produced one from the tote bag and handed it to him. "Call even if you find something that might not be useful," I said. "You never know what's going to make the difference."

"I'll do that," Kunkel said. "But you must promise to let me know if you find Ms. MacKenzie. Is that fair?"

"Sure," I said. "Is there a reason you're so interested in finding her?" I couldn't help but remember the other men Julia had apparently entranced.

The professor looked away, suddenly, and I was afraid I knew what was coming. "We . . . were seeing each other for a time," he said. "I never knew why she left so abruptly."

Yup. That was what I'd thought.

Twenty-four

The ghost "meet-and-greet" was scheduled for nine thirty Saturday morning, just after most of the guests had returned from finding some breakfast in town. Although it might've been more appropriately spooky to change the event to an after-dark activity, I wanted this to be as friendly and unthreatening an experience as I could offer. I did not want anyone to be overly frightened.

And I was worried about the guests, too.

Melissa, now an old hand at the spectacle about to begin, dressed in her best cute-little-girl outfit for summer—shorts and a striped T-shirt—and brought out a plate of cookies from a box I'd bought at the supermarket that morning. With all the sleuthing this morning, for all the good it had done me, I'd done a bare-bones run to the supermarket. But there were the cookies, as well as iced tea, iced coffee (both decaf and caffeinated) and bottled water.

I had changed clothes as well, from the business suit I was

wearing as a detective disguise to a much cooler, much looser summer dress that actually let in air. The smile on my face was a combination of guesthouse hostess friendliness and welcome relief.

Don Petrone, resplendent in a white seersucker jacket and aqua ascot, stood at the entrance to the library, where the "event" was scheduled to take place. He smiled his charming smile as I walked in carrying a pitcher of iced tea and placed it on the table at the rear of the room.

"So here come the ghosts, huh?" he asked. "How do we know when they're here?"

It was a logical question. "I'll let you know, but also, we'll make sure Paul and Maxie make themselves known as visually as they can. You won't see them, but you'll know they're there."

"Sounds great," said Don, who had thankfully thought everything sounded great since he'd arrived. I'd take a van load of Don Petrones every week if I could get them, but his refusal to perspire no matter what the weather would have been infuriating in a man any less charming.

"Just about five minutes," I told him, although he hadn't asked, and Don nodded graciously. I still needed napkins and paper plates for the cookies, so I headed back to the kitchen, but was stopped halfway through the den by Francie and Arthur Westen, who had come in through the front door in anticipation of our ghostathon and looked a little wilted and a little worried.

"We're not late, are we?" Francie asked. "We didn't miss the beginning, did we?"

"Not at all. Things will get started in about five minutes. Why not take a seat in the library and have a nice cold drink?"

Francie led Arthur in the direction of the library, still hustling as if I'd said they had no time at all. "We want to make sure we get seats together," she told him as they hurried, clearly overestimating the popularity of the event.

The final two Senior Plus Tour members, Mrs. Fischer and

Mrs. Spassky, ambled in with a minute or so to spare, happily chattering away with excitement about "finally getting to talk to the spirits of the house." It wasn't terribly crowded in the library—with the five guests, Melissa and me—but it wasn't an empty room, by any means.

The cookies were very enticing, the drinks were cold and the air-conditioning (another reason I'd chosen this room, because it was more efficient here than in larger areas) made the place comfortable. Paul dutifully stuck his head through the ceiling at one twenty-eight, the rest of his body still on the second floor somewhere. Even inverted, he was a trouper.

I couldn't say the same for Maxie.

After watching the walls, the ceiling and the floor for a not-so-good five minutes, I hissed up at Paul, "Where's Maxie?"

"I don't know. She isn't in any of her usual spots," he replied. That went beyond unusual; it had happened just once, the day before, and I thought I had made it very clear to Maxie exactly how unacceptable that behavior had been. Apparently not clear enough, it was starting to seem.

I walked out into the hallway as Francie said loudly, "It's time, isn't it? I'm not wrong, am I? It is time for the ghosts."

"Just a moment," I told the group, hopefully sounding pleasant and upbeat. I gestured to Melissa to come to my side, and she was there quickly, looking concerned.

"Go outside and see if you can spot Maxie on the roof," I told her. "ASAP."

She nodded. That is one good ten-year-old, my daughter. Out the door she went into the tropical heat wave.

I put on my game face and walked back into the library. "Sorry for the delay," I told my guests. "We're having a little trouble locating one of our resident spirits." Truth be told, I could have gone on just with Paul, but he'd been so weak and discombobulated the last couple of days I wasn't sure he'd hold up by himself. Maxie was, if not reliable, energetic.

"The ghosts are missing?" Francie piped up. "How can a ghost be missing?"

"I wouldn't say *missing*," I told her. "I'm guessing she's just a little late, to tell the truth. Sometimes people on the Other Side lose track of time a little, you know?"

Paul rolled his eyes at that one. It looks odd upside down, in case you were wondering.

Melissa ran back into the house, and I met her at the library doorway, where we could whisper to each other. "She's not there," she told me. "I ran all the way around the house, and I didn't see her anywhere."

"Try the basement." It was a long shot, but if Maxie really didn't want to be found, she might go to an area of the house where she didn't normally spend much time. Melissa nodded, and was gone before I could turn around.

Inside, the mob was getting a little restless (except Don, of course, who was drinking an iced decaf with Splenda and having what appeared to be a jovial conversation with Mrs. Spassky). I clapped my hands and smiled my most ingratiating smile.

"While we search for our missing friend," I said, without grimacing—I think—"why don't we start with some questions for the spirit who is actually in the room at the moment?"

I looked up. Paul was, indeed, still in the room, responsible soul that he was, but hanging from the ceiling, about a third of him visible from the chest up, or down, depending on how you wanted to think about it.

"How do we know where he is?" Mrs. Fischer asked. "I'd hate to be asking a question to the wall."

"I'll tell you what," I said. "We'll see to it that our friend up there writes his answers out for you; then you can not only see where he is, but that I'm not tricking you in any way. Paul really is up there."

But he was looking somewhat panicky.

"I'm not sure that's a good idea, Alison," he told me. "I'm not sure I can write like this."

"Like what?" I asked. A couple of the guests looked confused, then nodded, oh yes, I was talking to the ghost.

"In my current state. I get a little queasy trying to concentrate on things that are over my head, or in this case, under my head."

"How can you get queasy? You haven't eaten in two years." This get-together with the ghosts was starting to look a little lame to the guests, I was sure.

"Don't ask me how it can happen; I'm just telling you the facts," Paul said, looking profoundly unhappy. "There must be some other way I can verify my presence with these people."

Melissa stuck her head in just far enough to say, "Not in the basement. Trying the attic."

Before I could say "Paul would have told us if she was in the attic," my daughter was gone up the stairs. There was nothing to do but face the increasingly disappointed-looking faces of my guests.

"I'm afraid it's difficult for Paul to write anything at the moment," I told them. "Let's try to think of another way we can convince you he's here."

They stared at me for what seemed like an hour. I started trying to form a new sentence in my mind, but was coming up completely blank. You might just have well asked me to recite the lyrics to "Roundabout," by Yes. Which, I'm pretty sure, has lyrics.

"We could just take your word for it," Don Petrone said, smiling as usual. His teeth were so white I found myself trying to determine if they were natural or not. "I trust you, Alison."

"I don't think this is an issue of trust," Francie sniffed. "We're paying extra for this vacation in a house that has ghosts in it. Now, I've seen things flying around the room, and I've heard some spooky noises that I think were probably recorded, and the whole thing has been about as real as the haunted house at Disneyland. Then there was a woman here yelling up at a 'ghost' who just threw books around, just like before. So when we were supposed to have this one-on-one meeting with the ghosts, I thought this would be the chance to prove it. And now all I'm hearing is excuses."

I wanted to be annoyed with Francie, since hers was exactly the reaction I'd been dreading, but the fact was that she had a point. So I looked at her and said, "I understand just why you feel that way. And I'd like to ask you if there's anything that could happen right now that would convince you there is the spirit of a man in the room who has in fact passed on. What can we do to prove it to you, Francie? Name anything."

Melissa, from the library door: "Not in the attic. Trying farther into the backyard." And gone again.

"Why not pour some ink or paint or something on his hand and let us see him?" Mrs. Spassky tried. "Then we'd know there was someone there."

I groaned inwardly. "I'm afraid it doesn't work like that, Mrs. Spassky," I said. "Paul's not invisible; he's dead." I looked up to him for some sign of a solution; Paul was usually so good about helping out when he could. Now, he looked helpless, and unable to straighten himself out, literally.

"Give me the pad and pen," he finally pushed out through clenched teeth. "Tell them I'll answer one question, and that's all I can do on paper."

I passed the suggestion on to the group, and they agreed this would be sufficient to convince them of Paul's existence. So I picked up the legal pad and felt-tipped pen I had ready for the session, and reached up toward Paul, who was quite near the ceiling and faced away from me. "Here," I said.

Paul reached down with his right arm, and the space between the pad and his hand was about two feet. I stood on my toes, and asked him to lower himself a bit, something that under normal circumstances wouldn't have been in the least difficult for him.

"I don't think I can," he said. "I'm feeling really weak."

Noting the fabulous timing for that announcement, I looked

at my one loyal friend in the crowd. "Don," I said, "may I borrow your chair for just a moment?"

Don looked startled, but as usual, nodded and smiled. He stood and pushed the chair he'd been sitting on toward me.

I positioned it under the area where Paul was suspended, and stepped up onto the seat. That bridged the gap between our hands, and I pushed the pad into Paul's hand.

And he dropped it.

Mrs. Spassky looked at the pad on the floor, frowned, and stood. She walked out of the room without saying another word. Mrs. Fischer was not far behind her.

"Just one minute," I said, stepping off the chair to gather the pad off the floor.

"I'm sorry, Alison," Paul said. And he vanished.

I stood there, feeling shocked and alone. There was nothing left to do but tell the group that we'd have to reschedule this event—but when I turned around, I saw that each and every one of them was already leaving the library. I didn't even bother to make the announcement.

Melissa walked in just as Don Petrone, the last holdout, turned to me, shrugged, and left the room silently. She sat down next to me and put her hand in mine.

"Having a bad day?" she asked.

"I've had better. Where's Maxie?"

Melissa shook her head. "I can't find her anywhere, and that's weird," she said. "I know she hides from you sometimes, but I can always find her."

"She's lucky she's dead," I said. "Because after this, I'd kill her when I saw her."

"You don't mean that," Melissa admonished me.

"Not literally, no."

"Why couldn't Paul do the show?" Melissa asked.

I didn't want to worry her—she already knew Paul was upside down; telling her he was weak would have alarmed her—so I said, "The upside-down thing. He kept dropping stuff and it looked like he wasn't there." Which was pretty much true. And before Liss could ask why he couldn't do other stuff, my cell phone buzzed, indicating I'd gotten a text message. My heart leapt a little, but I exhaled when I took a look.

The message was from Phyllis Coates at the *Chronicle*. And it read, simply, "GET OVER HERE. SOMETHING'S FISHY WITH THE ARREST."

Twenty-five

"Since when are you interested in a murder in Seaside Heights?" I asked Phyllis.

Her office, overstuffed with paper and never roomy to begin with, was looking especially wilted today. It might have had something to do with the two table fans she had running and the lack of air-conditioning.

"I told you, it's a slow news cycle for us except for the borough boards making sound and fury signifying nothing. Even if stuff was happening here, the borough would want me to shut up about it because it would hurt the tourist business." Phyllis, who gave up smoking roughly around the time I was born, still liked to have a pen dangling out of her mouth where a cigarette once lived.

"Would you shut up about it?" I asked.

Phyllis snorted. "Of course not. But there really isn't anything going on, and now a woman from the area's been arrested for the Seaside Heights murder, so that makes it sort of interesting to my readership. But when I saw the report from the ME, it was beyond clear that someone is railroading this Katherine Malone faster than Amtrak could do it. Something really is rotten in the state of Seaside Heights."

"What about the medical examiner's report smelled bad?" I asked. It hadn't occurred to me that the obvious frame job someone was working on Kitty would extend that far.

"Fragments of metal in the skull? Any implement made of steel, like that wrench, would be ten times too hard to leave that kind of residue. A match made by examining those fragments against the weapon? Come on. You know how many wrenches are made with that kind of steel? And the idea that it's still there, waiting to be picked up and put into an evidence bag, after *two years*? I'm miles away from the county prosecutor's office, and I can smell the crap from here."

That was pretty much what Paul had been saying, but sometimes the idea that another person has reached the same conclusion independently can make you feel more confident about what you've already heard. "Your source in the ME's office might know something," I suggested.

But this time, she shook her head. "He won't talk about this one, no matter how I try to persuade him," she said, adding a little extra juice to the word *persuade*. "And believe me, I've tried."

"Do me a favor and don't tell me more," I suggested.

Phyllis chortled. "Anyway, it's clear that somebody is setting up this Malone woman as the killer, and for reasons I can't begin to fathom, the cops are going for it," she said. "I've done a little digging, and I really don't think this Detective Martin Ferry in Seaside Heights is a bad cop. Maybe not too much initiative. He seems honest enough, and his record of clearing cases was really good until he lost his partner."

"Yeah, all he does is talk about his ex-partner," I told her. "Was she killed in the line of duty or something?"

Phyllis cocked an eyebrow. "You don't know?" she asked with a tone so incredulous it occurred to me that I'd be diminished in her eyes if I told the truth. So I grinned with what I thought was a wiseguy expression.

"Of course I know," I said. "I was just having some fun with you."

"Good. Anyway, I only called you here because you showed some interest in this murder the day we went to Veg Out, and I wouldn't want to think a professional investigator would miss that detail."

"Don't be silly," I said. Mostly, I meant that referring to me as a "professional investigator" was silly, but there was no reason to tell Phyllis that. Now all I had to do was find out about Ferry's ex-partner.

"Anyway," Phyllis went on, letting me off the hook for the time being, "Ferry was doing well until he was on his own, and even now, he's not doing badly. But cops are competitive, and maybe he feels like he needs to clear this two-year-old homicide to keep his reputation alive; I don't know. I'm grasping at straws because this thing doesn't make a lick of sense on the surface."

It still didn't explain why she'd texted me so urgently. "I haven't found out anything you don't already know," I pointed out.

Phyllis picked up the thread. "You know something I don't. What's the motive? Why do the cops think Katherine Malone wanted to kill this biker guy? Was it the drugs?"

The drugs? "Big Bob was married, very briefly, to Kitty Malone's daughter," I told her. "And she really didn't like him. Supposedly, she thought he was trying to rekindle the relationship, although I think that's a crock." Then, even risking Phyllis's diminished opinion of me, I asked, "What drugs?"

She didn't even blink. "I'm told that there was some speculation 'Big Bob' was involved in a cocaine deal of epic proportions that never really seemed to take off," she said. "The cops say he was supposed to deliver a massive amount of blow to a buyer one night, but he never showed up."

That was, to say the least, news to me—everyone at the

Sprocket had been adamant that Big Bob never abused anything but the occasional beer. I shook my head to get my thoughts straight. "Big Bob was a drug dealer?" I said aloud, but not necessarily to Phyllis.

"Not before that night, no," she answered. "That's the weird part. But the narcotics cops I spoke to swear they got wind of some mammoth coke deal that was about to happen, and then it didn't, and nobody knew who the supplier was, but Bob Benicio was supposed to do the deal. He didn't show up, and nobody ever heard from him again until his bones showed up under the beach in Seaside Heights."

"That doesn't make sense," I told her. "If the cops thought Big Bob was in on some big drug deal, why didn't they look for him after he disappeared? Nobody seems to have given a damn about him until they found his body, two years later."

Phyllis, as always sifting through papers that probably had significance in some other story she was preparing to write, seemed to find what she was looking for in a stack and took the pen out of her mouth to underline something. "That's not entirely true," she said. "There was actually a pretty massive search for Benicio by the county cops at the time, but, of course, they never found him. They just kept it quiet because they didn't want his buyers to know the cops knew who they were. It all went nowhere because Big Bob was several feet under the boardwalk."

This turn in the investigation was really throwing me for a loop. It completely shattered the image Maxie and Luther had given me of Big Bob, and seemed to bolster the one that Kitty had apparently held. Big Bob was Bad News.

"I've got to go," I told Phyllis. "I'll let you know if I find out anything."

"Where are you going?" she asked, a slight smile on her face. This was what she'd wanted after all—to get me working on this investigation so she could ask me about it later.

"To someone who might know something," I said.

* * *

Shore Cycle of Lakewood, Luther Mason's "bike shop,"
was not what I had expected. I'd pictured a small store with
a garage in the back, where Luther and an assistant would
provide advice for motorcycle enthusiasts while standing
around a hot wood-burning stove during the winter. So I
was not exactly prepared for what I found.

The place was enormous, taking up the better part of a
half acre (I could judge in comparison to my own backyard). The parking lot alone was bigger than I'd pictured
the entire operation, and there were at least thirty motorcycles, serious-looking ones, parked there.

The big glass-enclosed showroom, more reminiscent of
an upscale car dealership, was so spotless I considered asking Luther the name of his cleaning lady. Four salespeople—
yes, there was even one woman selling hogs—patrolled the
floors. Business appeared to be brisk. Luther was nowhere
to be found, but when I asked a salesman (whose name was
Dan and whose jeans were pressed) where to locate him, I
was given directions to "the top floor." To be fair, there
were only two levels, but it sounded good.

I found the proprietor in his "office," which was really
an enclosed cubicle made of glass that overlooked the sales
floor. No doubt when a prospective customer was getting
hesitant about the outlay of cash, the rep on the floor would
bring him up to "see the manager," and Luther would close
the sale.

"I'm impressed," I told him when he welcomed me into
the "room." It was quite spacious inside, and the view of the
much larger space around it added the illusion of greater
depth. "You didn't let on it was this large an operation. A
bike shop, indeed."

"Well, it sort of started that way," Luther said. "When I
bought the original place, it was about half this size and

looked like a garage with an auto parts store in front of it. But I knew what real bikers wanted to be treated like, so I took every dime I ever had and turned it into this. It's working out pretty well."

"I'll say."

"So how come I haven't heard from you?" Luther asked, hurriedly adding, "What's going on with the investigation?" in case I thought he meant anything else. He seemed determined not to mention our venture into lip-locking—after all, it was just one kiss—and I was in a business state of mind as well, so I didn't disagree.

"I need more of your insight," I told him. "There's some suggestion now that Big Bob might have been involved in some very large drug deal around the time he died, and that could be why he was killed. Did you know anything about that?"

But the look in Luther's eyes had already given me the answer: He was shocked. "Big Bob?" he asked. "I never saw that guy venture beyond a couple of beers. I can't imagine he was involved in drugs."

"Apparently a lot."

Luther shook his head. "Couldn't be. I would have known, or one of the other guys. And it's just so outside Big Bob's character. He wasn't even all that concerned about money. As long as he was making a living wage at the grill during the season and picking up maybe some construction work with Wilson when he got some during the off-season, he was content. A lot of guys have these big dreams, you know, where they're gonna win the lottery and go live on some island in the Caribbean. Not Big Bob. He was happy with his life the way it was. I can't see him getting involved in something like that."

"What about Wilson?" I asked. "Could he have gotten mixed up with a bad deal?"

Luther considered a moment. There was a knock on the door—Luther's cubicle was the only one that had a door—and after a moment, the receptionist stuck her head in and said, "John's going to need you in a minute, Luther."

"Okay." She withdrew and Luther turned back to talk to me. "Wilson was a different story," he said. "He had the dreams, and he didn't especially care how he got where he wanted to go. I don't know about anything else, but I saw him smoke some weed every now and again. Hell, the fact is I smoked some weed every now and again in those days. Wilson was certainly less worried about doing the right thing than Big Bob."

"Could he have gotten Big Bob involved in a deal if Wilson thought it was his ticket to the good life? Would Big Bob have done that for a friend?" I asked.

Luther shook his head slowly. "I honestly don't know," he said. "Big Bob was pretty scrupulous, but if a friend really needed his help? Maybe. I can't call that one." He stood up. "One of my salesmen needs me," he said. "Can you hang on for about twenty minutes?"

"I can't," I answered. "A friend of mine is . . . ill, and I need to get back."

"I'm sorry to hear that," Luther said. "But I hope your friend is better soon. Let's walk down together."

We did, and on the way, I brought Luther up to date with the Seaside Heights investigation. I hadn't realized Luther was unaware of Kitty's arrest, and he became absolutely incensed when he heard that she was not being released after her arraignment.

"How is that possible?" he asked. "The woman's never done anything wrong in her life, and now they're holding her in county? It's ridiculous. Maxie's mother didn't kill Big Bob. I've only met her a couple of times, but I know she'd never do that."

I agreed, but I told Luther about the million-dollar bail and the 10 percent cash equivalent. "She just can't put her hands on anywhere near that kind of money," I told him.

Luther didn't look happy. "I don't understand how she got arrested in the first place," he said. "What makes them think she put a wrench into Big Bob's skull?"

"It's clear that somebody is framing her. It's such an obvious case that I'm shocked the cops are going for it," I said, echoing Phyllis, "but that's what's going on. They're buying this ridiculous story—hook, line and sinker—and letting Kitty pay the price while the real killer gets a laugh out of it."

Luther looked concerned. "It's not right," he said. "What can we do about it?"

"We have to find the real killer and get him to stop laughing," I suggested.

"I like that," Luther said. "I'll come over tomorrow, and we'll do that." Then he walked toward a man wearing a Shore Cycle denim work shirt, who introduced Luther to his customer, a kid maybe twenty years old whose girlfriend was eyeing him more than her boyfriend, something Luther pretended not to notice.

I marveled at him. Sometimes, people aren't at all what you expect.

Twenty-six

"Where *were* you?" I said—okay, bellowed—at Maxie. "You left Paul and me hanging out there to dry. There's absolutely no excuse that could possibly be sufficient."

She stared at me and said nothing.

"Well?" I demanded.

Maxie "sat down" on the dwindling pile of drywall sheets at the far end of the attic. I had measured very carefully, so there wouldn't be a significant amount of drywall left over when the walls were hung. The last thing I needed was to have to haul all that stuff back down to where it had originated.

Paul had been up here when I'd arrived, which was something of a relief, given the way he'd left the last time I'd seen him. He looked even less solid than usual, and said nothing. But when Maxie had showed up, and it had become obvious that we were going to have a heated discussion, Paul literally sank into the floor and disappeared.

Maxie continued the silent treatment.

"What's your excuse?" I said.

She drew in her lips and raised her eyebrows. Having to deal with a lunatic like me was clearly a trial for her. "What difference does it make?" she asked. "You just said no excuse would be good enough, so let's just assume I don't have one."

"Oh, that's great," I said. It was way easier raising Melissa than raising Maxie would ever be. I'll be puttering around this house in my nineties, and she'll still be twenty-eight going on fifteen. "Do you have any idea what kind of damage you've done?"

"Yeah, so the quaint little tourists didn't get to talk to the spooky ghosts," she mocked. "The world will probably come to an end now." She yawned theatrically.

"You know, it must be really easy when you don't have to think about anyone but yourself," I said. I turned to the wall, where I was lightly sanding a seam between two sheets of drywall with the hand sander attached to my shop vac. There was very little dust, but it was fairly loud, so Maxie had to shout to be heard over the work. What a shame.

"Yeah, I have it real easy!" she screamed.

Halfway through her sentence, I turned off the vac, so her words echoed around the room. Her eyes narrowed, and she stuck out her lower lip.

"You know, I never signed on for this vaudeville gig you worked up with Paul," Maxie growled. "He gets to keep his mind active with this gumshoe stuff, and you get us to help put your guesthouse on the map. What do *I* get out of it?"

Without thinking, I shot back, "You get to stay in my house for the rest of eternity!" And I immediately felt bad about it. Maxie has a talent for making me say things that I'm going to regret later, sometimes as soon as they leave my mouth.

She looked absolutely stunned. "You think that's what I want? To stay in this place until time finally ends?"

"No, Maxie, I—" I was backpedaling, but not fast enough.

"Forget it! You don't ever have to see me again if you don't want to!" And before I could say another word, she had vanished in a blink. I looked around the room, called "Maxie?" timidly and realized that I'd rarely felt quite so alone. I gave up the sanding and went downstairs.

But once I arrived in the den, where Don Petrone and Albert Westen were playing gin rummy (Don grinned when I walked in, but Albert barely acknowledged my presence), Maxie was there, talking confidentially to Melissa in the corner closest to the kitchen door. And when I got closer, I noticed the one thing I really didn't want to see.

Melissa was crying. I was the only one who could tell, because she was concealing her face, but we mothers have a sixth sense about such things. Besides, Don and Albert were concentrating on their cards.

I rushed to her just as Maxie finished saying, "not what I wanted," and glared at me.

"What's going on?" I asked Melissa. "What's wrong, baby?"

It took Melissa a while to get herself under control, and when she did, she quietly told me, "Maxie . . . Maxie says she's going away and never coming back, and she says you told her she had to go. Why did you say that?"

I think I might have literally seen red. "I *didn't* say that," I announced loudly for Maxie to hear, "and I *wouldn't* say that, ever." Don and Arthur looked up. Arthur pursed his lips and shook his head—*Nice try, lady, but there's no ghost there*— and Don just smiled. Don would probably smile if someone dropped a bowling ball on his foot.

I was feeling a level of anger I hadn't reached since the pre-divorce era, and I looked up at Maxie, who was hovering with a smug grin on her face, arms folded in a gesture of defiance. I didn't care who heard me anymore. "How *dare* you lie to Melissa like that? Try and make me look like the villain to my own daughter? What kind of monster *are* you?"

"It's okay, Alison," Don said, not looking up from his rummy hand. "We believe there are ghosts in the house, honey."

"You've wanted me out of here since the day you found out

about me," Maxie shot back, her eyes slits and her clothes changing into the more aggressive black leather she seemed to unconsciously sprout whenever she was angry. "Well, I'm giving you what you want. You can explain it to Melissa any way you want, but the fact is, I'm leaving because of *you*."

"You can't leave!" Melissa wailed. "You're my friend!"

"You know, it's really sort of in bad taste to get your daughter all upset just to convince us," Albert told me.

"I'm not . . . Look. I can't prove it to you right now, but I'm having a pretty heated argument with one of the ghosts right now," I said.

"Say something, Mom!" Melissa begged, gesturing toward Maxie.

"She's not going anywhere, Liss," I told her, staring at Maxie the whole time. "You forget—she can't leave the grounds of this house. She's just saying that to be mean."

"You think so?" Maxie yelled. "You couldn't find me when you wanted me to put on your little spooky show, could you? Where do you think I was?"

You know how, just when you think things can't get worse, they inevitably do? From behind me came my ex-husband's voice.

"Lissie, honey! Don't worry—I won't leave you again!"

See what I mean?

I turned to see The Swine, arms open, inviting Melissa to come over and shield herself from me in his comforting embrace. Liss, to her everlasting credit, looked at him as if he must have lost his mind, and managed to croak out, "It's not about you, Daddy."

The Swine looked absolutely stupefied. "It's not?"

Then I looked up at Maxie, who had spontaneously changed into a pair of ripped jeans and a shirt bearing the logo of Roadside America, a tourist attraction in Pennsylvania. "You can make yourself invisible whenever you want, but I know you can't just leave," I told her.

"That's not fair," said my ex. He's so vain; he probably thinks this book is about him.

"You watch me," Maxie spat back. And she turned to head for the wall.

"Maxie!" Melissa yelled. And Maxie did turn back, saw her expression, and suddenly looked sad. She hesitated.

"Who's Maxie?" Steven asked.

But at that moment, a voice from the direction of the front door shouted at her, "Maxine! What do you think you're doing?"

We all (except the two card players) turned and saw my mother standing at the doorway to the den, a look of sincere concern on her face. "Why is Melissa crying?" Mom asked.

"It's . . . She . . ." Maxie pointed at me.

Mom turned toward the door and said something I couldn't hear. She nodded her head.

And then Kitty Malone walked through the door and, looking a few feet to the left of her daughter, called out, "Maxie, you stay right here, and let's talk this thing out."

Twenty-seven

The ensuing pandemonium lasted a good few minutes, with Maxie coming down from the ceiling to try to embrace her mother, and Kitty seeming to feel the physical presence of her daughter. Mom walked to Melissa to comfort her and find out what the tears were about, and I rushed to Kitty with a thousand questions on the tip of my tongue.

Don and Albert simply nodded to the two ladies and went back to their game of rummy.

My biggest concern was The Swine, who, after realizing (with much prompting) that Melissa *wasn't* crying about him, became justifiably suspicious about all the people talking to the ceiling. But then he sidled up next to me and said, "Is this a spook show?"

"Yes," I told him, mentally thanking him for giving me the out. "Can you get Lucy out of here?"

"Where is she?" he asked.

"I have no idea. Go look." And he was out the door.

It turned out that Mom and Kitty had just met on the doorstep, both having arrived independently. Mom was brought up to speed on Kitty's ordeal, which she found horrifying, and having known Maxie's mother for a grand total of forty seconds, declared that the charges were completely baseless. Mom and gray areas have met, but they're not close.

Kitty clearly found Mom fascinating, and was especially jealous of the fact that my mother can see Maxie, but she can't.

When the excitement died down, those of us in on the situation (minus Melissa, who was told she'd be brought up to date shortly, and took the news well, stomping up the stairs to her room in protest) reconvened in the kitchen, with Mom continuing to pass on messages from Maxie to Kitty because it was simply faster than Maxie trying to communicate directly via pad and pen. I considered getting Maxie a phone so she could text her mother.

Paul, somehow having been alerted to the situation— maybe he'd run into Melissa as she huffed by—materialized in the ceiling, head down of course, and listened very carefully, stroking his goatee fiercely throughout.

Mom, disturbed by Paul's "less than right side up appearance," expressed concern, but Paul deflected it, saying he was just seeing the world from a new perspective because he could. Mom's eyes narrowed, as she was clearly having some trouble buying that story, but she turned her attention to Kitty, who said she wasn't sure why she'd been released, but was relieved anyway.

"They never moved me to the other prison," she told us. "They never even suggested that they were going to move me. So I was pretty much in the same place you saw me, Alison, and being treated quite well for someone they thought was a cold-blooded murderer. They sent out for Chinese food for me last night."

That was all nice detail, but as Phyllis would have told

Kitty, she was burying her lede. "But how did you get out?" I asked.

"Well, that was the strange part," Kitty said.

"The strange part?" Maxie asked, still not looking at me when she could avoid it. "This whole thing has been insane from the beginning."

We did not pass that comment along to Kitty, who simply continued, "Maybe two hours ago, Sergeant Packer—you didn't get to meet him, Alison, but he was very nice—came in and told me I'd made bail. It took about an hour or so to process the paperwork and get me back into my street clothes, and they even drove me back to my house, but I knew Maxie would be worried, so I came right here."

Everyone in the room took a moment to absorb that information. "So you paid a hundred thousand dollars in cash? Where did you get that kind of money, Kitty?" I asked, my head reeling.

Kitty examined my face for a moment, then burst out laughing. "*I* didn't come up with the money, Alison!" she said. "Goodness, no. I'd be lucky to find 10 percent of *that* in an emergency. No, the bail came from someone else, and that's something I wanted to ask Maxie about." She looked up, and Maxie moved into the spot where Kitty was staring, perhaps just to feel like her mother could see her for a moment.

That's the thing about Maxie: Just when you're all set to hate her, she acts like the girl she was, one who died much too young, and the sympathy gene kicks into gear. It's really annoying.

"Tell her I'm listening," Maxie told Mom, still deliberately ignoring me in the process. Okay, so she wasn't *always* a sympathetic character.

Mom passed on the message, and Kitty said, "The bail came from Luther Mason. You remember him, don't you, honey? Wasn't he a member of the motorcycle gang you were involved with?"

Maxie rolled her eyes like a practiced teenager (Melissa

had already perfected her technique at ten, because she's precocious) and took the time to write "IT WASN'T A <u>GANG</u>" on the pad to show her mother. Then she said out loud, "Sure, I knew Luther. Luther's the guy who asked her"—that was me—"to find out who killed Big Bob."

"Wait a minute," I said. "Luther Mason put up your bail? A hundred thousand dollars?"

"That's what they told me," Kitty said, nodding. She looked pretty surprised herself. "He didn't even stay long enough for me to thank him. Apparently, he just showed up, paid the money and left."

Luther? I mean, the motorcycle dealership was very impressive, but a hundred thousand dollars lying around with nothing to do? Luther never failed to explode my expectations. He must have left for Seaside Heights right after he'd seen me.

"That's amazing," Maxie said. She wrote on the pad for a while and then showed Kitty the message: "SEE? BIKERS ARE NOT SUCH BAD PEOPLE."

"No," Kitty agreed. "I guess you're right. But I can't imagine what made Luther suddenly show up and get me out of jail. I can't have met him more than three times in my life. He came by just a few days ago, and that's when I told him about you, Maxie. Why he'd come out and give all that money, it's mystifying."

"I know," I told her. "Luther's my client. I just saw him a few hours ago, but he didn't say a word about—"

Mom cut me off before I could finish the sentence. "You saw Luther just before he bailed out Kitty?" she asked. "Did you tell him about her bail?"

"Well, yeah, but I didn't ask him to—"

Maxie's eyes widened. "*You* did this?" she asked me, addressing me directly for the first time since our blowup. "You got my mother out of jail?"

Paul's eyes narrowed. I think. It was hard to tell with him in that position. He might have just been getting sleepy.

Maxie swooped down and hugged me as best she could. It

was interesting how the sensation differed from when Paul had touched me; whereas he felt like a warm breeze, Maxie's touch was closer to a paper fan on a hot summer day like today. Light, pleasant, but not really all that different than the way you felt before.

"Hang on," I told the room. "I'm happy Kitty's free now, but it wasn't my doing. I don't have the money. I didn't ask Luther to put up the bail. This is his good deed, not mine."

"Don't be modest," Mom said. She thinks I am the second brightest spot in the universe—just behind Melissa—and that everything I do is absolute perfection. Yeah, I know it sounds great, but it wears at the nerves, let me tell you.

"I'm not being modest. Look, I'll prove it to you." I pulled my cell phone out of my pocket and dialed Luther's number. When he answered, I began with, "You bailed Kitty out of jail! That is just so . . . I'm at a loss for words. It's probably the first time I've been at a loss for words in years." (Actually, it was since the moment The Swine told me about Amee, and I overcame that feeling quickly.)

I put the phone on speaker so the room could hear Luther say, "I was glad to. She didn't deserve to be in jail, and I had the money."

"Yeah, that's some kind of bike shop you have there, with a hundred grand lying around in cash," I told him.

"Cash?" Luther laughed. "I don't have money lying around in piles, Alison. I wrote them a check that will pay through an account I have just for emergencies. I'm pretty sure Kitty's not a flight risk, so I don't have to worry about losing the money."

"I'm right here," Kitty said into the phone, louder than was necessary. "This is Kitty Malone, Luther. I can't believe how generous you were. I really can't thank you enough."

Luther seemed slightly cowed by the new voice in his ear. "It's perfectly okay, Mrs. Malone," he said after a pause.

Kitty said, "But I have to ask—why? Why would you lay out that kind of money for someone you've barely met?"

Luther let out a long breath. "You know, ma'am," he finally

sighed, "I think maybe I wanted to change your opinion of the kind of people your daughter hung out with. I knew Maxie, and I liked her. And I thought maybe because you saw how we dressed or because you watched her ride away on the back of Big Bob's bike, you thought we were out of the Hells Angels or something. I wanted you to know that we're decent people like anybody else. Big Bob might not have been the son-in-law you were hoping for, but he did love your daughter in his own way. I think maybe you didn't give him a real fair break. And I wish I had said that to Maxie, too, when I had the chance."

Kitty's eyes welled up, and Maxie had already turned away from us, her hand to her mouth. Kitty gulped, shook her head to herself, and when I offered her the phone, she took it. "It was never about the way he looked or the bike," she told Luther. "He hit Maxie. And that wasn't ever going to be okay with me. You don't get a second chance on that. Can you understand, Luther?"

"Yes, ma'am, I can," came the answer. "I didn't know that until Alison told me, but I do understand how you feel."

I took the phone back from Kitty and decided to rally the troops. "Now that we're all here," I said, "we need to mobilize. We need to figure out how to keep Kitty out of jail, and find out who really did kill Big Bob. We need to go to . . ."

Paul started to gesture in my direction, so I turned toward him. He checked to see if Maxie was still looking away, gathering her thoughts, and she was. So Paul silently pulled his index finger across his throat, the universal signal for *stop*. For some reason, he didn't want me to say any more in front of the group.

"Uh, to see if we can find some stuff out. So I'll call you to keep you informed. Okay, Luther?" I said. I must have sounded like a lunatic who couldn't make up her own mind.

"Um . . . sure," Luther answered, sounding justifiably confused, and we ended the call.

"What do you think we should do?" Kitty asked.

"What I'd like you to do is go home and relax," I said. "You've had enough of an ordeal for the time being."

"Where are you going to be?" my mother said.

"In Levittown, Pennsylvania," I answered, "looking for a man named Wilson Meyers. Do you know him?"

Kitty shook her head. "I heard about Wilson, but I never met him. He didn't seem to be one of the main . . . people in that group." She looked where she thought Maxie was hovering, and got a good look at the karaoke machine. Kitty did not comment.

Maxie looked over at me. And our eyes met for a second without any rancor. It was hard to know what that meant, because she almost immediately vanished.

Kitty regarded me carefully. "I'm going with you," she said.

"No, you're not," I said. "Leaving the state will violate your bail agreement, and Luther will lose his money."

Kitty looked determined, but beaten on that point. She nodded. "I wouldn't know Wilson if I saw him, anyway," she said.

"Neither would I," Mom said. "But I'm going anyway. *I'm* not out on bail." She nodded conspiratorially at Kitty, who grinned.

A long argument ensued, and it turned out that Kitty Malone was almost as difficult to dissuade when she got an idea in her head as my mother.

"You and Maxine need to sit down and clear the air," my mother said.

We were driving through White Horse, New Jersey about noon the next day on I-195, not far from the "Trenton Makes" Bridge (bearing lettering that read "Trenton Makes / The World Takes," which harkened back to another era), which would take us into Pennsylvania. We'd be in Levittown in less than half an hour.

I had decided specifically not to call ahead to Meyer Wilson, despite Lieutenant McElone having given me a phone number taken at the time of his speeding ticket (seriously, twenty-nine?). If Wilson was hiding out from something and didn't want to be found, calling him ahead of time would be sort of counterproductive.

On the other hand, if he wasn't home now, what would Mom and I accomplish?

"First of all, I'm not sure Maxie actually sits down these days," I answered her. "And the air, while certainly not clear at the moment, is breathable. Why should we have another screaming match in an attempt to explain the last one?"

I had eschewed the GPS for this trip, as it was almost all on the major highway, and Mom, MapQuest pages in hand, could navigate. Sometimes that British woman who tells me to "go straight on" when I hit the highway sounds snotty.

"I'm just the grandmother, but to me it looks like the tension between you and Maxine is upsetting Melissa," my mother suggested. That's as close as she'd come to criticizing me, and it packed a wallop. I drove silently for a long moment.

I'd been thinking about this latest flare-up with Maxie since it had happened, and I was ready to say what I thought out loud for the first time. "The fact is, Maxie and I aren't ever going to be friends. I don't mind Maxie, and I'm perfectly fine with her staying in my house, largely because Melissa likes her so much. But we see things"—I'd almost said *life*—"in different ways. Maxie is all about rebellion and doing things that provoke, and I just want to raise my daughter and run my guesthouse. I'm trying to get by, and she's trying to get attention. That doesn't mean we'll always be at odds with each other, but it does mean we're never going to have the same point of view."

Mom wasn't entirely in my line of sight, but I didn't want to turn my head while driving to see if I'd upset her. So I wasn't really prepared when she chuckled lightly under her breath.

"You know what?" she said. "I think the problem between the two of you is that you're too much alike."

"Alike!" I belted out. "How on earth am I like Maxie?"

"You know what you want, and what you have to do to get it," Mom answered. "You've always been that way, even when you wanted to get that . . . What was it? That little lightbulb oven you wanted when you were six."

"The Easy-Bake Oven," I said, trying not to roll my eyes while driving. "That doesn't make me like Maxie."

"You both have a little bit of a temper. You do what you think is right and you don't worry too much about what other people think. And you both have something that Melissa responds to. Stop me when you think I'm wrong."

I didn't say anything because the thoughts were bouncing around in my head too fast. Me, like Maxie? She'd been a thorn in my side since I'd met her, and already it felt like we were eternal combatants, destined to be at odds with each other on every issue, every decision, everything that ever came up. And with Maxie, "ever" could end up being a very long time, indeed.

"I'm more grown up than Maxie," I said in my own defense. "I'm just trying to get on with my life after all that's happened."

"I know," Mom said, nodding. "But you had the advantage of being able to mature. You had a young daughter and a husband who wasn't going to be much help. You *had* to grow up. Maxie didn't get the chance, and she never will."

"It seems like every time I think I have her figured out, I find out something that changes my view of her," I said. "I didn't know she went to design school."

Mom nodded as we got on the Trenton Makes Bridge. "Maxine told me about that one day when I was babysitting Melissa. She got a full ride from a very good college, too," she said. "She was the only student from New Jersey who did, because they loved her designs so much."

"Why did she leave school?" I asked. "Was it Big Bob?"

She shook her head. "No, she met him after she left school. She dropped out because she got into a fight with one of her professors over a design project, and the school backed the professor."

"What didn't they like about the design?" I asked.

"It wasn't very . . . tasteful. You probably don't want to know the specifics," Mom answered. She was right; I probably didn't.

We got off the bridge and drove in silence for a while, other than Mom reading the directions to me. In very little time, we were pulling up in front of a cute little house that had clearly been seriously renovated since the original Levittown homes, all of them looking the same, were designed after the Second World War. It had what appeared to be recent brick facing, new windows, and a blue Ford Focus, the car reputedly driven at breakneck speeds through suburban streets.

There was no motorcycle in front of the house.

"This doesn't exactly look like the home of a fugitive biker," I said to my mother.

Mom looked cautious. "Don't judge a book by its cover," she said.

"You think he's dangerous?"

She raised an eyebrow and looked at the Focus. "I'm pretty sure you can outrun him in that thing if you have to," she said.

"Let's hope I don't have to find out," I said. I got out of the car. "Do you want to come in?" I asked through the open door as July closed in around me. Air-conditioned cars are wonderful, but I really couldn't afford to buy one right now. I had stuck to the seat in areas I'd not thought about in years.

"Well, I didn't drive all this way to sit in a hot car," Mom answered, and in a moment, the two of us were standing across the amazingly quiet street from a house with the address for "Meyer Wilson."

We stood there for a while, considering. But we couldn't come up with anything more creative than walking over and ringing the doorbell, so that's what we did. For the record, it was my finger on the doorbell button. Then Mom and I breathed in a bit and waited.

From inside the house, we could hear a woman's voice yell, "Door!"

And a man's answered, "What?"

Woman: "There's somebody at the door!"

Man: "Who?"

Woman (exasperated): "I don't know!"

Man: "Well . . . ?"

A few seconds later, the door opened, and a woman, presumably the one who had been trumpeting our arrival, stood in the doorway. As any human with a functional nervous system in this heat would be, she was wearing shorts and a tank top, and she eyed us warily. "Can I help you?" she asked.

That was the question I had driven here to have answered.

"We're looking for Wilson Meyers," I said, in what I hoped was a businesslike tone. "Does he live here?"

The woman's face grew suspicious. "No, Meyer Wilson lives here," she said. "I don't know any Wilson Meyers." But there was something in her eyes that made me think maybe we were in the right place after all.

"I'm a private investigator," I said, flashing the license I'd gotten ready for just such an emergency. "I just want to ask him about someone he used to know. He's not in any trouble." That I knew of for sure.

But it didn't matter, because the woman's eyes had widened at the words "private investigator." She turned her head toward the inside of the house and hollered, "Meyer!"

I could barely see into the living room of the house, which was a little cluttered but clean. From inside, wearing a pair of blue-jean cutoffs and a "Car Talk" T-shirt, came a thin man, shorter than I'd expected, slightly balding, fairly sunburned and wearing wire-rimmed glasses. He was drying his hands on a dishtowel. And that confirmed my suspicions: Obviously, Meyer Wilson was a completely separate person from Wilson Meyers, so Mom and I had just made the drive from the New Jersey Shore in a sweltering Volvo for absolutely no reason. The ride home would be even more delightful, because this was clearly not the biker who had so spooked everyone back at the Sprocket. We had caught ourselves a wild goose. I was sure of that.

Until the woman said, "These ladies say they're detectives, and they're looking for Wilson Meyers," and I got a look at his face.

The guy looked absolutely stunned. And more than a little frightened.

Wilson—because that had to be who he was—took off the glasses and regarded the two women standing on the other side of his doorstep.

"Detectives?" he said. He looked at Mom. "Really?"

"I'm the private investigator," I told him, and handed him a business card to prove it (like you couldn't just print them up if you wanted to). "My name is Alison Kerby, and this is my associate, Loretta."

Mom waved a hand. "Associate," she mocked. "I'm her mother. Can we come in? It's really hot out here." Mom believes honesty is the best policy, and I believe Mom should shut up every once in a while.

Wilson shot a glance at his girlfriend/wife/caretaker and stood aside. "Of course," he said. "Please come in."

It was indeed a relief to get into the house, whose central air-conditioning could be heard as a low hum throughout. Wilson gestured us into the living room and offered us some lemonade, which I gratefully accepted. The woman he finally introduced as Alice went into the kitchen to retrieve it, still giving us a wary look.

"Do you want something to eat? I could get the grill going." Wilson seemed to be trying to make this a social visit. "I'm really good on the grill."

I declined the offer and introduced myself, not mentioning that the deceased version of Maxie was inhabiting my attic. "Now, you really are Wilson Meyers, aren't you?" I asked, keeping my voice down in case Alice did not know the real identity of the man she lived with.

The guy seemed to think about it for a moment, then nodded and stole a quick worried glance toward the kitchen door. He didn't say anything.

"I'm not here to get you into trouble, Wilson," I told him. "But I'd appreciate it if you could answer some questions honestly for me."

"It's about Big Bob, isn't it?" Wilson asked. "I figured as soon as I heard there was a detective here."

Mom and I looked at each other. "You know that he's dead?" I asked.

Wilson nodded. "I saw the newspaper article on the Internet," he said. "They found his body, right?"

That sounded ominous. "That's right," I told him. "Do you know anything about what happened to him?"

Wilson stared at me for a moment, then drew back in shock. "You think *I* had something to do with what happened to Big Bob?" he said.

Wouldn't you know it—that was the moment Alice returned from the kitchen with a tray bearing a pitcher of lemonade and four glasses already filled with ice. "What's going on?" she asked.

"They think I killed a friend of mine two years ago," Wilson shrieked. "They tracked me down just so they could accuse me."

"That's *not* what we think," I assured him. "We're trying to find out what happened, and we thought that since you left at right around the same time, you might have some idea of what was going on with Big Bob back then. Why someone might have wanted to murder him."

"I don't know nothing," Wilson said, folding his arms across his chest.

"Nothing?" I asked. "You were pretty close to Big Bob in those days. Then he gets killed and you leave at almost the exact same moment. Seems like a big coincidence."

"I don't know nothing," Wilson repeated.

"If he says he don't know nothing, he don't know nothing,"

Alice reiterated for us, in case there had been some misunderstanding of Wilson's initial statement.

I felt my face scrunch up as I thought. Clearly, Wilson *did* know something, but what that could be might go in any number of directions. Just striking out in the wrong one could shut him down entirely as a source of information.

Wilson must have taken my silence as a sign of disbelief, which was probably accurate. "Look," he said. "I've got a nice life here. I've got a job at the Walmart as an assistant manager. I've got a nice wife." He gestured toward Alice, who looked baffled. "People like me. I don't do any of that stuff anymore. I didn't do anything to Big Bob. So why don't you just leave me alone?"

I looked at Mom, and she got the hint. She leaned over and spoke confidentially. "Wilson," she said, "they arrested someone for Big Bob's murder and they put her in jail."

Wilson turned white, which was impressive, given the redness the sun had bestowed on his face and bald head. "Who'd they arrest?" he asked.

"Kitty Malone," Mom said. "She's a very nice woman. Do you know who she is?"

Wilson's voice came out as a wheeze. "Maxie's mom," he said.

Twenty-eight

It took some more coaxing, but the thing Wilson Meyers really needed was time. Once he had actually taken in what we had told him, he was ready to cooperate. But he was clear that anything he told us could not be shared with anyone who carried a badge for a living.

"No cops," Wilson insisted. "I came out here to get away from the cops, and I don't want to have to move again. And I'm sure not going to jail. I didn't do anything, almost."

Alice was looking suspicious. Clearly, this was the first time she'd heard any of her husband's story. "Well, what *did* you do?" she asked with an edge to her voice.

But Wilson's gaze stayed on me, presumably because he was afraid of facing his wife. "Okay, here's what I know," he said. "About a month before all this stuff blew up, I got wind of a possible way to make money, and I was behind on some payments, you know, so I was looking for something quick.

"Big Bob comes to me one day, and he tells me someone he

knows has found—that was the word he used, *found*—a whole bunch of coke, maybe five or six pounds of the stuff, and is planning on selling it, but he needs a middleman. Big Bob asks me if I'm interested."

"So it was Big Bob approaching you?" I asked. "Do you think he was lying about it being someone else who 'found' the drugs, or was there someone else involved?"

"Oh, there was another guy, all right," Wilson said. "Big Bob really didn't want to do it at all. He kept talking about calling the cops. But he knew how bad I needed the money, and he didn't want to see me . . . Well, it wouldn't have been good if I couldn't pay some people back, let's say."

I could only imagine. But that part of the story wasn't pertinent right now. "Okay, Wilson," I said. "You're supposed to be the third man in this scheme, along with Big Bob and the other guy. Was the other guy someone you knew?"

Wilson shrugged. "I never found out. He wanted to keep himself invisible, you know. No way to trace him if things went wrong. But I figured it was Rocco, you know? Because he was really the only one who'd ever done time or anything."

"That doesn't mean he was involved in anything bad," Mom told Wilson. "Kitty Malone's in jail now, and I know she's innocent." She had picked up on my not mentioning that Kitty was out on bail. It made the situation seem more urgent, and kept the pressure on Wilson to talk to us.

Wilson shook his head sadly. "That's bad," he said. "Kitty's an older lady, too, small, not built for it. She can't make it in prison. And why would she kill Big Bob, anyway? Him and Maxie were broken up."

Alice's mouth hung open, and I hoped we weren't ruining their marriage. I leaned forward. "Did things go wrong?" I asked.

"They must have," Wilson said. "It was my job to line up the buyers, and I had some, just through connections I had around the shore, you know. The night comes when we're supposed to do the deal, and for days, Big Bob has been mopin' around, acting like the weight of the world was on his shoulders. 'It's not right; we shouldn't do it,' stuff like that. When it gets to be that night, he asks me how far deep am I in, and can I get by without the money from this deal. He really was a good guy, you know."

"How much money are you talking about?" I asked, trying to keep Wilson focused.

"Oh, a lot," Wilson said. "Close to a million each."

The house around us was a nice suburban place, but it didn't represent that kind of a nest egg. "So what happened?" I asked. "I'm guessing you didn't get the money."

"Hell, no," Wilson agreed. "I'm lining up the buyers, and we agree to meet at three in the morning. So I'm supposed to meet up with Big Bob at two, after he and the other guy, whoever, got their hands on the coke. I go to where we're supposed to meet, just off the boardwalk at Seaside Heights, and I wait. And I wait. And I wait some more. It gets to be three in the morning and no Big Bob. I don't know how to get in touch with the other guy. I figure something went wrong, or they're cutting me out, but Big Bob wouldn't do that. So when my cell phone starts ringing after four a.m. and it's my buyers, I don't answer. It finally ends up six in the morning, and nobody's bringing the blow. So I throw my cell phone into the ocean, get on my hog, and ride away from there as fast as I can without getting busted. Never looked back."

Alice sucked in her lips and nodded. "So now I understand why you never wanted to talk about where you came from," she said. "Meyer, honey, you must have been really scared."

I didn't have time for the family drama. "That's the night Big Bob died," I said. "So you never found out who the other guy in the drug deal was?" Whoever it was must have been the one who'd killed Big Bob, and probably would have killed Wilson after the deal was done to get all three shares of the money for himself.

"Never did," Wilson said. "But I had my suspicions."

Finally! "Who?" I asked.

"Like I said, I always kind of thought it was Rocco," Wilson said. "He was the only guy who was mean enough and smart enough to pull it off. Little Bob wouldn't have done it. Wouldn't even have thought of it."

There weren't many more questions after that: Wilson and Alice clearly had a lot to talk about, and we had found out all he could tell us. I wasn't sure if it had helped, but Paul would know if it was progress.

We made our farewells and thanked Wilson for his help. He walked us out to the Volvo. As we opened the doors and let the car air out a moment, I asked Wilson, "What did you tell Big Bob?"

He looked puzzled. "When?"

"When he asked you if you really needed the money, and if he could cancel the deal," I explained. "What did you say to him?"

"That's the funny part," Wilson told me as we reached the Volvo. "Normally, I'd have done anything to get that much money, but Big Bob seemed so sad and upset, I told him it was okay with me if we forgot the whole thing. I guess he went ahead with it anyway."

"Probably not," I said as I started the car. "Thanks, Wilson." And I drove away in my non-air-conditioned car as fast as I could. At twenty-five miles per hour. From what I'd heard, the cops around this area were nuts about speed limits.

Twenty-nine

We considered that all the way back to my house, and there was very little talk in the car. I drove Mom back to my house, but she begged off and said she needed to think and might call later. I think the trip had drained her more emotionally than she'd expected. Not that it would convince her she shouldn't horn in on my business when I asked her not to; that wasn't going to happen.

I did my customary sweep of the house. It was just about dinnertime for most of the guests, so the only ones left in the den were Don Petrone and Lucy Simone, who looked sad, probably because Steven had gone out with Melissa and hadn't invited her. I said hello to Don and Lucy, asked if they needed anything—they didn't—and went upstairs to change my clothes and then to the attic to check on the ghosts.

But before I made it to the pull-down stairs, I caught a glimpse of Tony Mandorisi at the far end of the hall past my bedroom door. Tony, in full contractor mode, was measuring the wall space and nodding gleefully to the beat of whatever was playing on his iPod.

"What's all this then?" I asked in my best British bobby voice as he wrote the dimensions down on a small pad of Post-it notes he keeps in the pocket of his cargo shorts. He turned and saw me walking toward him, and held up his hand.

He took the headphones off. "No peeking," he said. "I've figured out our access problem, and you're going to love the solution. But you don't get to see ahead of time. It's a birthday present."

"My birthday was three months ago," I reminded him.

"Did I get you anything?"

"No," I admitted.

"Well, there you are. Now, let me get to work." And the headphones went back on. There could be no further discussion.

I left him to his secret plans, and before confronting my two troubled spirits, I decided to go back into my bedroom and call Luther with the news of the trip to Levittown.

"It looks like there was a drug deal," I told him. "And it's possible that Rocco was involved."

Luther was silent for a moment. "I have a hard time believing it. Wilson said that?"

"No, not exactly. He was guessing. But I wanted to hear what you thought, because you know Rocco so much better than I do. What do you think?"

Again, there was a significant pause. I pictured Luther, not the way he looked at his business, where he was playing the role of Your Friendly Motorcycle Dealer, but as he looked the day I first met him, in blue jeans and a black leather jacket, more relaxed (and a little menacing, as I remembered it). That was better. I actually liked that guy more.

To be honest, I'd been thinking about that kiss and wondering if I hadn't pulled back too soon.

"I can't say that Rocco and I have had a lot of deep philosophical conversations," Luther admitted. "He has a nasty streak, no doubt, but that's putting an awful lot on his head with very little to back it up. I never even saw him so much as have a cross word with Big Bob."

"Do you know where he lives? Can we go there?" I asked.

"I've never seen his place," Luther said. "But maybe I can find out where it is. Give me about an hour, and I'll call you back."

"Tell you what," I said. "Can you come over when you find out?"

"So we can strategize?" Luther asked.

I sort of bit the side of my mouth gently. "That, and maybe so we can try that kiss again when I'm ready for it."

"I'll be there," he said without hesitation.

And almost immediately after we hung up, my phone buzzed again with a text. I decided not to look once I saw it was from a number I didn't recognize. Since it wasn't Melissa or Mom (or Jeannie saying it was "time"), I didn't want to know.

I walked back out to the hallway, scrupulously avoiding any glance at Tony, and pulled down the attic stairs. Once upstairs, I took a look around both to assess the progress in the room (not far enough along) and to see if I could find two ghosts. I only found one, and he was upside down.

"This is getting really tedious," Paul said of his inverted status.

"I know the feeling. Yeah, I imagine the novelty wears off pretty quickly," I agreed. I gave Paul the update on the Big Bob investigation, during which he appeared to be listening very carefully. When I told him I'd also informed Luther, he murmured that he wished I hadn't done that, and let it go. I never know what to say when Paul gets jealous.

"You've met this Rocco," he said. "Do you think he could have killed Big Bob?"

I'd been running that around in my mind ever since Wilson had suggested it. "I can't decide," I told Paul. "I only met the man a couple of times, but I've been trying to picture him as the mastermind behind an enormous cocaine deal, or bashing in Big Bob's brain with an adjustable wrench, and I'm not really seeing it. Everybody keeps telling me he has a mean streak, but to me, he seemed pretty benign, if a little rough."

Paul's goatee was getting quite the workout on this one. "I've found that your instincts about people are usually pretty accurate," he said.

I thought, *You have*? But I kept the comment to myself.

"If you're not convinced that Rocco could kill Big Bob, we should look into the possibility of other suspects," Paul continued. "Do you think Wilson could have done it himself?"

I tilted my head to the left, which I do involuntarily when thinking. "I don't know. There seem to have been two Wilson Meyers—the one before he left the shore, and the one after. I've only gotten to see the one after. *He* seems like a guy who would have a hard time stomping on a really nasty caterpillar."

"Give me time," Paul said. "I'll work it out."

"I'm not eliminating either of these two as suspects," I said. "I've been wrong about people. I married Steven, after all."

"Good point." Thanks, Paul.

I decided to ask him something that could prove dangerous. "What does Julia MacKenzie look like?" I said. "It would probably help me along if I knew what to look for."

"That was an interesting segue," he said. "Are you having trouble with the search?"

"You know the rules. Now help me out."

Paul got a sad smile on his inverted face. "She is not classically beautiful, but she has such a warm smile and such deep eyes that it's impossible to think a negative thought about her."

"That doesn't tell me much," I said, but I was noticing what I'd hoped for. I'll tell you in a minute.

Paul nodded, trying to get into business mode, but still with the faraway look in his eyes and the goofy grin on his face. "About five-foot-three. I couldn't tell you her weight; I'm a very bad judge of such things. But she is not so thin you worry about her health, nor overweight."

"Hair?"

"Brown. Not black, not blonde. Brown. A very elegant color."

"Eyes?"

"Also brown," Paul replied. "Very, very deep and inviting. Nose, to be honest, a little bit larger than the rest of her features, but that kept her from looking perfect, more human. She is a very human woman."

And then he looked at me, and saw that I was grinning broadly. "What?" he asked. But before I could answer, he noticed. "I'm right side up!" he said.

I nodded. "You started straightening when you were talking so fondly about Julia," I told him. "It seemed to take you back to a calm—and upright—place."

I think Paul was going to thank me, but just then was when Maxie pushed her way into the room through the ceiling and descended between Paul and me. "You won't *believe* what just happened!" she crowed.

It seemed to me that what had just happened *here* was pretty remarkable, and Maxie was going out of her way not to notice. "Look!" I countered, and gestured toward Paul.

Maxie glanced at him, then back at me. "Yeah, but wait! I just . . ."

That was just rude. "Maxie," I admonished. "*Look* at Paul."

She made a face that indicated I was being a pill, took a quick look at Paul again, and then looked back. "Do you want to hear my news, or not?" she asked flatly. "Frankly, you've sort of killed the moment, thank you very much."

"To tell you the truth," I said, "I *don't* want to hear your news, because you're being a pain. Do you see what just happened?"

She made the kind of noise I expected to hear out of Melissa in three or four years and shouted, "I get it! He's not upside down anymore! Big yip!"

"Calm down, ladies," Paul tried, but it was much too late. His feet were starting to rise.

"Paul," I said. "Take it easy."

"Not sure I can. This must be stress related." And he was horizontal, although not upside down, again.

Maxie rolled her eyes and vanished again, so Paul and I looked at each other. "You know, being in this house with the two of you isn't always a wonderful dream," he said. "I need a break." And he rose up through the ceiling as if he was on a platform.

Ghosts. A bunch of ungrateful little babies, if you ask me.

Fortunately, two floors below the doorbell was ringing, and that could only mean one thing after such a short period of time—Luther was serious about getting that second kiss.

Sure enough, when I reached the front door, he was standing there, just a little spruced up from his usual out-of-the-office appearance: He was wearing the black leather vest he rode in, and had on clean jeans and a pair of boots that matched the vest. Even his mustache looked groomed and prepared. Luther was ready.

I wondered if I was, too.

"That was quick," I said.

"Well, I was given an incentive," he answered. "Can I come in?"

I stepped aside, and Luther walked into the foyer so I could close the door to keep in some of the cooler air. He grinned a very ingratiating grin at me. "How should we start?" he asked.

"Well, let's talk about Big Bob and work our way up," I suggested. "Business before—"

"Gotcha," Luther said. "You're still on the clock, aren't you?"

We went into the front room and sat, alone, as the sun did its best to stay in the sky as long as possible, but for the past three weeks, it had been losing just a little bit each night.

"Did you get Rocco's address?" I asked him.

"I did. Now, what should we do with it?"

"Here's the thing," I said. "I just don't get Rocco killing Big Bob."

"No, you're right," Luther said. "I've been thinking about it since you told me Wilson said that, and it just doesn't add up. There's nothing that says Rocco was even involved in the cocaine deal. So is Wilson going only on a guess?"

I considered what he'd said. "Yeah. Wilson . . . Well, Wilson isn't the sharpest tool in the shed, is he?" Actually, Wilson wasn't erudite, but he was pretty good at self-preservation, if nothing else. I wanted to see if Luther agreed.

He chuckled a bit. "No, but Big Bob always liked him. He said Wilson had potential, but nobody could see it. That was exactly the kind of thing Big Bob would say."

It was funny: I'd never met Big Bob Benicio, and hadn't even heard of him until he'd been dead for two years. But after talking to everyone I could find who had been part of his life, I felt like I knew him a little. And it was starting to really annoy me that someone had killed him.

"He was quite a guy, wasn't he?" I asked.

Luther's head rolled back a little as he remembered. "He sure was. Bob and I were about the same age, but I always felt like he was sort of a little brother. I met him when we were just about twenty-two or twenty-three, and we just saw the world the same way. It hurts when someone like that gets taken away from you."

"So, gut feeling: Who do you think killed Big Bob?"

His nostalgic smile went away. Luther looked away from me and made a face that indicated he'd been over this subject a million times in his mind and still couldn't put it to rest. "If I had to guess right now, I'd say it was somebody we haven't thought of yet. Someone who really needed to get that cocaine and really didn't care what he had to do to get it."

That was the moment my stomach dropped. I stood up and started toward the den, which is the largest room in the house. Someone must be in there.

"What's wrong, Alison?" Luther said. He stood up behind me. "Are you okay?"

I kept walking and made it to the archway between the two rooms. "Yeah, I'm all right," I said. "I just felt the need for some more air."

"Alison." There was something in his voice.

I turned around. Luther's eyes were cold and narrow, but his grin remained friendly and flirtatious.

"What gave me away?" he asked.

Thirty

I retreated quickly into the den, where I'd expected to see Don and Lucy, if no one else, but the room was empty, probably for the first time in a week. My luck.

So I reached for the number-one source of security and access in the twenty-first century, my cell phone, before realizing I'd left it on the dresser in my bedroom before going up to see Paul in the attic.

So far, this was not turning out to be my evening.

Luther didn't rush to follow me; he seemed preternaturally calm as he walked into the den. "Seriously, what was it that tipped you off?" he asked, his voice as casual as if asking for a glass of water.

But he was holding a tire iron in his right hand. And I wasn't sure where that had come from.

"You mentioned the cocaine deal. Twice," I said. "You didn't know about that."

He knit his brow. "Sure I did. You told me about it at least a couple of times."

I shook my head, still backing up and hoping to make it to the French doors, or at least to stall until somebody—anybody—walked into the room. Except Melissa. "No. I said 'drug deal.' You went straight to cocaine. You couldn't have known that from what I'd told you. It could have been meth; it could have been weed. What happened with that deal? Why didn't you deliver the drugs?"

Luther's face twisted at the mention of his former accomplice. "I wasn't ever going to give that stuff to someone else to sell," he sneered. "He came up with buyers for three million, and I sold the drugs—sorry, the *cocaine*—all by myself for five."

"And that's how you got the money for your little 'bike shop,' wasn't it, Luther? You didn't inherit any money from your mother." Under my breath, as quietly as I could, I started saying Paul's name. Sometimes, he responds to that. Depending on where he might be on the property and what kind of mood he's in. Now I'd annoyed him to the point that he was probably at the far end of the backyard and unable to hear me unless I screamed. Even Paul couldn't get back fast enough to stop Luther from getting violent at that distance.

There was, of course, no response. And all I could think was, *Even if I get out of this alive, I'll bet Steven sues for custody of our daughter.*

The Swine.

"My mother died when I was fifteen," he said, walking forward just as slowly as I was backing up. "She left me no source of income and bills totaling thirteen hundred dollars."

Someone had to be around to hear my cries, if I screamed. But the guests were generally not physically equipped to take on Luther—I was probably a better bet than any of them—and both ghosts appeared to have evacuated for the time being.

Wait, though: Tony was upstairs, all contractor muscle and sinew, working on his secret attic-access project. He was a floor up and all the way on the other side of the house, but if I made enough noise, it might be possible to attract his attention. Again, speed was going to be a problem. Any help was at least six rooms away, while Luther was only a few strides from tire-iron distance.

And it was so damn quiet.

"How did you become a killer?" I asked Luther. Keep him talking, and he might not remember to kill me. "Big Bob didn't care if he got the money or not."

"What Big Bob cared about was irrelevant," Luther said. "*Wilson* cared. He needed the money, but Big Bob was all broody about the whole thing for days, telling me we should give back the coke—can you imagine? I come across this huge stash of cocaine from a friend who stole it, sold a big chunk of it, and skipped to Argentina. I'm sitting on dynamite, ready to change everybody's life forever, and there's Big Bob actually suggesting we should call the cops! Then I realized I could have all the money from the drugs for myself. Why have partners who can talk?" He hefted the tire iron and picked up his pace a little.

I froze for a moment. If only I could alert someone . . .

Just a few feet away, to one side of the sofa, there was a chance. But I had to distract Luther. "There were other things that gave you away, you know," I said. That seemed to matter to him.

He looked genuinely surprised, and stopped. Good. "What?" he asked, all innocence.

"The time you came to pick me up on your bike," I said. "When I came out of the house, you were working on those bolts with a pair of pliers."

I inched my way toward the sofa as Luther said, "I told you those were custom bolts. That was true. No regular wrench would accommodate them."

"No, but an *adjustable* wrench would," I pointed out as I reached behind me in a move I hoped was subtle and unnoticeable. "And I now realize that it was weird you didn't have one in your kit. But of course, you had already used your adjustable wrench to kill Big Bob, and now it was sitting in Kitty Malone's basement to better frame her. You went to see

Kitty just before you came to Harbor Haven and met me. Did you call the cops from a pay phone on the way to the *Chronicle* office?"

My hand found its target, and hit a switch. It would take a moment or two to warm up, but if I lasted that long, I might have a chance.

Luther sneered a little and shook his head. "This is the information age, Alison," he said. "I sent them a text from a prepaid phone before I came here the day you and I had our picnic. And they bought it—hook, line and sinker."

"But you went to the Seaside Heights cops and talked to Detective Ferry about nobody doing anything with the Big Bob investigation," I pointed out. "And you bailed Kitty out of jail. That seems counterproductive."

"Oh, I don't know," Luther answered. "Nobody was going to suspect me after I did that, were they?" He grinned. It wasn't that attractive anymore. "Even if I lost the hundred grand, she'd just look even guiltier, and it wouldn't occur to the cops to look at me as the killer. A good business investment," he said.

Oops. "Why Kitty?" I asked him. "Why frame her? What did you have against her?"

"She was convenient. Once the police ID'd the remains as Big Bob and said he was murdered, someone had to take the rap, and she'd been vocal about not liking Big Bob. I just had to move the wrench out of my toolkit and into her basement."

"And all the time *you* were the murderer," I said.

"You make it sound so dramatic. It's not a profession you pick up. I hit a guy with a heavy wrench, and I killed him. I'm glad I did it, but I'd never done it before, or since. Until now."

He made a quick move forward, and I had to take my chance whether enough time had gone by or not. With my left hand, I grabbed the microphone from a stool next to the sofa and gave full voice to the power of the karaoke machine amplifier.

As "Time in a Bottle" began to play, I substituted my own lyrics: "Help! Anybody! I'm in trouble! In the den! Help me! Luther Mason killed a man! He's trying to kill me!" Okay, so it didn't rhyme, but I hoped I'd gotten the point across.

And for a second, I thought it had worked: I saw the outline of a transparent face poke through the ceiling, but it pulled back as quickly as it had materialized, if it had really been there at all.

"That was stupid!" Luther growled, and he lunged forward to grab the hand that held the mic. Even as he yanked it away and turned it off, I kept shouting for help. But it didn't seem like anyone would get there in time.

Well, he wasn't getting me without a fight. I ducked down to avoid any blow from the tire iron (which was not yet coming), and kicked at his shins with as much power as my sandaled feet could muster, which wasn't much. Luther stumbled, but otherwise there didn't seem to be much effect. Still, at this point, I was all about keeping him at bay for as long as possible until someone could walk in. Anyone except Melissa.

I saw a face at the entrance to the den, and for a second held out hope again. Until I recognized the face as Francie Weston's. Francie was in her seventies and not going to win any track meets or boxing matches anytime soon. Though she *could* dial a cell phone.

"Call nine-one-one!" I yelled.

"He's not a ghost," Francie sniffed. "You're not fooling anyone."

Some people are impossible even when you're trying to get them to save your life.

"I'm not pretending he's a ghost!" I yelled as Luther turned to regard Francie. I saw his eyes estimate the distance between them. He was trying to figure out if he could reach her after I was dead. "He's a killer! He killed Big Bob! Run!"

Luther got a funny smile on his face. It wasn't attractive.

"Who's Big Bob?" Francie wanted to know.

Luther turned his attention back toward me, and grabbed

my flailing arms and held them. I knew he'd have to let go
with at least one to hit me, so I relaxed, trying to distract him
from his task.

"Why did you even bother getting me involved?" I asked
him.

"I dropped the wrench off in Kitty Malone's basement
when she was going to get us some lemonade and sandwiches
in her kitchen. And I talked to the cops in Seaside Heights.
But I needed eyes and ears. I came to Harbor Haven because
Maxie used to live here. Figured she might have had a friend
or two I could exploit, get someone to go to the cops so I could
find out how much they knew. Kitty didn't have any names,
but she mentioned you lived in the house now. So I went to the
newspaper office to see the story about her murder, see if any
friends were quoted. Somebody not associated with me or the
biker bar. The office wasn't open when I got there, but then I
got really lucky, heard you talking about being a PI and how
you were interested in Big Bob—it was perfect," he said. "I
didn't think you'd actually figure it out." And for a moment,
his expression softened. "I'm really sorry, Alison."

"You don't have to be sorry. Really. Just don't do this." Was
that movement I saw behind him?

"I have to," Luther said. And he let go of my left arm
with his right hand, and raised the tire iron. But he held me
so tightly with his left that I couldn't duck. I tried to block
with my arm, but it wasn't going to work. There just wasn't
time.

I was about to close my eyes so I wouldn't see it coming,
but before I could, I saw something swing through the air
behind Luther, and suddenly he fell backward as his legs gave
out from under him. In his place was a pool cue, which seemed
to dance in the air by itself until I saw Maxie's hand turn into
the light. She brought the cue down on the prone Luther three
more times.

"You killed Big Bob!" she screamed. "And you're trying to
kill my friend!"

By that point, however, I don't think Luther could hear her anymore. To be fair, he never really could.

"My goodness," Francie said. "There really *is* a ghost." She turned toward the front room, shouting, "Arthur! A ghost!"

I looked at Maxie, holding the now-broken pool cue in her hand. She wasn't breathing hard, for obvious reasons, but she still looked like she had exerted herself pretty mightily.

" 'Your friend'?" I asked.

Her attention turned to me. "Don't let it go to your head," she said.

"I wish I could give you a hug," I told her.

Maxie grinned. "You're running on adrenaline. In a few minutes, you'll go back to hating me."

"I've never hated you."

She took her eyes away in an apparent determined effort to avoid any sticky sentiment. "What are we going to do with him?" she asked.

"If you wouldn't mind going to my bedroom for my cell phone, we're going to hand him over to the police," I said.

"You want this?" Maxie asked, extending the cue. "In case he wakes up."

"I doubt that'll happen, but thanks," I said, taking it. Regarding Luther, I told her, "We should tell the cops that it was your mom and not mine who was in Pennsylvania with me today."

She had already turned to go, but looked back. "Why?"

I pointed to Luther, lying on the floor. "He'll lose the money he put up for bail." Maxie was still laughing when she disappeared into the ceiling.

Thirty-one

Detective Lieutenant Anita McElone arrived even ahead of my mother, which is a real feat if you know my mother. Of course I hadn't called Mom (although you'd think her "Mom Radar" would have kicked in, but no), so McElone had time to cuff Luther behind his back before he completely regained consciousness, and had taken my statement, which indicated that I had knocked him out with a pool cue after he'd tried to kill me with a tire iron.

Tony had gotten there first, of course, apologizing because he'd been listening to his iPod and had headphones on when I was executing my brilliant karaoke gambit that had almost gotten me killed.

"Something pulled off my headphones and pushed me really hard, a couple of times, toward the stairs," he reported. "Must have been one of your . . . friends."

He was standing quietly to one side now as McElone and two uniformed officers had taken charge. He looked downright embarrassed that he hadn't been there to rescue me "like a man should." Please.

"Exactly why did you have a pool cue in this room when the pool table is all the way on the other side of the house?" McElone asked. She had actually seen the game room a few months earlier, so I was impressed she remembered where it was located in my floor plan.

"I guess someone just left it there," I told her. "Lucky for me, I guess, huh?"

McElone's eyes indicated that she didn't believe me. "I guess."

From the entrance, though, Francie Westen was still braying, "It was a ghost! She didn't hit him with the pool stick! The *ghost* did it!"

Maxie and Paul both appeared near the ceiling, but said nothing. Maxie was intent on Luther, and looked like she wanted to hit him again. Paul, at about a 45-degree angle, was more cerebral, staring at the detective to see how she would handle the moment. Tony was on his cell phone, no doubt informing Jeannie of the developments.

McElone, who is not fond of my house or the unusual things she's seen happen in it, shuddered a little and looked at me. "A ghost?" she asked.

"Some of the guests take the brochures a little too literally," I whispered.

Two uniformed officers were leading an understandably groggy Luther out of the house. He was alert enough to murmur, "You can't prove anything. You don't have any proof."

"He confessed," Francie argued. "I heard him."

"He can be charged with attempted murder and assault, if nothing else," McElone said. "I assume you'll testify?"

"Try and stop me," I said.

"There's something else," came a voice from the front room. Detective Martin Ferry of the Seaside Heights police walked in wearing a short-sleeved shirt with a pocket and a tie that was very undone. He regarded Luther for a moment, and gestured to the uniformed officers to stop for a moment, so they stood there while Ferry regarded some more.

"See, we never really suspected Katherine Malone in this homicide," Ferry said, looking at Luther but talking to McElone and me. "Mr. Mason here was way too clumsy in his frame job. I mean seriously, Luther. Did you really think we'd believe that Mrs. Malone held onto that wrench for two years and then left it out for us to find? That all those anonymous tips were from a concerned citizen with no ax of his own to grind? And a gentleman biker coming to the cops to complain we weren't doing enough? Please. We could smell this one a mile away. We suspected you the whole time."

"How does that become another piece of evidence against our pal here?" McElone asked him. I assumed she had called Ferry as a courtesy, since Luther's arrest was for a crime (trying to kill me) that took place in Harbor Haven.

"Did you think we didn't know about the drug deal, Luther?" Ferry went on. "We knew. The FBI had a guy on the inside, and we knew every move you were going to make, but we didn't have your name. And then you changed the plan at the last minute. Bad move, Luther. You got the Feds mad at you. And if you think they haven't been looking into this case the whole time, you are dead wrong."

"You've got no evidence," Luther mumbled. I'm not sure Ferry heard him. "I didn't kill Big Bob."

"We have enough," Ferry told him. Then he turned toward McElone. "The real kicker came when he bailed out a woman he didn't even know with a hundred grand he just happened to have lying around. So we did some research into Mr. Mason's financial records, and waddaya know, he managed to buy his business, knock it to the ground and rebuild it to the tune of two million bucks *right after* the coke deal went down and Bob Benicio got killed. Pretty big coincidence, huh, Luther?"

"I didn't kill Big Bob," Luther repeated, a little more fervently.

"Well, how about this," Ferry countered, turning to me.

"You wanted to find someone to take the fall for the crime after the bones were found. But you'd only met Mrs. Malone a couple of times. How could you make her the perfect patsy?" He turned toward me. "Who did you tell about Mrs. Malone saying she'd like to have killed Benicio?" he asked.

"I didn't tell any . . . Wait! I told Luther," I said. "The night we went to the Sprocket for the first time, because I was so shaken by what Kitty had said. You're right—but he's the only one I told. And Kitty didn't say she wanted to kill Big Bob. She said she wished she could have done it herself."

Luther's eyes got meaner, as he must have seen the trap springing around him. And he was looking at me when he spoke, slowly.

"I. Didn't. Kill. Big. Bob."

Ferry, meanwhile, was going on with his taunting, circling around Luther as he spoke. "So the night the drug deal was supposed to go down, the two of you went to Seaside Heights. At first, we thought you made him dig his own grave, but that wasn't it, was it? Under the boardwalk was where you had buried the cocaine. That's what the two of you dug up, right?"

Luther remained silent.

"Then what happened? Your pal backed out? Or you just got greedy? One way or another, you already had the big, heavy wrench with you. And for whatever reason, you decided to bash his head in, right?"

Again, there was no response from Luther. But he kept glaring at me.

"Did he fall into the hole after you'd gotten the drugs out, or did you kick him in?"

Maxie reached for the pool cue, but Paul held her back, shaking his head.

"What's the matter, Luther? You don't want to brag about your brilliant plan?" Ferry shook his head in Luther's direction in a disapproving gesture. "A shame, really."

"You have no evidence," Luther repeated, louder this time. "You have a crazy old lady who thinks she saw a *ghost* hit me with a pool cue, and some connect-the-dots circumstantial stuff. I'll be out in ten minutes. I didn't kill Big Bob, so you can't prove that I did." He looked nastily at me when he said that last part.

"You've got a little something else," I told Ferry. I walked to the karaoke machine. "You've got this." I pushed the play-back button, and got exactly the section I was hoping for, as "Time in a Bottle" played in the background.

"It's not a profession you pick up," Luther's recorded voice said. "I hit a guy with a heavy wrench, and I killed him. I'm glad I did it, but I'd never done it before, or since. Until now."

"The machine has a record feature," I said to Luther. "You were never in better voice."

"I want to talk to my lawyer," Luther said.

Cops hate hearing those words because it means they'll get no more from the people they arrest, and there will be no formal confession, at least until the attorney is involved. But in this case, Ferry and McElone were grinning pretty broadly.

"Get him out of here and let him call his lawyer, for all the good it'll do him," Ferry told the uniforms, and Luther was led out of the house. As he walked out, he looked at me, and I'm not sure if his expression was one of menace or regret.

"I didn't kill Big Bob," he told me. "And you know it."

And suddenly, I wasn't so sure. But by then, Luther was out the door.

"We'll have to confiscate that karaoke machine," Ferry told me. "That confession will play beautifully in court."

"Will I get it back?" I asked. "It's gotten very popular around here." Just the previous night, I'd heard Mrs. Spassky doing her best version of "Don't Get Around Much Anymore."

"We'll buy you a new one," Ferry assured me. Then the detective got a smug look on his face. "You thought I was a monster, didn't you? Locking up some little old lady who probably couldn't have even lifted that wrench high enough to kill that guy? Just a mean, stupid cop I was, huh? Steel shavings in his head." He laughed at my stupidity.

All right, maybe I deserved a little of that, but I'd just barely missed getting killed myself, so I wasn't in an especially charitable mood. "Kitty's not that old," I told him. But that just sounded silly. "You could have let me know," I suggested.

"How could I know you were legit? You were hired by the guy who turned out to be the killer."

I was about to answer, but McElone beat me to it. "You could have asked me," she said to Ferry. Then she nodded in my direction and added, "She's a pain in the butt sometimes, but she's not crooked."

That was a nice gesture, in an odd sort of way, but I was just coming to grips with what had happened. "We need to get in touch with Kitty Malone and tell her she's off the hook," I said.

"Her lawyer already knows," Ferry said. "I'm sure she's been informed, or will be shortly." I glanced up at Maxie, who smiled. She did not actually say thank you, but then, this was Maxie.

"Can my statement wait until tomorrow, detective?" I asked Ferry. "It's been kind of a long day."

He looked a little concerned with the wait, but nodded. He took another look around the room, but any crime that took place here would be the property of McElone, for which I was oddly grateful. He walked over to her and took her hand.

"Good working with you again, Anita," Ferry said.

McElone smiled. "Always fun, Martin," she responded. Ferry let go of her hand and left the house.

"You?" I asked. "You're Ferry's ex-partner? The one he never stops talking about?"

McElone actually looked a little embarrassed. She nodded. "Before I came to work in Harbor Haven, I was with the Seaside Heights department. Martin and I worked together there."

"It figures," I said.

"Don't underestimate us cops," McElone told me. "Some of us actually know what we're doing."

She left soon after, and perhaps five minutes later, guests started wandering back into the house. Tony didn't want to leave me unprotected again, but I convinced him that the danger was in handcuffs, and he should go home to his pregnant wife.

The sun was just beginning to go down, and Francie Westen was regaling Don Petrone, Mrs. Spassky and Mrs. Fischer with the remarkable story of how she had seen the ghost (my involvement became completely peripheral in her version) when the front door opened, and in walked Melissa, followed by The Swine

Liss gave me a really good Melissa hug when she came in, and without saying anything, she gave me the impression that The Swine had done something especially Swine-like, making me the favored parent again. The Swine, for his part, was mostly withdrawn.

"The service at that place was terrible," he said.

"Dad stiffed the waitress," Melissa told me in a disgusted tone. "Just because she left the lemon out of his Diet Coke."

"I specifically asked for it," The Swine insisted.

"You sure did," Liss responded. That was *my* child.

Steven sat down heavily to show how misunderstood he was, and we, being more mature, ignored him.

"How's your evening been?" Melissa asked me.

"Nothing special," I said.

Thirty-two

Kitty Malone showed up later that night to show us all (mostly Maxie) that she was all right. I left out much of my story until Steven and the guests were out of the room. It's funny; I don't have to shield my ten-year-old daughter from the truth, but my ex-husband and my adult customers (not to mention my mother, who called and got the edited version) are better off not knowing about certain things.

I had to drive to Seaside Heights to be debriefed by Detective Ferry after the spook show the next morning (Paul, at only a slight angle, wrote answers to questions and played bongo drums, while Maxie repotted a plant I was killing on the window sill), and I decided that since I was close enough, I might as well revisit Julia MacKenzie's old address in Gilford Park and see if her landlord (who had never called me back) might be in this time.

So once Ferry finished asking me the same six questions for an hour and a half, I hopped into my Volvo and made the trip over. Along the way, I tried to come up with a plan B. If I couldn't wrangle a current address out of the landlord, how *would* I find Julia MacKenzie, breaker of numerous hearts? I couldn't stand to let Paul down now and possibly send him into a literal tailspin from which he might never recover.

Because for Paul, "never" is not an abstract concept.

I pulled up once again in front of the two-story house—like many of these shore homes, a little bit less than perfectly kept up—and noticed only one car in the two-car port in front. That wasn't great news, but I hoped that it was the landlord's car and not one belonging to his new tenant upstairs, where I'd seen the young mother having a "vacation" the last time I was here.

I was just about to get out of the car when I saw something in the passenger seat that literally made me scream, if briefly. It took me a good few seconds to catch my breath, and then I could only squeeze out the words, "What are you doing here?"

Maxie, resplendent in a pair of long black jeans (what did she care how hot it was?) and a black T-shirt that bore the legend "This Space Available," was in the passenger seat. And when I say "in the passenger seat," that's what I mean. Like at home, she was not as much sitting on the seat as nestled *in* it, half obscured and half bouncing up and down. I'd never seen one of the ghosts in such an enclosed space before, but they can't actually stay very still. They're not *really* there.

"This is what I was trying to tell you yesterday," she crowed. "I can move around now! Almost anywhere I want to go. I mean, I haven't tested the limits yet, but as you can see, here I am!"

Not entirely sure I wasn't having a bad dream, I reached over to touch Maxie and, of course, couldn't. But that same light breeze I felt when she had hugged me was there. "How?" I managed.

"I don't really know, but it's been coming for a few days. You know, after I got used to the idea I couldn't, I never tried. But when you got me mad the other day, I just went outside and kept going. After a while, I realized I wasn't on the property anymore. So I started to explore."

I breathed in. Oxygen is a good thing, especially when

you've been seriously startled. "So that's where you were when we were searching for you the other day."

"Exactly. Isn't it crazy?"

That was one word for it, yes. "Why are you here?"

She tossed her hair, in a gesture of freedom, I guess. "Because I can be!" she said. She rubbed her hands together. "Okay. What are we doing here?"

I hadn't told Maxie about the Julia MacKenzie thing because Paul had seemed to want the matter to remain confidential, and frankly, the idea of Maxie teasing him about it was a little too plausible and a little too upsetting. But I just wasn't quick enough to come up with a realistic lie to tell her, so I gave her the essentials as I understood them.

Maxie, whatever her faults (and if you have a couple of days, I could list them for you), is a smart ghost and, at heart, a good friend. She listened to Paul's story and grasped its intellectual and emotional impacts immediately. When I was finished, she had a determined look on her face.

I got out of the furnace-like car and walked to the door of the ground-level apartment, and Maxie lifted herself out through the Volvo's roof and hovered nearby as I rang the doorbell. As before, there was no answer. But this time, I wasn't prepared to go away without some kind of lead, some clue, some . . . something. I rang the bell again.

Nothing. The car in the port was either not the landlord's or he was purposely not coming to the door for someone he did not recognize. There was only one way to be sure.

I looked at Maxie, and tilted my head toward the door. "Would you mind?" I asked.

"Sure," she said, and vanished through the door into the apartment as I waited on the doorstep. After about a minute she reemerged and shrugged. "Nobody home," she said. "But that guy's a pig."

"Messy?"

Maxie gave me a significant look. "No."

I had hit a wall in the Julia search again, and slunk back to the car, feeling very much like I'd let a friend down the one time he'd actually asked me to do something that mattered to him. Maxie hung back; she's not especially good at bolstering other people's confidence. "Maybe *you* should hire a detective," she suggested as I reached the Volvo.

I didn't answer. I knew Maxie was trying to help, and having established this new level of détente between us, being snide or yelling at her would have been counterproductive. Besides, I was feeling too dejected.

But then, from upstairs, I heard a voice shouting, "Jason! I told you to put the milk away when you're done with it!" And I stopped dead in my tracks.

I recognized that voice.

Walking over from the car toward the far side of the house, I once again had to shade my eyes to look up at the second-floor deck, where a woman in a sensible two-piece bathing suit was calling in toward the apartment upstairs. "And put your bowl in the sink, please!" she added.

Man, I could be stupid sometimes. I called up to the woman. "Excuse me?"

She stopped and looked down at me. It was slightly later in the day than the last time I'd come by, so the sun wasn't directly in my face, and this time I could see her far better. She was not heavy, but not stick thin. Her hair was brown, not black or blonde. I couldn't really tell from here, but I was willing to bet her eyes were brown and very deep for a man to look into. And she had lied to me about leaving as soon as she'd heard Julia MacKenzie's name.

"Can I help you?" she asked, recognizing me too late.

"The jig is up," I told her, despite my not knowing what a jig was or why it's better for it to be down. "You might as well let me come up there to talk, Julia."

"Do you have any idea what it's like being a single mother trying to date?" Julia MacKenzie asked me. Before I had a chance to tell her that, yes, I did, she added, "Men don't want to know about your kid. They don't want to know about the kid's father. They don't want to think you've ever been with anybody else. They want to think they're the center of your life." She shrugged. "So I let them think they were."

"How many of them?" I asked after a gulp of iced tea. If it was 95 degrees downstairs, it was a 100 easy up here on the deck, with no shade at all.

Maxie, hovering over a lawn chair with her legs crossed, seemed fascinated. She stared at Julia and actually emulated a few of her movements, drinking from a straw and turning her head to talk to her son, Jason, a spirited four-year-old currently splashing in a wading pool a few feet away. It was like Maxie was trying some of Julia's mannerisms on for size, deciding what to keep and what to discard.

Once I had recognized Julia's voice as the woman I'd spoken to in this same spot before, it had all made sense. She'd told me, during our previous conversation, that she and her family—her preschool son, as it turned out—were leaving the next day. And yet, here she was. That meant she hadn't told me the truth, and there was only one reason for her to do that.

I'd told her I was there representing a man who had worried about her after she'd vanished, but I refused to give her a name. She might have heard that Paul was deceased; the news had been in at least one newspaper at the time, and the story had gotten even more media after the murderer had been found. Frankly, Julia hadn't seemed all that interested in which man was concerned. They tended, she said, to all blur together in her mind.

Julia's eyes were indeed deep and soulful but also, from my point of view, a little dreamy and unfocused. "I don't know. It depended on the day or the week. For a while, there were only two, and then at one point as many as five. It was easy to find men who would be interested in the girl I pretended to be. What was hard was finding a reliable rotation of babysitters."

"I don't get it," I told Julia. "You could have told at least *one* of these men about Jason. *One* of them might have been perfectly fine with a woman who had a child. Why not look for that one, instead of trying to charm all those other guys?"

Julia lit up a cigarette and blew some smoke in the direction away from her son. "You had to know Jason's father. Hell, *I* should have known him. We hooked up for one stinkin' night, and when I call to tell him I'm going to have his child, he tells me he took precautions so this had to be my fault. So I had the baby, and after I got my figure back, I decided I'd get guys to take me out to nice places and buy me nice things, and I'd give them what they wanted, which was the idea that this girl they thought I was could find them fascinating. It worked for a while."

"But then you stopped. Pretended to move away. Changed your last name to Lamont. Why did you do that?" I asked.

"Lamont is Jason's father's name; would you believe it? But it was easier to disappear and not have to talk to all those guys anymore. At the time, it was because Jason was having problems in nursery school, and I needed to be around more, so I couldn't go out at night so much," she said. "And I didn't have money for new clothes all the time, stuff like that. I'm working at his preschool now as a teacher, and you don't make much." She stubbed out the cigarette, which was less than half smoked.

"But the fact of the matter, now that I can look back a little, is that I got tired of it. Of them. All the men—they'd believe anything you told them. Anything. And they'd get so *attached*. One of them was going to ask me to marry him, I was pretty sure. Then I never heard from him again."

I had to fight the impulse to grab her by the throat and tell her what she'd done to more than one man, but fight it I did. "Which one wanted you to marry him?" I asked as casually as possible, with Maxie making significant eye contact.

Julia looked up to one side, thinking. "The teacher? No. It might have been the blond one, or the one with the goatee." She shook her head, trying to knock the memories loose. "Honest, after a while they all just sort of become the same."

We talked a few more minutes, but I wanted to leave as soon as I could. And take a shower, preferably. But I had another trip to make.

"Where are we going?" Maxie asked me when we got into the car (only one of us through the usual "open the door" method).

"Levittown, Pennsylvania," I answered.

Thirty-three

Alice Wilson looked less than thrilled when she saw me on her doorstep again. If she'd seen Maxie there as well, I'm willing to bet she would have looked even more annoyed. Or maybe I'm projecting.

"What do you want *now*?" she humphed. "Haven't you upset Meyer enough?"

"Meyer? Who's Meyer?" Maxie asked. I'd been very careful about not telling her who we were visiting on the ride to Levittown, which, believe me, had not been easy. Now, I simply ignored her.

It occurred to me that I'd probably upset Alice more than her husband on my last visit—he'd seemed glad to get the burden off his mind—but I didn't say that, either. See how much restraint I showed?

"It will just take a few minutes," I lied. "But if I could see your husband alone . . ."

Alice did not seem pleased but let me (us) in. She screamed,

"Meyer!" like before, and when he appeared, she simply turned and walked out of the house without speaking. I decided at that moment not to add "marriage counselor" to my business card.

I turned back toward our host, who was wearing what is so charmingly referred to these days as a "wife beater" and a pair of khaki shorts with too many pockets. He looked confused and tired. "Ms. Kerby," he said. "I'm really not interested in telling you anything more."

But it was Maxie's reaction that really made the difference. The second he'd come to the door, she had dropped three feet in altitude, and was now up to her knees in living room carpet. Her eyes were wide and her mouth dropped open. I'm sure if a nose could register amazement, hers would have done that, too.

"Big Bob!" she croaked out. "I thought you were dead!"

I looked him in the face, with my suspicions corroborated. "You can drop the act, Mr. Benicio," I said. "I know who you are."

Big Bob Benicio offered me an iced tea, which I declined. "I don't get it," I said. "Why?"

"Why what?" Big Bob seemed genuinely incredulous.

"Why"—I waved my arm around the room—"this? Why did you become Meyer Wilson here in Levittown, Pennsylvania? What *really* happened back in Seaside Heights two years ago?"

He lowered himself into an overstuffed easy chair that most certainly would have reclined if he'd wanted it to, but didn't now. "Everything I told you yesterday was true," he said. "Except you have to substitute me for Wilson Meyers in every sentence. I was the one who was supposed to contact the buyers, and Wilson was the one who was working with someone else to provide the cocaine."

Luther's insistence that he specifically hadn't killed Big

Bob—not that he hadn't killed anyone—had stuck with me. And the pieces had started to fall into place when I'd realized that "Meyer" was shorter than the Wilson Meyers I'd been told about. You can do a lot of things to make yourself look different, but you can't change your height. I hadn't planned on Maxie being able to make the trip, but when she recognized Big Bob, that had confirmed my suspicions.

It took a good deal of insistence to convince Big Bob that it was Luther Mason who had killed Wilson Meyer. He insisted it couldn't be true even after I told him Luther had confessed— and that Luther had also tried to kill me. Big Bob continued to stare off every few seconds, shake his head, and say, "Luther."

Maxie, still in shock, gaped at Big Bob and assessed what she saw. She giggled. "You lost almost all your hair," she chortled.

"So, what happened?" I asked.

It seemed to wake Big Bob from his reverie. "Everything I told you. I waited for them to call, they didn't, my buyers were going to come get me, and I bolted. Rode my hog for a while, about two hours or so west, and then I realized I was too noticeable on that thing, that the cops were probably coming for me, so I sold it to a guy in a used car lot in West Chester, swapped it for a car and ended up here."

Big Bob stopped talking, and it took me a moment to realize he thought the story was finished. "But that wasn't all there was to it, was it?" I asked. "I mean, why would the police be after you? How would they know to look for you?" I thought I knew the answer, but I wanted to hear him say it.

Instead, Big Bob started to cry. Maxie looked angrily at me. "What did you *do* to him?" she demanded.

I couldn't say anything to her, so I patted Bob on the arm. "What's the matter?" I asked.

"It . . . was my fault," he sobbed. "What happened to Wilson . . ."

"Wilson Meyers was the body found in the sand at Seaside, wasn't he?" I asked.

Big Bob nodded. "My fault. I should have known. I didn't figure it out until I tried calling Wilson that night, and his cell phone never answered. First couple of times didn't mean anything, but after a while, I realized he wasn't ever going to answer. I knew he'd been scared. I figured something went wrong and they killed him."

Maxie looked confused. "But the police said it was Big Bob. They said there were fingerprints and dental records that proved it." I resolved to point out to her—as soon as we were out of earshot—that Big Bob sitting there in front of her was proof that he was alive. Then again, she was sitting there in front of me. Everything's relative.

"Because you were the FBI informant?" I asked Big Bob. "That's why you think it was your fault?"

Maxie actually sat down on nothing, eyes wide, and gasped.

Big Bob nodded. "I didn't want to deal drugs to anybody."

Maxie wasn't looking at anyone in particular when she said, "I forgot. He had a brother who died of an overdose."

"I got in touch with a guy I knew, a cop, who used to come into the grill where I worked. You know, the cops came by a lot to get free food, and we gave it to them," Big Bob said. "I liked him, and I told him about this great big drug deal, tried to get him to stop it. He brought in the FBI."

"But nobody knew Luther Mason was involved," I said. "They only knew about you and Wilson."

Big Bob shook his head and mouthed "Luther" again, and then he sucked in his bottom lip and nodded. "I didn't give them Wilson's name. I don't know how they found out about him. I told them I wouldn't inform on my friends, my riding partners," he said. "I'd only give them the buyers. They'd have to take it or leave it."

"They took it," Maxie said.

"You told them about the buyers and when the deal was supposed to go down. Did they make arrests?" I asked.

Big Bob shrugged. "No idea. Like I told you, once it got

that late and I figured everybody was after me, I chucked my cell phone in the ocean and rode away. But the FBI found me, a couple of months after I got here. They were perfectly happy to leave me here, since I couldn't help them on the drug bust anymore. Made me change my name so the third guy—Luther, you're saying—couldn't find me. They called me again when the bones were found. Said they were going to put it out that it was me in the ground there, maybe smoke out the killer, because he'd know it wasn't me. But you were the only one who came out, and I didn't tell them that. I don't want to move again, and everybody here knows me as Meyer Wilson."

"Why that name?" It didn't seem to fit—why provide a trail to follow with such an obvious clue?

"I guess I felt I owed it to him," Big Bob said. "I felt guilty about a lot of stuff. About informing to the cops. About running away. About Maxie . . ."

Maxie stared at him.

"Maxie?" I asked.

"I hit her once. Never been able to live with that memory. Now she's gone, I hear, and I'll never get to tell her I'm sorry." Big Bob's head dropped.

Maxie's voice was very faint. "I forgive you," she whispered.

The front door opened, and Alice marched back in. She took up a stance in the living room, hands on hips, face twisted into a defiant expression.

Before she could utter a sound, I stood up, shook Big Bob's hand and said, "Thanks for the help, Wilson. I promise I won't be bothering you again."

That took the wind out of Alice's sails. She sputtered a little, dropped her hands and opened the front door for me to walk out.

As I was walking to the car, I heard Big Bob call out from inside, "Say hello to your mom!"

Maxie floated behind me and passed through the driver's side door to take her position in the passenger's seat. She even unlocked the driver's door from the inside for me before I could use the key.

I settled into the seat. "What tipped you off?" Maxie asked. "How'd you know Wilson was really Big Bob?"

"He said your mother was an older woman and too small and frail to handle prison," I told her as I started the car and lowered the window. "Wilson never met your mother, but Big Bob would know what she looked like."

Maxie closed her eyes as if she was about to take a nap, and made a contented sound. "I'm so glad he's not dead," she said.

"I think I am, too," I told her.

Thirty-four

"She was devastated when she heard what happened to you, but in the two years since, she's managed to pull herself together," I told Paul.

Maxie and I had agreed not to tell anyone—*anyone*—about finding Big Bob. Let him remain Meyer Wilson. He didn't need the police and the FBI reentering his life. He didn't need to hear from Rocco and Little Bob, and they didn't need to know their pal had been informing, if not specifically on them, at least to the police, most of whom they didn't trust. It was a secret only Maxie and I would keep. So it was time to concentrate on Paul.

He was completely right side up now, and also somehow seemed more solid than he had been before. Less transparent. Almost more like a living man, but not really. He leaned forward from his perch on my bedroom dresser and listened with the intensity he usually paid to my recounts of interviews related to investigations.

"I was afraid the news would hurt Julia," he said with great concern. "She was so fragile. But she's doing better now?"

"Yes. She's . . . I don't know if I should tell you this part . . ." I was especially proud of that touch, which I had practiced three times in the car on the way home with Maxie. She knew she wouldn't be allowed to see the actual performance, so she insisted on being there for the dress rehearsal.

"It's all right," Paul said, as I'd anticipated. "I want to know."

"She's met another man," I told him, feigning concern over his reaction. "She doesn't know if it's going to be serious yet, but she has hopes. She says, though, that he couldn't ever replace you."

Paul sat back, which put his shoulder blades through the wall but kept most of his head in the room. It's disconcerting when he stops realizing how he looks. "Do you think she's happy?" he asked quietly.

I hadn't seen that one coming, but I had prepared for a similar question. "Well, I don't think she'll ever be completely over you, but I think she can still lead a happy life," I said. "She's a very . . . resilient woman." There were other words I could have used, but the idea here was to make Paul feel better.

"I really appreciate your doing this for me, Alison," he said after a moment's reflection. Then he seemed to rally; he sat up straighter and his voice took on a less hushed tone. "And I'm very impressed. Without any help from me, you found a woman who'd seemed to have vanished."

"She just couldn't face anything after what happened to you," I told him, mentally crossing my fingers behind my back. "She needed time to recover."

"So did I, I guess. Did you give her the ring?" he asked.

I produced the box from my tote bag. "I thought it would be cruel to tell her about that. Do you want it back?" I held it out to him.

Paul considered, then shook his head. "Hang onto it," he said. "I don't think I'll be needing it anytime soon."

Before we could get too maudlin, I decided to go downstairs and check on my guests, all of whom were leaving in another hour or so. Their luggage was all stacked up in the foyer already. I breezed through the game room (Don Petrone gave me a dapper nod, playing pool by himself and still wearing his blazer—the man had no sweat glands), the library (Mrs. Fischer and Mrs. Spassky were engrossed in what looked like a very serious game of chess), the front room (nobody there) and the den (Francie, still raving about her experience with the ghost to Albert, who was beaming with his wife's bravery and the story they'd be dining out on for weeks) and got a good number of thank-yous and a few genuine embraces as everyone prepared to board the Senior Plus van that would be showing up in the driveway very soon.

So I made it to the kitchen without having to fix anything or help anyone. And that's why I was throwing out the broccoli I'd bought at Veg Out—now sadly wilted and quite useless, serving as a reminder of my first meeting with Luther, not to mention my awful nutritional program and inability to take decisive culinary action—when The Swine informed me that he'd also be leaving, the next day.

I don't think I even turned around to face him; it had been so obviously coming that I felt like I'd already had this conversation with him. And perhaps I had.

"Given up on the Robin Hood 'take from the rich, invest for the poor' plan?" I asked. I took a carton of lemonade out of the refrigerator, which now contained a half gallon of milk for cereal, a few eggs, a bag of baby carrots and four chocolate yogurts. I think the dairy compartment had some cheese, and there was a package of hot dogs in the meat section. And this, dear reader, was an improvement from the usual. Pity me.

"Not at all," The Swine responded. "I'm still going to do that; I think it's my calling. But, you'll recall, you told me you need me out of here tomorrow to accommodate the guests you have coming in. And I need to get back to California and take care of the things I had going on there." Like Amee, for example. I wondered what he was telling her.

"So you're going to be setting up a Wall Street business from Los Angeles?" I asked.

"Mission Beach, actually," he said. "It's near San Diego."

San Diego. Of course. "This wouldn't have anything to do with Lucy Simone, would it? She lives near San Diego."

I continued to look away from him so I wouldn't see the sly little bad-boy grin (Smile Number Thirty-Six). "Not specifically," Steven said, and he sounded even a little embarrassed trying to sell that one to me. "But I do find her interesting, and I imagine we'll be seeing each other once I get out there."

"Because you'll be living together?"

He let out his breath and made it sound like it was my fault. "I never could put one over on you, Alison."

"Yeah, you could. At least once. What are you telling your daughter?" I asked.

"Melissa?"

"Do you have other daughters I don't know about? Yes, Melissa. She's gotten used to having you around and acting like a daddy. What have you told her?"

"I, um, figured I'd talk to you first," he said. He shifted his weight from one foot to the other, like a third-grade boy who's been caught with a comic book stuck inside his arithmetic text.

"You mean, you figured you'd get me to tell her for you. Not this time, Steven. Do your own dirty work." I poured myself a glass of lemonade and didn't offer him one. That'd teach him.

He stood up straighter, as if called to attention. "I had no intention of slinking out of here without talking to Melissa," he said. And he turned on the heel of his overpriced running shoe and left the kitchen with an air of moral superiority.

"Just one thing," I said before he hit the door. He stopped and turned to face me. "Just tell me, once before you go, the real truth. Why did you come here in the first place?"

Steven's face betrayed his thought process: First he looked like he wanted to be sly and tell me once again how he'd just wanted to see his wife—sorry, ex-wife—and daughter. Then his mouth dropped a little, and he said, "It was about the TV footage."

I had no idea for a second what he was talking about. "The tape from *Down the Shore* that they shot here in April?" I asked. What the hell could *that* have to do with him?

He nodded. "I have a buddy who knows a guy who heard about this crazy show set in a haunted house. But the cops wouldn't release the footage, and this guy thought it was a shame that the public wasn't being allowed to see . . ."

"He thought you could sell it for a lot of money," I corrected him.

Steven hung his head. "Yeah. And I figured if I came and just asked about it, you'd stonewall me. So I came to visit—I really did want to see Lissie—and along the way, well, it was obvious something was going on in this house."

"I told you, it's a marketing ploy."

"Now who's lying?" he asked. He didn't give me time to answer. "Anyway, I think it's probably best not to release the footage. I don't want Melissa to have to deal with that kind of exposure."

"Do you actually mean that?" I asked.

"Alison. How could you even ask me such a thing?" Shaking his head, The Swine turned and walked out of the room.

It's how he manages to live with himself. Which, thankfully, was something I didn't have to do anymore.

The bowling machine was broken, so Little Bob was giving me his full attention. But even after having been told the story three times, he still shook his head in disbelief. "You sure?" he asked. "Luther really killed Big Bob?" The idea just didn't make any sense to him; you could see it in his eyes.

I would have put my hand on his shoulder if I could, but I'd have needed a step stool just to make an attempt. "I know, Little Bob," I told him. "He had me fooled, too."

Earlier, under stress (I had brought Jeannie with me), Lieutenant McElone had confirmed what I already knew about the drug bust gone sour two years earlier. Luther had murdered Wilson Meyers and stolen the drugs. Big Bob was the FBI informant (a detail I was keeping from the bikers in the bar), and the police had known he was alive, even that he was in Pennsylvania. They figured as long as he was safe, there was no reason to publicize the fact that he was alive, so the county's medical examiner had been "persuaded" to issue a report saying the bones found under the boardwalk were those of Big Bob Benicio. They'd hoped putting out the wrong information would make the killer do something stupid, and it worked. He'd hired me.

But I wasn't allowed to tell anyone for fear of endangering Big Bob even to this day. The drug buyers had never been found, and the Feds, although keeping an eye on the investigation into Big Bob's "death," had not wanted to make—and I apologize in advance—a federal case out of it. But now Luther was finding out just how much trouble he was in, and just how long he could expect to be in jail. Now he'd be charged with Wilson Meyers's murder, not Big Bob's. But nobody here had to know that.

"Luther killed Big Bob?" Little Bob asked again, and shook his head sadly.

Maxie, who had insisted on coming along to see some members of her old crowd even if they couldn't see her, actually floated above our group in the Sprocket, looking wistfully at Little Bob and Rocco. She'd tried to talk me into telling them she was there, but I was very clear that if her new ability to travel around with me was going to work, the one rule would be that no one besides me would ever know she was present.

Tonight, no one but me and six spirits in the bar knew Maxie was here. Two of them had hit on her as we passed through the main room, and she had rejected them quickly and efficiently with the pronouncement that she didn't "date dead guys."

Paul had been a little taken aback when told about Maxie's now freedom, but, after a day, he seemed actually happy for her. "I can't say envy doesn't come into play here," he told her when we'd explained it to him, "but that doesn't mean that maybe I won't be able to do the same thing soon."

"Absolutely," I'd agreed, and I had to admit it seemed this latest episode had improved his motor skills to Maxie's level, at least. This morning he had actually been juggling three oranges from a fruit basket Phyllis Coates had sent as "thanks for the great story" she was running on Big Bob's murder, an "exclusive interview with the gumshoe who solved the case." Maybe moving outside the property would develop differently for Paul. As I'd discovered since buying 123 Seafront, anything is possible. Even stuff you wish wasn't.

"Is Luther going to jail?" Little Bob wanted to know, clearly hoping that if he weren't, that would mean a mistake had been made and Luther really wasn't guilty. Of course, the whole "trying to kill me" thing was pretty strong proof from my point of view, but it was possible I was biased.

"He's already there," I informed the huge man gently. Luther's attorney had taken a look at all the evidence, the tape, and the fact that there were witnesses (all right, one witness) who had seen him come after me, and advised him to take a plea bargain offered by the FBI: a life sentence with the possibility of parole after twenty years. McElone had told me that was "a sweet deal" considering that he'd killed a man in cold blood, then later attempted to kill a woman (me) to cover it up. The fact that a federal informant had been lost to them as part of the same operation did not help Luther's case, but again, they were letting the local officials be the public face of the prosecution. Various other charges regarding the false evidence given to police officers and all the drug offenses (only some of which could be proven after two years) had contributed to the plea deal. "He'll be there for quite some time."

Little Bob sighed and shook his head again.

"But that's not why I came here tonight," I told them. I held my beer mug high. "Here's to Big Bob," I said. Rocco, Little Bob and three other bikers who had known Bob Benicio raised their glasses to the ceiling. So did Maxie, although her glass was imaginary. "I never met him, but he sounds like he was a nice guy who didn't deserve what he got. Let's hope he found what he was looking for in the next world."

"Wherever that is," Maxie said. The other ghosts and I were the only ones who heard that.

Those of us who actually had physical glasses in our hands drank to Big Bob's memory. Then I hugged Rocco and Little Bob—which was an experience, since his arms were so long I think they circled me and still touched his hands to his shoulders—and told the group I had to get back home.

"I have a special guest in my bed tonight," I said, just to get them to cheer me out, although Little Bob looked a little shocked.

Melissa had asked to sleep in my room that night. It was one of the rare nights we had with nobody else in the house, and she had gotten used to a little more activity around the place. It seemed eerie when it was just the two of us.

"Dad already left," she informed me when I got back from the Sprocket. "Lucy was going to the airport, and he decided it would be better if they flew out there together."

She snuggled next to me. The air-conditioning seemed more efficient somehow when we were alone in the house, and we were under a comforter and a top sheet, but her feet, she took great glee in demonstrating, were icy cold. Ten-year-olds are strange beings.

"I know he can be disappointing sometimes, but he's still your dad, and he always will be," I told her.

"I'm not disappointed," she said. "I pretty much expected it."

"Sure you did."

There was a long pause. "You know . . . I kind of spied on you for him."

"What do you mean, you spied on me?" The light was out, but I looked at her anyway. I could sort of see the outline of her head, but not her expression.

"All that stuff about why you married him and how you wished he would still work to help people," Melissa said. "Dad asked me what would make him more . . . what would make you like him better, so I asked you some stuff, and I told him what you said. He wanted to know about the TV stuff they filmed here, too. I didn't know anything about that, but I told him what you said. I'm really sorry."

I hugged my daughter close. "You don't have to be sorry, honey. You wanted your dad to come back and make us a real family again. I understand."

"We *are* a real family," she told me. "But I wanted to see what it would be like if he lived with us again."

"And what did you find out?" I asked.

She paused for a long time, thinking that over. "I really love Dad," she said. "And he's fun to be around. He always wants me to be happy, and he always acts like just another kid to play with. There's just one thing."

Melissa didn't say anything after that, so I asked. "What thing?"

"I just wish he didn't always end up being such a swine."

The next morning, Melissa was already out of the room when I woke up. We'd have a whole day to ourselves, since the new Senior Plus guests wouldn't arrive until tomorrow. I decided the best thing was to get some work done in the attic. I was in the middle of putting down a hardwood floor over the ply-

wood that was there, and would stain that after it was down
and prepped. But when I got out into the hallway, I was met
with a crowd.

Melissa and Mom were right outside the bedroom door,
looking surprised that I had emerged from there. "I was *wondering* where you were," Mom said. "Melissa thought you
were in the attic."

"I don't know why she'd think that," I said.

"I called Grandma and she came over to take me for
bagels," Melissa said. "I thought you'd be upstairs. You *never*
sleep this late."

I would have asked exactly how late it was, but now I was
embarrassed. Luckily I'd put on my work clothes before I left
the bedroom, because behind my mother and daughter were
Tony and Jeannie, standing in front of a blue tarpaulin that
Tony had hung in front of his secret project. Maxie was hovering near the ceiling above Tony's head. I started searching my
mind for behavior of mine that might have triggered an inter-
vention, but came up short.

"I was tired," I said.

I walked toward Tony, who was wearing a grin so wide I
was afraid it would meet at the back of his head. "I assume
this means you've finished your fiendish plan," I said to him.

"I have," he admitted. The grin got a little wider.

"I don't know what it is, either," Melissa told me. "Tony
said it was for my room, so it had to be my surprise, too."

I have never had to question Tony Mandorisi on any home-
improvement project, ever. The man is an unsung genius. So I
had no trepidation when I told him, "Okay, then—let's see it."

"Stand back," Jeannie warned.

I couldn't imagine what might be behind that tarp. A staircase to the attic would take up far too much room and eat up
almost the entire hallway. Fireman's poles seemed impracti-
cal, as they really only work in one direction. I had not seen
any construction going on outside, which would have required

permits from the borough and cost far more than I could afford.

But Tony, I knew, wouldn't let me down.

So it was with great anticipation that I pulled on the rope that Tony indicated, which let the tarp loose and dropped it to the floor. And with a little disappointment that I saw what was behind it.

"It's . . . a closet," I said.

"A closet!" Jeannie shouted. "You think my husband spent the last two days up here building you a *closet*?"

Melissa, of course, caught on much more quickly. "It's an elevator!" she yelled, and launched herself at Tony for a hug, which he supplied.

But he shook his head. "It's not exactly an elevator, Liss. It's a dumbwaiter."

Melissa looked up, and I knew she was confused. "Is that a joke, Tony?" she asked. "It doesn't sound like a very nice name for something."

"I can't help what it's called, Liss," Tony answered. "But I think it'll help you get up and down from your new room once it's finished."

Walking closer, I could see how the contraption was going to work. Deeper than it first looked, it would be possible to hoist up at least some small furniture items or boxes for some-assembly-required pieces. And the chains mounted inside would raise and lower Melissa slowly and safely, but also add an element of fun to the process that just running up the stairs would not be able to offer. The accordion grate she'd have to close to prevent her falling out would keep her safe.

"You're a genius," I told Tony, and gave him a hug of my own.

"Didn't I tell you?" Jeannie glowed, rubbing her ever-growing belly.

Melissa tried out the dumbwaiter first; then, after having deemed it "awesome," and noting how easy it was to raise, she insisted on giving her grandmother a ride up. Mom looked momentarily wary, but refused to concede that her grand-daughter could do anything that wasn't perfect, and took the ride.

The rest of us went up the pull-down stairs, which Tony had suggested I leave intact, "for emergencies, and just because you won't always want to pull everything up with your arms."

My attic, soon to be Melissa's bedroom, was still about as far along as Jeannie, but it was definitely getting there. The walls were up and smooth, the windows installed, the paint bright yellow (the final decision having come after Melissa had compared color cards for a day and a half), the border wallpaper hung around the crown molding and the skylight installed. But there was still no air-conditioning up there because the ductwork I needed was lying in a carton in the basement. It would be the first equipment the dumbwaiter would deliver.

"It's beautiful," Mom said after climbing out of the dumb-waiter with a big grin on her face. "You've done a wonderful job up here, Alison."

Paul and Maxie, floating near the skylight, smiled down at us.

"I had help," I said.

FROM
CASEY DANIELS

A HARD DAY'S FRIGHT
A Pepper Martin Mystery

Cemetery tour guide and reluctant medium Pepper
Martin is enjoying quite a reputation on the ghostly
grapevine. So when a free spirit from the sixties needs
closure, she knows just who to haunt . . .

PRAISE FOR
THE PEPPER MARTIN MYSTERIES

"Pepper is a delight."
—MaryJanice Davidson, *New York Times* bestselling author

**"Gravestones, ghosts,
and ghoulish misdemeanors delight."**
—Madelyn Alt, national bestselling author

**"Entertaining . . .
Sass and the supernatural cross paths."**
—*Publishers Weekly*

penguin.com
facebook.com/TheCrimeSceneBooks